The Lost Pipers of CraigDhuin

And Other Adventures

A John and Mary Braemhor Mystery

by

Owen Magruder

For information, email **Cozy Cat Press**, cozycatpress@aol.com or visit our website at: www.cozycatpress.com

COZY CAT
P R E S S

ISBN: 978-1-939816-99-3

Printed in the United States of America

Cover design by Paula Ellenberger
www.paulaellenberger.com

1 2 3 4 5 6 7 8 9 10

To Nellie

Chapter 1

The morning mist rose beneath John Braemhor's apple trees like the bridal wreath of Hera's nuptials. Clothed in white and barely visible through the mist, the smallish trees bent their heads from the weight of their fruit. They stood as sentinels, protecting the garden from the demystifying, reddish-orange glow of the rising sun. But to no avail. The day could not be held back, and the warmth of the sunlight burned away the white shroud and exposed the bountiful harvest the trees bestowed on the Braemhor household.

John looked out admiringly at the reddish orbs hanging from the limbs and marveled at the cycle of life of which the trees were emblematic. *Why, when life is so full and giving,* he wondered, *must the dark side of human nature constantly challenge its beauty?* Mary's voice broke his philosophic reverie.

"John, the post is here," Mary called from the front hall.

John went to the front door to pick up the letters that had just arrived.

Letter from James, he observed as he sorted through the half dozen envelopes. He handed it to Mary. James lived in the Colonies, as John referred to the United States, just across the river from New Boston in the village of Hiramville, with his wife, Jennifer, and John and Mary's two grandchildren. They had relocated there from New Boston last year in order to find a more academically-oriented school district for the children.

"Anything new?" John asked as Mary scanned the letter.

"Not really. The children are flourishing in their new school. Both James and Jennifer remain happy in their professions. They are very pleased with the new house. . . . Oh, yes, Jennifer has joined the area symphony orchestra. . .and listen to this. The neighbors think a house across the street from them is haunted!" Mary hesitated to mention the last item, because she knew it would just activate John's investigative antennae.

"Haunted, you say. How so?" John was intrigued.

"Seems the owners have been unable to keep it let. Renters move in, but within a few weeks they all leave, saying they can't abide to live there any longer. No one will say why exactly, but the last couple did say that the wall clocks were acting strangely."

"How strangely?" Now John was really intrigued but tried to hide his interest in what Mary was describing.

"James doesn't say, just that the last couple left in less than a week. The owners are as puzzled as the neighbors. And, you'll like this, John, they wonder when we are coming to visit."

"You made that up," John observed.

"I did," Mary admitted, "but I can see your interest in the haunted house behind your casual questions, and besides it has been some time since we've seen the children. A trip to the Colonies?" Mary let a knowing smile float across her face.

Before John could answer, the phone rang. He raised the receiver, "Dunmoor Cottage, John Braemhor here."

"Ah, I'm glad I caught you. DI Ferguson here. Ron Ferguson. May I have a word?"

"Of course, Ron. How are things around Loch Ness this season?"

"Not too well. We've had two more disappearances."

"People can't stay out of your fairy circles again?" Braemhor smiled as he recalled the last time he and Mary helped Ferguson with a series of disappearances thought to be connected with the fairy circles under some of the trees of the region.

"Nothing like that this time. We are losing some of our best pipers, and the circumstances appear to be far more ominous than beckoning fungi. It's all happening right near Loch Ness, practically on the grounds of the CraigDhuin ruins. A number of the tour buses that stop at the ruins bring a piper with them, and while the tourists walk the castle grounds, he places himself on a small hillock across the A82 from the ruins. He pipes while the tourists walk. Very picturesque. Except that on two recent occasions, the piping suddenly stopped and the piper disappeared. The driver and some of the passengers searched the area, but to no avail. The piper was gone without a trace."

"Without a trace?" Braemhor was intrigued.

"Yes, and this is even stranger. A number of locals and some tourists claim to have seen, around the mound where he had stood, large, wet prints in the ground the size of—you're not going to believe me. . . ."

"Try me."

"A dinosaur's foot! Over a foot across!"

"Wait, Ron, if they saw anything, it must have been ancient, fossil tracks—which would be scientifically interesting in itself. But, Ron, though dinosaurs did inhabit western Scotland, that was over 150 million years ago."

"No, John, they claim these impressions were fresh. Imbedded in the hillside. Six inches or so in depth."

"You want me to believe that ancient dinosaurs, sauropods, 50 feet long, weighing about 20 tons and 150 million years old arose from Loch Ness, walked across open terrain, crossed a paved highway and devoured a lone piper on the hill without 40 tourists, who were walking on the same grounds, seeing it?"

"Not really, John," Ferguson smiled. "Neither I nor any of my men could find anything of the sort, but the locals are convinced that it was a hungry Nessie, lured by the pipes, who ate the piper, pipes and all."

"Ron, first, sauropods were vegetarians and would not have eaten a piper, pipes and all. I think you're dealing with a case of crowd hysteria. It makes you understand why eye-witness accounts of crimes are so notoriously unreliable."

"I agree, but you see what I'm dealing with. Try convincing a group of local Nessie lovers," Ferguson concluded.

Braemhor picked up the unspoken question in Ferguson's tale. "Still, the story is fascinating. Maybe Mary and I will take a holiday and come up to Ft. Ewen and explore a bit."

"I was hoping you would say that. When could you get here?"

"Day after tomorrow. I'll call you when we get there." Braemhor hung up and turned to Mary, who had been listening to his half of the conversation.

"I would like a trip to the Colonies very much, but first we need to go back to Ft. Ewen." John told Mary the details of his conversation with Ferguson.

"I know you don't believe that Nessie is eating the pipers." She knew her husband would not buy into such a fantasy. "That's a story as strange as the fairy circles, and you remember those fables had very real explanations."

"Of course, and like the fairy circles, the disappearance of pipers near Loch Ness has some sort of logical, realistic explanation, but so far Ferguson has been unable to solve it. Worse yet, the tale is feeding the wildest imaginations of the local Nessie clubs in the region that Nessie is a real monster. Probably assume the story will be good for business."

"Good for business?"

"Of course, the more mystery they can conjure up, the more tourists will want to come to Ft. Ewen and the CraigDhuin area."

"But how can a possible crime attract tourists?"

"Excitement. People love excitement, even if it involves putting themselves or their loved ones in imminent danger. I'll bet you could even sell tickets to some to stand with the piper and see Nessie slosh across the castle grounds and devour the piper."

"Oh, John, people are fascinated with the unknown, but you're exaggerating."

"Probably so," John admitted, "but shall we go Nessie chasing?"

"Do I have a choice?"

"Not really, but you have to admit that the beauty of the region around Loch Ness is breathtaking. How do our reservations look?"

"None until next Friday." Mary had already consulted the Dunmoor register.

"So we won't have to bother Aunt Rita to look after the Cottage?"

"Let's save her for our trip to the Colonies. Besides, I understand she's quite busy at Dunmoor Castle managing wedding reservations for the old keep." Mary's parents had begun opening Dunmoor Castle

Estate for wedding parties in the refurbished 15th century keep as well as pheasant hunting on the extensive grounds. Aunt Rita was only too happy to take an active part in the family's plans to move the Estate into 21st century modernism. She even embellished her role by telling tourists that some of the pheasants on the grounds were really reincarnations of family members from Robert-the-Bruce's time. They had helped King Robert in his quest for Scottish independence, and so they should be careful not to shoot the birds that had a golden crown atop their heads. All said through the puckish, restrained smile for which she was known in the family.

* * * * *

Next morning, John put their valises in the boot of the Vauxhall and they headed towards Glasgow and the A82. It was the same route they had taken last year when they were assisting DI Ferguson with the mystery of the disappearances in the fairy circles near Ft. Ewen on Loch Ness. Once again, their route took them past the serene and placid Loch Lomond with its unsurpassed beauty. Yet to Mary its undisturbed surface seemed to be mantled with a quiet foreboding that had a sinister tranquility about it. Mary always thought that there was something about the loch that both attracted and repelled her. She would have far more believed that an ominous, gigantic lizard-like behemoth resided *there* than in Loch Ness.

At Fort Lochiel John and Mary went straight to Ferguson's office in the Town Hall on Cameron Square. The clerk pointed them down the hall to the door now labeled "DI Ferguson," where he awaited them with his usual broad smile. "Good to see you both again," he opened.

"Anything new since we spoke?" John asked.

"Only that the tour buses have stopped bringing a piper with them, and we've been inundated with the curious wanting to catch a sighting of Nessie as she roams the CraigDhuin grounds looking for her next meal." Ferguson enjoyed his own dark humor.

"Are there any tour companies that do not employ a piper?" John asked quickly.

"Only one, a small company—Magnum Tours—that does not bring a piper with them to entertain the customers. I was thinking along the same line, Mr. Braemhor. Thought maybe the competition for tourists might have driven someone to do something foolish. But, no, Magnum is clean. They are a Fort Ewen Mom and Pop outfit, not a large, evil corporation. You can talk to them, if you like, but I don't think you'll find much."

"We might do that, just to cover all possibilities. Corporations don't have to be large to do evil. What about local preservation groups that might resent the flood of tourists around CraigDhuin?" John had already given some thought to possible motives for the apparent crime of the disappearing pipers.

"In fact, are you sure there has been a crime committed?" Mary asked. "Maybe the pipers were tired of their jobs and left of their own accord."

"I thought of that, too, but why would they just leave and not tell anyone? Even their families are perplexed. . .and very distraught."

"Understandably so. Well, if you can give us the address and phone of Magnum Tours, we'll be off to Fort Ewen and the Nessie Hotel."

Ferguson handed John a slip of paper with the information about Magnum and rose to see him and Mary out. "Call me if you find anything or if you need anything."

It was a short trip from Fort Lochiel to Fort Ewen and John was quietly thoughtful most of the way.

"What do you think, John?" Mary queried.

"I'm not sure what to think yet. It's like the fairy circles, no body, just a disappearance—two in fact—the pipers were piping on the hill, then stopped and no one has seen them since. Your question, "Is there a crime?" was very apt. I don't really know what to think at this point."

"Do you suppose Heinrich Zauberin would be of any help?"

"Zauberin, from *The Witch's Cauldron*? Interesting you should mention him. I was just thinking about him. He certainly seemed to have his finger on all of the local goings-on the last time we were here. He's probably laid in a supply of Loch Ness monster books, if I guess correctly. Let's go there before we check in at the hotel, shall we?"

"Good idea. Maybe he'll have a new book on the fairies I can get for Rita." Mary concurred with John's plan.

* * * * *

Zauberin's shop was as they remembered. A plethora of tarot cards, amulets and other magical trinkets to amuse non-critical thinkers. His corner library of book offerings now contained, as John predicted, books on the Loch Ness monster, some containing pictures which strangely resembled the sauropods of millions of years ago. Zauberin himself was the same gaunt, skeletal giant, attired in the same black and white garb with gold trim down the outside seams of his onion-skin tight trousers.

"Mr. and Mrs. Braemhor! What a pleasant surprise! Still chasing the fairies in their circles?" A faint smile rippled in the corners of his blue-black lips.

Still reminds me of something out of Dante, Mary thought.

"Not this time, Mr. Zauberin. I thought your brother in Fort Lochiel would have told you of our arrival."

"Oh, he did. He did. But I don't want to reveal all of my secret sources of information so quickly." This time a more genuine smile flashed across his parchment-like countenance. "How can I help you this time?"

"What can you tell us about the disappearing pipers?"

"Well, you people certainly have a thing for disappearing individuals, I must say. First in the fairy circles and now at the CraigDhuin ruins. I thought this was a local mystery, but your antennae must be particularly tuned in on tales of vanishing people. Next thing I know, you'll be chasing invisible men."

John ignored the banter. "Come, come, Zauberin. You know all of the occult and mysterious events going on near Loch Ness, or your shop would not be so thriving. I notice you now have a collection of books on Nessie that you didn't have before. So stop the repartee and tell me what you know."

Zauberin suddenly melted under Braemhor's interrogation. "You're right, Mr. Braemhor, my livelihood is based on knowing all of the strange, mysterious and unexplainable things that happen hereabout, the better to fool the public with. So, here is what I know so far about the disappearing pipers. Homeland Tours bring a piper when they visit

CraigDhuin; they put him on the hillside across the A82 from the ruins. He plays traditional Scottish pipe tunes while the tourists wander the castle grounds. Adds to the Scottish flavor of their trip.

"Two weeks ago the piper suddenly stopped playing *Johnnie MacDonald's Reel* in mid-tune. The tour guide for Homeland crossed the A82 to investigate, and there was no sign of the piper. Then, about a week ago Highland Fling Tours had the same thing happen. Their piper was in mid-tune too when the sound suddenly stopped. The driver went to see what had happened and, as before, no piper."

"And he was playing. . . ?"

"*Johnnie MacDonald's Reel.*" A sardonic smirk lit Zauberin's face.

"You seem to think that's significant," John observed. "Is it because the MacDonalds contended with Clan Kenlaine for possession of the castle in the 16th century?"

"Oh, I forgot, you and your wife are Scottish history buffs. Yes, it crossed my mind that there might be a connection."

John just shook his head. "When will the Scots ever stop fighting the feuds of centuries ago?"

"Oh, I hope they never do. It would be so bad for business." Zauberin appeared offended by the idea.

"Well, Mr. Zauberin, we best be on our way. We'll be at the Nessie Hotel if you think or hear of anything else that might be helpful." John took Mary's arm and guided them both towards the door.

Mary turned back as they left. "We'll be back for some more books later." She smiled. Zauberin beamed.

"I'll look forward to it, and happy Nessie hunting." Zauberin turned to straightening the books on his library's shelves.

* * * * *

The drive to the Nessie Hotel was brief and the loch was clothed in the mists of evening, the moon just beginning to make its presence known on the horizon across the lake. The wind had picked up considerably and was now a howling gale sweeping across the hills, the castle ruins and Loch Ness itself.

"Notice anything about the loch, Mary?" John asked as he turned into the hotel car park.

"Only that it's as beautiful as always. . .and a very strong wind has come up."

"Look across the loch, at the shoreline. More of it is visible than usual."

"You're right, the loch does seem to be down." *How many other people would have noticed?* she thought. Even after so many years together, Mary was always surprised by John's extraordinary powers of observation. "I wonder why?"

"Don't know. We'll ask Mr. Duncan."

Inside the reception, Harold Duncan, the proprietor of Hotel Nessie, greeted them with his broad smile and room-filling, roaring voice. "Aye, I wondered when you would get here, Mr. Braemhor, Mrs. Braemhor. Your usual room?"

"Fine," Mary answered.

"Hear about the mystery of the disappearing pipers?" A small, knowing smile flashed across Duncan's face. "It has all of the locals atwitter. First Carl Rhodes and now Sam Erlandson, both retired pipe majors, one with the Seafield Highlanders, the other with the Glencairnie Pipers. Playing on the hill above the ruin when, poof, they were gone. Strange—and scary—business, I'd say."

"Why scary?" John asked as he signed the register.

"Supposing it was Nessie. Now don't get me wrong, Mr. Braemhor; I'm not a superstitious man, but it's got me thinking. What if there is some truth to all of the stories of Nessie living in the loch?"

"Surely, Mr. Duncan, you don't believe in a millions of year old sauropod wandering the castle grounds in the 21st century?" Mary challenged him.

"No, ma'am, I don't, but. . .but. . .I just don't know what to think." Duncan was clearly embarrassed by Mary's query.

"It is a puzzle, there's no doubt about that," John broke in. "Maybe time will give us some more logical answers, but for now I think we'll settle in and then have another of your restaurant's delicious offerings." He picked up his and Mary's valises and started toward the stairs to their usual room. Then he turned. "We noticed the loch seems very low this year. What happened?"

Duncan shook his head. "Don't know, but just about a month ago the whole water table in the area dropped. 'Course there has been some work on the Great Glen canals of late. Maybe that was the cause."

"Maybe so," John mumbled as he and Mary went upstairs to their room.

* * * * *

Later, over dinner, "Well, John, what about the missing pipers?" Mary asked.

"Not much to go on yet, but it sounds like the locals are convinced that a million year old plant-eating dinosaur is devouring human pipers. It's amazing what people want to believe. I would have thought that. . . What is that??!!"

The room suddenly was awash with a very loud, high-frequency sound. "What *is* that?" Mary shouted above the din.

"Sounds like two pieces of metal being rubbed together." John quickly moved toward the door to the outside.

"Or Mr. Zauberin running his fingernails down a chalkboard," Mary added as they exited the hotel and into the howling wind.

"It's out here somewhere," John said as he scanned the dusk-filled evening and pointed, "towards Loch Ness."

By the time the hotel reception and restaurant had emptied, guests poured out into the night as the moon rose behind the Kenlaine Tower on the CraigDhuin grounds a half mile south. Most of the guests were befuddled, not knowing what was happening. One man offered the opinion that it was a jet plane in trouble and about to crash. At that announcement two of the women began crying and screaming—almost as loud as the sound itself. "It's Nessie, it's Nessie!! Oh, God, this is the end. We'll all be eaten. Run! Run! For God's sake, run!" Part of the crowd exploded down the road away from the sound like toothpaste suddenly squeezed from a tube.

John pulled Mary out of the way of the surging mob, and they stood in a corner of the car park watching the chaos and crowd hysteria.

"Interesting how people react to the unknown. . ," John quietly observed, "when they want to believe in the supernatural."

At that moment, someone else shouted, "It's Nessie's love song responding to the pipes."

"That was a week ago," chided a woman. "You've had too much to drink."

"Week ago or not, she's still searching for the pipes that sing the siren song of the monster," was the slurred response.

"Now there's a thought for you, John." Mary smiled. "All these years our Scottish bagpipes have been singing love songs to Nessie. Rita would love it, don't you think?"

"No doubt. Let's see if we can find the source of the screeching." John led Mary to their car across the park. But just as they were about to get in, the sound whined its way to silence and Nessie stopped her "love song."

At that moment, Harold Duncan appeared with five or six of his guests in tow, returning them to the hotel, calming them with soothing words and telling them the safest place would be inside the hotel. He, himself, looked as if he had witnessed a fright, but his apparent calm—to the guests—brought at least the few guests with him to their senses and they followed him, like the children of Hamelin, back to the half-timbered hotel. John and Mary fell in line and followed Duncan and his charges into reception.

"What do you make of it, Mr. Braemhor?" Duncan, obviously shaken, turned to John and Mary.

"Has anything like this happened before?" John answered Duncan's question with a question of his own.

"Not in my lifetime. And it was so loud. And started so suddenly. I just hope I can find all of my guests and get them safely back into the hotel."

"Perhaps we can help you. They can't have gone too far," John offered.

"I'd be much obliged if you would. You're right, they can't have gone too far. They all ran north up the A82."

"Mary, you get the car. Duncan and I will search on foot, and maybe with the three of us we can bring all of the guests back." John and Duncan started walking north on the A82. Within the hour, all of Hotel Nessie's guests were accounted for and back in the hotel restaurant calming themselves with Duncan's offering of free coffee and scones. Only three very frightened and distressed elderly female guests were brought back in the car.

Once all of the guests had returned to their rooms, John and Mary sat down with Mr. Duncan to review the evening. Duncan was still upset, but much better composed than earlier. He had gotten a bottle of Ebony Label from behind the bar and was supplementing his coffee. It seemed to help sooth his nerves. He looked at the Braemhors. "I really appreciated your help rounding up all of my guests tonight."

"It was really nothing. We just wanted to help," Mary said.

"Well, it was a big help. But what do you think it was?" He looked straight at John.

"Hard to say."

"It seemed to rise and fall with the wind. Reminded me of a high-pitched pipe organ, but certainly not as melodious," Mary observed.

"That's another thing. We don't usually have such high winds around Loch Ness. The wind itself seemed strange." Duncan's agitation appeared on the rise again.

"Maybe it was Nessie breathing in and out." John tried to add some levity to the situation that was once again becoming tense with imagined foreboding.

At that, Duncan's smile slowly returned to his face dispelling the lines of tension that had temporarily wiped away his usually cheery countenance. "Maybe so. Maybe so, Mr. Braemhor, but I don't want to ever again live through such a night. Things like this almost make me believe in Nessie—but not quite." The twinkle had returned to his eyes by now.

"Well, it is getting rather late. Perhaps we all could do with a good night's rest, now that the sounds of Nessie have subsided. Shall we go up, Mary, and leave Mr. Duncan to close up for the night. It will be a bit easier to search for the origins of that horrible sound in the daylight tomorrow." John rose and nodded to Mary.

"I agree. I've had enough adventure for one night," Mary concurred.

* * * * *

"What are you looking for, John?"

"My windbreaker. I was sure I packed it. . .ah, here it is."

"Why do you want your windbreaker? I thought we were going to bed." Mary was slightly perplexed.

"You go to bed; I want to do a little exploring."

"Where? It's almost midnight."

"Won't take me long. I just want to walk the castle ruins quickly. Something you said got me thinking about the origins of that earlier sound everyone else attributed to Nessie. I won't be long, not more than an hour." John smiled as he pulled on his hiking boots and his windbreaker, and picked up one of the several torches and his walking stick. With that he left the room and walked quietly down the corridor to the stairs.

Fifteen minutes later, John crossed the moat bridge at CraigDhuin and circled the grounds around the Kenlaine Tower. Once he reached the loch side of the tower, the footing became more treacherous. *Glad I brought my walking stick,* John thought as he slithered down the embankment and began exploring the edge of the loch. With the water level down he could, with his torch, easily see the rock levels that supported the tower, in fact, the entire castle. As he moved along the water's edge he began to hear a low moaning sound that seemed to rise and fall with the wind, which had subsided considerably from earlier in the evening. The sound was eerie and reminded him of music by Ravel. For fifty yards or so there was nothing particularly remarkable about the landfall.

Another twenty-five yards further on he saw what he thought he might find. In the rock face were a series of pits and indentations. *Just as I thought! Small cave openings.* And the closer he got to the openings the louder and more bacchanalian became the moaning. *Just like Ravel's* Daphnis and Chloe. Then suddenly it stopped. John, too, stopped and looked around. Then he realized what had happened; the wind had died down and was no longer bursting upon the shoreline. John, a smile of knowledge on his lips, climbed up the cliff face and walked briskly back to the hotel.

"John, it's 1:00 a.m. Where have you been?"

"I told you that I'd be back in an hour. And it was an hour well-spent."

"What have you learned?"

"I've solved one mystery—the Nessie siren song. Remember you remarked that the sounds we heard last evening, the ones that created chaos with the hotel guests, sounded like a high-pitched pipe organ?"

"Yes?"

"Well, how does an organ produce sounds. . .by passing a column of air across pipes of varying lengths and diameters. So I got to thinking. Last night was very windy, at least until the sound ended. I wondered if the passage of the high wind had anything to do with the production of the sound, which everyone else took for Nessie singing a love song.

"Also, remember we noted that the water level of the loch seemed to be unusually low. So I began to wonder if the low water level had exposed any natural apertures in the rock base under CraigDhuin, small caves that had trapped water over the years. Just as I suspected, I found several small holes in the rock face of the exposed shoreline—probably formed over many years. The closer I got to these openings, the more I heard sounds like a moaning pipe organ. There, then, is the natural explanation for the supernatural sounds we heard. Not a sea monster at all but the natural consequences of natural phenomena interacting as they had not done for many years, so long as the water level of the loch stayed at its normal level.

"That's too bad," Mary observed.

"What?" John was not quite following her thinking.

"Think of all of the local folk that at last thought they had a real sign that Nessie actually exists. Local Nessie clubs will be very distressed." Mary smiled.

"Well, they can continue to believe in the supernatural while we get some sleep. We can disabuse them tomorrow," John mused as he got into bed.

* * * * *

Next morning the room phone rang as John was shaving. Mary took the call. "Yes, yes, I'll tell him." She hung up. "John, Ron Ferguson is at reception."

Ten minutes later, the Braemhors greeted the young DI. "Had breakfast yet?" John asked.

"Yes, I did in Fort Lochiel before I came up."

"Then come in and have some coffee with us," Mary invited.

As they sat in the restaurant, Ferguson opened the conversation. "I understand now we have another mystery. Nessie has started singing at night. It was all over the news this morning. Our local Nessie lovers are absolutely delighted. It proves the existence of the Loch Ness monster—to them."

"We hate to disappoint the local fable lovers, but I solved that one last night." John smiled and proceeded to tell Ferguson what he had learned at the castle in the early morning hours.

"Well, that will certainly save me some blind alley searching. How do you think of these things? I must admit that wind in rock crevices would not have occurred to me."

"Oh, it would have had you been here last night. The strength of the wind was quite remarkable, and Mary had commented that the sound was similar to a pipe organ. It just fell into place, and with a little searching on the Castle grounds the supernatural got a natural explanation. Now, do you have anything new on the disappearing pipers?"

"Well, yes and no. The owners of Magnum Tours—Angus and Margaret Ross—contacted me yesterday. They said they had been receiving some strange and they thought threatening calls since Erlandson and Rhodes disappeared."

"Threatening? How so?"

"The caller, apparently a man with a harsh, raspy voice, simply said that Nessie was on the prowl and they were next! Mrs. Ross was quite upset."

"I can imagine," Mary said as she turned to John, "Maybe we should go to see the Rosses today."

"After I walk the grounds of the disappearances. Care to walk with me?" John turned to Ferguson.

"I walked it when the disappearances first occurred, but a third walk may be instructive." Ferguson smiled as he and John rose to go to the hill opposite the CraigDhuin ruins.

Mary looked up at John. "Perhaps I could interview the Rosses while you two are out near CraigDhuin. I have their address. I'll call them first."

"Excellent idea. Let's meet back here for dinner, say, near one?"

"One it is, then." With that, Mary went to their room to phone the Rosses and arrange a meeting later in the morning. John put on his windbreaker, took up his walking stick, and he and Ferguson went to the latter's car for the short ride to CraigDhuin.

"What are you looking for, John? And why the stick?" Ferguson asked as they left his car in the car park by the castle ruin and crossed the A82. He planned to learn all he could by observing Braemhor's investigative approach to the "crime scene."

"Not sure myself, but I need to get a better feel for the terrain. And I often carry a stick; it makes an excellent probe."

"Last night was instructive. What I found made me speculate that the land under the castle ruins might be riddled with ancient caves, centuries old and forgotten by modern day archeologists. I wonder if there are any larger ones than those I discovered last night. They were barely pipe organ-size, but very effective for producing the sounds the heavy winds caused. Let's see what we can find, shall we?"

As they started up the hillside, John noted that the police ribbon was still in place, warning tourists and others to avoid the area. Ferguson lifted the ribbon, and they both ducked under and approached a small fenced off area around the spot where the two pipers had stood before their sudden disappearance. Both men walked slowly around the area. John quickly formed an imaginary grid around the piper's stand and slowly began walking his unseen grid parallels systematically from left to right, slowly closing in on the fenced space. With each step he probed the earth with his walking stick and then moved on in an exaggerated pace and probed again. Ferguson was fascinated and followed Braemhor's path as he narrowed the area converging on the piper's spot.

"It was as if the ground had just swallowed them up," Ferguson noted as they came nearer the fence. John continued probing gingerly with his stick until, quite unexpectedly, the earth yielded to his probe.

"Ah, ha. Very prophetic," John remarked as his latest thrust sank the walking stick a full six inches into the sodden ground. "Just as I thought. Now we're getting somewhere!" But his walking stick had, after a six inch descent, struck what felt like solid rock. *Probably the shale close to the surface,* John thought.

Ferguson was perplexed as he gazed over John's shoulder at the imbedded stick.

"We need a shovel," John said as he extracted his walking stick from the ground. "And don't walk any closer to this area," he added quickly, as he took a step backward.

"I've got a small entrenching tool in the car. I'll get it." Ferguson started for the car park.

"And bring a torch, if you have one," John requested as he dropped to one knee and began a careful search radiating out from where his stick had sunk into the sod. It did not take much digging for John to discover why his stick had penetrated the surface but six inches.

In a short time he outlined a region where the earth was not as solid as that of most of the hillside, which seemed to have an underpinning of flat shale-like rock—except around the place where the pipers had stood. *Fascinating,* he thought as he awaited Ferguson's return.

Ferguson came back promptly with an old, military-style entrenching tool and a yellow police torch. John took the former and began a shallow probe into the soil which confirmed what he had already learned. He was able to lift off a square area of sod that seemed to be resting on the flat rock below. Except that it was not rock, but a decaying, weather-petrified wooden plate. Ferguson was astounded. "What do we have here?" he asked aloud.

"If I am not mistaken, it is most probably an entrance to some sort of passageway under the hillside," John explained.

"An underground passage that someone did not want found," Ferguson observed.

"Precisely. But do you suppose that it was an escape route constructed in the early years of CraigDhuin to give the occupants a way to escape an extended siege?" John asked.

"If it is, I never heard of it and I thought I was fairly well up on the history of this area and the castle. It would certainly be an archaeological find of some importance, if it is."

By now Braemhor was attempting to lift the wooden cover but despite its age and fragility it would not move.

"Seems to be fastened on the underside." He looked at Ferguson. "We need to find out if there is a labyrinth of passageways under the hillside and perhaps under the castle ruins."

"Maybe the present curator of the site can help. John Kenlaine is a descendent of the 13th century Sheriffs of Inverness. His family has a long history with CraigDhuin and he, if anybody, should know of any secret passages in the area. His estate is just south of Inverness and I am certain that he would be interested in what we've found. Shall I contact him and see if he can be of any help?" The excitement in Ferguson's voice told Braemhor that he had a valuable ally in the young DI.

They quickly covered over the wooden door with the sod and went back to Ferguson's car to return to the Hotel Nessie.

* * * * *

Mary greeted the two explorers in reception. "Successful survey?" she asked.

"Very." John smiled and told her of their finding what looked like an entrance to some underground passages under the hill where the pipers had disappeared.

"So you think they were dragged underground the day they disappeared?"

"It looks like a real possibility, Mrs. Braemhor," Ferguson replied, and then he turned to John. "I'll call John Kenlaine and see if he can meet with us." He went to the guest phone on the reception desk to place his call while John and Mary went into the restaurant for some dinner.

John explained to Mary his and Ferguson's search in detail. Ferguson came into the restaurant after his phone call and told the Braemhors, "Kenlaine says he can meet us later this afternoon at the ruins. He has to come down from Inverness anyway to tend to some minor curator business. 'bout three, all right?"

"That will be fine," John responded. "Come have some dinner with us for now."

"I'd better not. I need to get back to Fort Lochiel to attend to some other police business before I come back to meet with you and Kenlaine. This is not the only case I have active." With that, he exited the hotel and got into his police cruiser for the short trip south.

"So you think there are passageways under the hill that might lead back under the ruins?" Mary was fascinated by the Gothic turn of the investigation. "Maybe Nessie is roaming under CraigDhuin, attacking unaware pipers as they serenade the tourists." She smiled.

"Probably not Nessie, but some human-form monster. Maybe it's a music perfectionist who can't stand the high-pitched whine of pipe music," John rejoined.

"But surely, John, a Scottish musician wouldn't mind the sounds of the native instrument of his homeland."

"Probably an American, then, they're not known for their appreciation of musical sounds, other than their own. But, seriously, you raise an interesting point. What could be offensive about a Scottish tune that adds flavor to a tourist tour? Unless. . . ."

"Unless what?" Mary quickly recognized that the conversation had turned serious again.

"Remember what Zauberin said the pipers were playing at the time of their disappearance?"

"Yes, it was *Johnnie MacDonald's Reel.*"

"And he seemed to think that that was significant."

"Because of the 16th century history of CraigDhuin."

"Yes. . . well, let's keep that in mind as this case unfolds. Meantime what did you learn from the Rosses?"

"Not a lot really. Mrs. Ross seems a very sweet person, and a very frightened person. The first call came shortly after the second piper disappeared and they have repeated every few days since. Always the same, a gravelly voiced male—sounds like an older individual—who quickly warns them that they are next and then hangs up. She said that DI Ferguson put a tap on her phone line, but that the calls were always too short to get a fix on their origins."

"Do they occur at any special time of day or night?"

"She said not, though more of them have come at night."

"So we have three—the main three—tour lines in the area all being attacked, two having their pipers disappear and the other receiving threatening phone calls. Sounds to me like someone is trying to put a stop to the local tour business. But why? Certainly they bring additional tourists to the area which should be good for the economy. And kidnapping, or worse, is pretty drastic. There must be something we're not seeing. . .yet," John added. "Maybe we'll know more after we talk to Sir John."

Chapter 2

The afternoon was beautiful, a rare sunny day with a mild westerly breeze. John and Mary decided to walk the short half mile to the CraigDhuin ruins for their meeting with Sir John Kenlaine. As they approached the ruins, John pointed out to Mary the hillside and the low fence marking where the pipers met their fate. Police ribbons cordoned off the entire hillside where John and Ferguson had been digging in the forenoon.

"That's a very long tunnel, if it comes all of the way to the ruins proper," Mary noted.

"Hopefully, Sir John will be able to enlighten us if such an ancient escape route even exists. But it seems to me that a tunnel from the cave to the lake would have been shorter and easier to construct, unless. . . ." John was thinking aloud.

"Unless what?" Mary always found it somewhat distracting when John did not finish his sentences."

"Oh, sorry. . .unless large caverns already existed under the grounds. We'll soon know." John and Mary traversed the bridge across the moat and headed towards the old Kenlaine tower remains. The inside was dark and dank; the moisture of the lake on which the castle stood and the general Scottish weather combined to give the old structure a humid wetness not so noticeable on the outside. They entered the first level of the ruin through a small chamber with stone balconies near the ceilings on the side walls. Before this room and beyond it were two massive iron gates suspended from the ceiling, capable of being lowered quickly and trapping anyone in this entrance chamber from either going forward or retreating. John noted that the gates were now held in place above the entrance room by large steel wedges to prevent them from descending on unsuspecting tourists.

In the next chamber, somewhat larger than the one in which attackers could be trapped, was a very large cistern and stairs going up to the living quarters in the upper reaches of the tower. These stairs were in a defender's well, coursing upwards clockwise so that any attacker would have to wield his sword or mace in his left hand and therefore be less effective—unless he were one of the rare left-handed warriors. The narrowness of the assent also diminished the effectiveness of a protective shield so that the attacker was extremely vulnerable to blows raining down from the defender above.

"Makes you wonder how any castle was ever successfully attacked," Mary noted.

"Warfare in those days was even more bloody and up close than nowadays. As you read history, you have to wonder if the gains made by so much bloodshed were really worth it," John opined.

"Or today," Mary concurred.

The stairs guided the Braemhors into a rather large room which had several open doorways leading, they supposed, to other rooms in the tower keep. These passageways were blocked by metal gates to preclude the tourists from wandering too far into the ruin's far reaches. One opening looked out onto Loch Ness with a sweeping view of the western shore. As they admired the vista across the lake, the voice of Ferguson captured their attention.

"I see you've found your way up to the main room of the keep."

"Yes, it is a beautiful view, and so peaceful," Mary responded.

With Ferguson was a man who looked every part the lord of the castle. "And you must be Sir John Kenlaine," Braemhor said extending his hand, then continued, "I'm John Braemhor, and this is my wife Mary."

The tweed-clothed Kenlaine smiled slightly as he nodded and took Braemhor's hand. "Glad to have some Scottish tourists for a change. Ron tells me you're investigating the disappearance of the pipers. Nasty business that. I hope you can help remove this dark cloud from our castle."

Kenlaine was of medium build, slender and straight as a sapling. His reddish-blond hair seemed to be trying to hold back the onslaught of grey and with some success except at his temples. His Vandyke which added a distinctive point to his face betrayed his age, as it had turned almost solidly white. "Ron tells me that you're interested in possible caves beneath the ground level quarters. I'm not aware of any, but there are areas of the castle that have never been explored in modern day, so anything is possible. I can show you some of the lower levels, but I warn you they're not pleasant, and may in parts be submerged in standing water."

"That's why we wore our rain boots." John pointed at his and Mary's feet.

"Ah, so I see. You did come prepared. And warm jackets also I see." He led the way down the circular stairs to the ground level. The entrance to that level from the outside was the dual room chamber, each room separated from the other by massive iron lattice-work gates. The interior room contained the large well

Mary and John had observed when they'd entered the castle earlier. Here, of course the inhabitants of the castle, when under siege, were able to obtain sufficient fresh water to withstand an interminable period until the attacking hoards either gave up in frustration or were defeated.

John observed the space between the two iron entry gates more carefully this time. The stone balconies near the ceiling of the room were accessible through a passageway from the inner (well) room so that invading marauders, caught between these two iron gates, were subjected to boiling oil and/or a rain of arrows from above.

Noting John's careful inspection of the isolation entry room, Sir John commented, "Even the MacDonalds were unable to penetrate the tower and thus failed in every attempt to take the castle. There were several bloodbaths centuries ago in this very entry where we now stand."

Mary shuddered at Sir John's last statement.

"To feed the castle's inhabitants, main food supplies were stored in rooms off of this area and in other spaces in lower levels," Sir John went on. "Come, I can show you some of those rooms. I see you have brought torches with you." He retrieved some oversized keys from his pocket, went to an iron plate door marked "Private," and opened it. The high-pitched screech of the rusted hinges added a sound effect worthy of the Gothic mysteriousness engendered by the ruins and their musty dampness. A stone stairway greeted the four.

As they descended, the damp, musty smells invaded their nostrils. *Like descending into a cold, wet inferno,* Mary thought. An old, frayed rope looped through iron rings served as a railing. Once down at the next level, their torches illuminated a rather large, cave-like chamber with areas of wetness on the floor and open doorways to several passages in the direction of the A82 outside. Most of these openings had large latticed iron gates—with ancient keyholes in their surfaces—obstructing further exploration. But the entrances of two were blocked by ancient iron doors also with keyholes.

"Where do they go?" Braemhor queried, examining one of the doors as he spoke.

"I don't have the slightest idea," Sir John said offhandedly, "but I have no keys that will fit any of these doors. I suppose they lead to other storage rooms from centuries ago."

"Was there ever a map made of the interior of the castle?" John pressed on.

"The only diagrams we have are of the upper tower and this one large room in which we now stand. No one's ever asked before." Sir John was becoming a little testy. "What is it exactly that you're searching for? DI Ferguson also asked about chambers below ground level."

Braemhor became very circumspect. "Nothing really. Just wondering how the dwellers of this ruin lived in the past. Both my wife and I are interested in Scottish history in all its detail."

"Well, as you can see they lived in very barren, cold and damp circumstances. Not much fun, I would say. The interior climate, including its smells, was not what we would think of as pleasant today." Then abruptly, "I'm afraid that's all I have to show you down here. Have you seen the family living quarters up in the keep?"

At that moment, Mary broke in, "John, what is that sme. . . ?"

"Yes, I think we would like very much to see the rooms in the upper part of the tower," John cut off Mary in midsentence.

"Well then, follow me and we'll go up again," Kenlaine hurriedly added and set off for the stairs which had led them down into this large storage room.

* * * * *

Sir John's tour of the rooms in the upper tower was brief and perfunctory. To Braemhor he seemed a man in a hurry to rid himself of this excursion through CraigDhuin. His original welcoming warmth had clearly worn thin. His exasperation became even more evident when they entered space on the second level of the keep that was obviously being lived in. It consisted of a small apartment, complete with a bedroom/living room area adjoined by a modern kitchen alcove. Sir John quickly regretted that he had inadvertently opened the door into this chamber. He became decidedly flustered and quickly pulled the door to before Ferguson and the Braemhors could get more than a brief look into the room.

He quickly said, as he hurriedly closed the door, "Sorry, those are private quarters."

"Private quarters? In a ruin?" It was Mary who questioned him this time.

"The on-site manager lives here," was Sir John's curt response as he hurriedly led them down the stairwell to the ground level. "I really must be going. I have other business in Inverness." They exited the keep, and Sir John strode off to the car park and drove rapidly away in his Bentley.

"That was instructive," Braemhor observed as he looked at Ferguson and Mary. "Shall we discuss what we've learned over supper?"

Back in the Hotel Nessie's restaurant the three sat down to shepherd's pie, the culinary specialty of the establishment, a hardy crofter's fare.

"What did you think of Kenlaine's behavior?" John started the discussion.

"Peculiar, I'd say," Ferguson answered between bites of his supper.

"He seemed so friendly and accommodating at first, then suddenly turned cold and distant. As if he didn't want us to learn any more about CraigDhuin, or at least about the lower reaches of the ruin," Mary added.

"And then upstairs, he acted as if he were trying to hide the fact that someone lives in the tower," John noted.

"Strange. It's common knowledge that Sir John's younger brother, Ian, is the on-site manager, and I don't see anything unusual about an on-site manager living on the premises. Makes his job easier, if he doesn't mind living in a centuries old ruin," Ferguson said.

"What do you know about Ian Kenlaine?' John directed his question to Ferguson.

"Not a lot really. He lived in Edinburgh until about three or four years ago when he joined Sir John in Inverness. Seems he's had some sort of rather severe medical problems for years. Spent a number of years as a patient in a small private psychiatric hospital in the Lothian area. Rumor has it that the two brothers' mother had similar problems and spent time in the Bangour Village Hospital."

"The Bangour Village Hospital? Wasn't that a new concept in hospitals for the mentally ill in the early 1900's?" Mary asked.

"Oh, yes," John added. "It was based on the Continental Colony idea, with a set of residential villas in which the patients resided, to give it a more homelike atmosphere. It was built in 1902 by the Edinburgh District Lunacy Board and finally abandoned early this century. Very innovative for its time. But what was the nature of Ian's problems?"

"Don't know. I only know the area gossip that he was hospitalized for some years before his brother, Sir John, brought him to Inverness. The family has been very tight-lipped about that part of the family history, naturally."

"John, something else has bothered me about our castle tour. Sir John was very cordial when we were down in the underground storage room, and then suddenly acted as if he wanted to get us out of that area quickly. Why?" Mary turned the conversation back to the ruins.

"I think it was because he noticed what I noticed," John responded.

"Which was?"

"The crumbs and small food scraps on the floor in front of one of the shuttered iron doors. You didn't see them?" John answered.

"No, but I did note the faint scratches on that door's hinges and keyhole." Mary smiled proudly. "And I also noted the food smells."

"About which I had to rudely interrupt you before you gave us away to Sir John."

"Sorry, but they were so pronounced."

"Yes, and fresh. And the scratches were fairly new too, not remnants of centuries ago. Like the door had been opened recently."

Ferguson had stopped attacking what was left of his pie and sat in quiet awe listening to these two well-seasoned sleuths review their observations. *I've still got a lot to learn,* he thought, *and where better than with the Braemhors.*

"What next, John?" Mary asked.

"I think I need to go back to the underground storage rooms."

"Why just you?" Mary was a little incredulous.

"Because I need you here in case anything goes wrong. If I, or we," he looked at Ferguson, "don't return in a specified time you can summon assistance."

"How will you get in?" Mary asked.

"The castle locks are not modern by any means. And locks in the days of the castle's construction were simple affairs, not particularly complicated. We should be able to pick them fairly easily. You didn't hear that, Ron." John turned to Ferguson.

"What? Oh, yes, of course. I'm eating my supper in an unofficial capacity. Right?" Ferguson fumbled his answer.

"Care to join me?"

"I think not. I don't think it would look good for a member of the constabulary to be caught trespassing on private property run by Historic Scotland," Ferguson declined John's offer.

"Right. Then I will have to assault the castle on the sly. If you get a call that someone is burgling the ruin, delay your arrival to give me time to vacate." John smiled at Ferguson. "I think I need to get my materials together and return to the ruin for some detailed exploration."

"And I need to get back to Fort Lochiel. Call me if you need anything or find anything new." Ferguson rose and took his leave.

"Nice young man," Mary observed.

"Right. And a good DI. Just needs a bit more seasoning," John added.

* * * * *

John and Mary went up to their room where John dressed in black trousers, a black turtleneck sweater, and a soft cap, and then gathered two torches, a strand of rope, and his lock-picking kit from the Vauxhall.

"If I'm not back by three, call Ron." He pecked Mary on the cheek

"I don't like this, John," Mary protested.

"I know, but it's the safest way to attack the castle."

"I still don't have to like it," Mary continued her protestation.

"Not to worry," John reassured her, then pecked her on the cheek again and exited the hotel to make the short walk to CraigDhuin.

As expected, Braemhor found the entrance chamber locked. The lock yielded quickly to his expertise, and he easily gained access to the cistern chamber. He went directly to the iron-plated door marked "Private" and handily picked its lock. The stone staircase led him down into the storage room Sir John had showed them earlier. He began to inspect the hinges of one iron door on which he had noted the faint scratches earlier in the afternoon. Sure enough, there were a few food scraps by the door. He immediately began to work on the lock in the door face. *Ah, this one will be more of a challenge,* he thought as it appeared that the original lock had been replaced with a more modern vintage, though it looked like the old locks in the rest of the ruin—black, iron and its surface uneven and ancient looking. *Clever bit of metal work. Made to look as old as the rest of the door locks.* The lock yielded, but just as it did, Braemhor heard the door to the stone staircase that led to the cistern room screech open.

Quickly he refastened the lock and moved to a corner on the same wall as the stairs, partially behind some large, jagged chunks of stone. Unfortunately the stone boulders were not enough to hide him completely, so placing his hands in his armpits and pulling his soft cap down over his face, he curled up into as small a ball as he could manage, hoping the blackness of his costume and of the room would protect him from discovery.

Looking through the mesh of his cap, Braemhor could barely make out the image of a person descending the stairs and then entering the room. The light of the individual's torch reflected minimally off the wet walls of the chamber. Braemhor, with difficulty, could make out that this person was very emaciated and small, and no more than five and a half feet tall. His unkempt shoulder-length hair looked like a hood over his face and head. He carried a torch in one hand and two metal plates in the other, which from the smell, Braemhor assumed to contain food. *I wonder if that is Sir John's brother, Ian*, Braemhor thought, hardly daring to breathe, much less move.

Fortunately, the individual did not cast the light of his torch about, but directed it to the lock on the door on which Braemhor had just been working. The intruder was muttering to himself, "I thought I told John to lock that door when he was done with the copper and his friends. He should never have brought them down here in the first place. He just doesn't think," the low, raspy voice grumbled.

At one point, just as he was about to open the iron door he suddenly turned and swept his torch light around the room. *Surprise will give me an advantage,* flashed through Braemhor's mind as he tensed, ready to leap from his hiding place and attack if necessary. But the glare of the torch's light passed above Braemhor and the stone that hid him. *That's a relief.*

Ian—at least that's who Braemhor thought he was— put down the two plates, opened the door and went through. His footfalls gradually diminished. Shortly, John thought he could hear the faint sound of several voices coming from the passage behind the door. *I think it's time for me to leave,* he thought. Then, *No, I'll wait and see what happens.* He raised himself up on his hands and knees and looked over the piece of stone that was hiding him. He was about to exit his hiding place and get closer to the passageway door, the better to hear the conversation beyond. But just as he did, he heard footsteps approaching from behind the door. Like a large black cat, he silently scurried back to his refuge and curled up once again behind the chunk of stone, pulling his cap over his face to create an entirely black image. Ian—if it was Ian—relocked the passage door, hurriedly strode across the room and up the stairs to the cistern chamber above. Braemhor waited until he heard the stairwell door being relocked, then crawled out of his hiding place.

Now what? he thought. *I'll give our food carrier another ten or fifteen minutes, then I think I'll try to find the sources of the other voices I heard.* He sat down on the stone he'd hidden behind and patiently waited until he was reasonably sure that Ian was not returning. He went back to work on the lock on the passageway door. Once it yielded, he carefully eased the door open just enough for him to squeeze through. Then he moved silently up the inclined passageway ahead, towards the voices in low conversation.

About another 100 yards farther, he came to another passage to the right. The voices stopped abruptly, and Braemhor froze in place. "Hello, Mr. Kenlaine," one of the voices called out.

"Sam? Carl?" Braemhor responded in a whisper. Both voices called, "Yes, yes, who are you?" The fear in the voices was palpable.

With that, Braemhor walked down this new passage and into the room to which it led. "I'm John, John Braemhor. I've come to get you two out of here, if we can manage it."

"Oh, thank God," the voice that was Sam Erlandson sighed.

"Who are you, sir?" was Carl Rhodes's relieved question.

"I'm a private investigator, here to help. Now let's see what your situation is." He flashed his torch about the room. It was small and damp but lacked the puddles of water on the floor in the large storage room. Against the back wall lay two tired, dirty looking individuals in kilts. Their pipes lay near the opposite wall. Neither had shaved for several days and grey stubble covered their faces. The circles surrounding their eyes gave them a certain ghoulish look, except for the big smiles that had broken out on their faces when they saw Braemhor. Both were chained to the wall by leg irons. "How did you get here?" he asked.

Both told the same story. They were playing *Johnnie MacDonald's Reel* on the hillock opposite the castle ruins when suddenly the ground beneath opened up and they fell five or six feet straight down into a stone passageway. Both had briefly lost consciousness, and by the time they awoke they found themselves chained in their prison room. Each had suffered mild concussions but they seemed to be in good health. Rhodes did have a badly sprained ankle from the fall. They assumed someone had dragged them down the inclined passage to the room where Braemhor found them. They were both cold and, John Braemhor surmised, probably suffering from hypothermia.

"How far away is the opening you fell in?" Braemhor was calculating which direction to try to get the two men out of their prison.

"Don't rightly know, but it could not have been too far, since that little guy must have dragged us here."

Unless he had help, John thought.

"I'd better see how far it is." John rose to explore the escape passage. "Wait here for me."

"Right, sir." Both pipers were very relieved by his presence and could now appreciate his dry wit.

Braemhor quickly moved down the passageway towards where he thought the trapdoor on the hillock across the A82 would be. Sure enough, only about 50 yards on, he found a small iron ladder ascending to an ancient wooden trapdoor above. *This won't be as hard as I thought,* ran through his mind as he returned to the room where the pipers were.

"Shouldn't be too bad," he said as he knelt down and began to pick the locks on their leg irons. In ten minutes they were both free. Erlandson stretched and stood up and would have fallen, had not Braemhor been there to steady him down again into a sitting position. "Whoa!" the dazed piper exclaimed.

"Better get up slowly and not try to do too much moving about. Easy does it. It'll take a bit to get your sea legs." Once Erlandson was standing up and seemed to be more stable, Braemhor asked, "Think you can walk to the trapdoor?"

"I think so, sir, but Carl here's going to have a harder go of it. His ankle's none too good."

Braemhor directed his torch to Rhodes's ankle. Sure enough, it was swollen and discolored with bruising. "Give me the tail of your shirt," he ordered. Rhodes fumbled with his shirt as Braemhor quickly took it and tore a long strip from it. "What?" he burst out as he saw Braemhor tear the shirt.

"We need to immobilize that ankle as much as we can," Braemhor explained, taking the strip of shirt tail and binding Rhodes's ankle as best he could.

"Now, Carl, think you can hop to the trapdoor, if I support your injured side?"

"Oh, yes, sir. I've been through worse in the big war. I'd hop a mile, if it will get me out of here."

"Okay then. Erlandson, you okay to walk now?"

"Yes, sir. But what about our pipes?"

"They can wait until tomorrow. First let's get the two of you out." Braemhor led them up the passage, supporting the injured Rhodes as he hopped along.

When Erlandson reached the trapdoor, his voice fell, "It's locked, sir. Oh, God, we're never going to get out."

"Brace yourself, man. Of course we are. Here, let Rhodes lean on you, and let me get to the lock. It can't be any more complicated that the ones I've already opened," Braemhor spoke commandingly as he squeezed forward, handing Rhodes to Erlandson as he did. He began work on the lock. He was right. It yielded quite readily, soon the trap was lowered, and the three men could see the star-studded night sky above them.

"Erlandson, up you go now." Braemhor took the rope he had brought from off his shoulder and handed one end to Erlandson. "Here, take this with you and get ready to lift your mate up to safety. I'll push from below. Rhodes, think you can hop up the ladder one rung at a time? Between the two of us we should be able to get up through the door."

Erlandson got into position outside on the hillock. Braemhor tied his end of the rope under Rhodes's arms and got him situated at the bottom of the ladder. "Now on the count of three, Erlandson, you pull. Rhodes, you hop, and I'll push. Ready? One. . .two. . .three, lift!" All three grunted, and Rhodes ascended the first rung. The next two rungs were the same. But on the fourth, Rhodes missed the rung and fell back with his full weight onto Braemhor's shoulder. But Braemhor held fast, and the three men recovered their positions and made ready for the next rung. Three more rungs and all three of the men were on the outside, puffing from the exertion but happy with the result.

"You should cut back on the pints, Rhodes," Braemhor looked at Rhodes and quipped as the three sat on the grassy knoll and caught their collective breaths.

"You know, sir, the whole time I was in there I kept thinking 'if I get out of here alive, I'm going to give up the suds. Me wife's been after me for years. Thanks to you, I think I will."

"Now you two rest while I get us some more help," Braemhor ordered and pulled out his mobile. His first call was to Mary.

"John, where have you been? I've been worried sick. I was just about to call Ferguson. It's half past two, you know?"

"Sorry, Mary. It took me a bit longer than I anticipated. Now, call Ferguson. Tell him to get here as soon as possible and to bring several officers with him."

"Where's here?"

"Oh, the hillock across from the castle. And tell him to bring an ambulance as well. No lights, no sirens. Tell them to come quietly."

"An ambulance! Oh, John, are you all right?"

"Yes, yes. I'm a little weary, but one of the pipers has a rather nasty ankle that needs attention. And both of them need a good clean up and some good food."

"I'll call right away," Mary said through a sigh of relief. Then she clicked off.

* * * * *

"There's a small copse of trees over there." Braemhor pointed. "Let's go over there while we wait. DI Ferguson from Fort Lochiel and some of his officers should be here shortly." He turned to Rhodes. "And I've summoned an ambulance so we can get your ankle properly cared for. In fact, it can take both of you to hospital for a checkup, some good food and a rest."

While they waited, Braemhor questioned them more about their ordeal. Both thought their captor was unstable. "He belongs in an asylum. Kept going on about how he was doing God's work and protecting CraigDhuin from the MacDonalds. I don't know what the MacDonalds had to do with it. It was like he had a personal gripe," Erlandson offered, to which Rhodes added, "It's like he thought we were personally there to do him harm."

Sounds rather paranoid to me, Braemhor thought as he listened. "Were there any other people involved, as far as you could tell?" he asked.

"Nooooo," was Rhodes hesitant reply, but then Erlandson pointed out, "One time, another one came in. Skinny with a little grey beard. Tried to calm the first one down. Told him, 'we don't want to hurt these fine men.' And then he said, 'yet.' I thought then that we were not going to get out alive. I was sure we were goners."

"Did he say anything else?"

"Only something about protecting the castle," Erlandson concluded.

"Interesting," John said, but he thought, *Sounds to me like the whole family needs psychiatric care.*

"Well, I'm glad we got you out of there when we did," Braemhor concluded as he saw Ferguson's green and whites approaching on the A82. "Stay here, I'll flag down our help." He rose and walked toward the road waving his arms.

"What have you got, Mr. Braemhor?" Ferguson stepped from his car.

"I've got your two missing pipers up there in that copse." He pointed. "Send your men to the moat bridge and have them stand by until you and I can get there. I think Sir John's brother is in the tower, and we need to catch him by surprise. Meanwhile, send the medics up the hill for our pipers. They can get them to hospital while we find Ian Kenlaine." Braemhor was like a general deploying his troops in preparation for a battle. His orders were crisp, clear, and authoritative. Ferguson marveled at his well-thought-out battle plan and the precise execution he expected. "I'll be there in a moment," Braemhor told him and turned up the hill once again.

In the copse, the ambulance personnel were loading the two pipers onto gurneys and preparing to take them down the hill. Braemhor smiled at them. "Now you two get some rest, and I'll stop to see you in a day or two."

"But what about our pipes, sir? They're still in the dungeon." Rhodes made this last plea as he was being loaded into the ambulance.

Braemhor smiled again. "Not to worry. I'll get them before the day is over and bring them to you in hospital."

"And, sir, thank you for all you've done," Erlandson spoke for both pipers.

Braemhor saluted them, quickly descended the hill and met Ferguson and his officers on the castle side of the moat bridge.

"What's the plan, Mr. Braemhor?" Ferguson had placed himself and his group completely in John's hands.

"I think we still have the element of surprise on our side. My guess, my hope, is that Ian Kenlaine is in his tower apartment unaware of our presence. Let's send two of your officers around the loch side of the tower— in case there's another entrance or exit I'm not aware of. Ferguson, you and I and. . . ." He looked at the sergeant who had not yet been assigned a task.

"Denton, sir, Sergeant Denton." The young man stepped forward.

"Yes, Denton. We three will make a frontal approach, but we must be quiet. We will have to ascend those defensive stairs from the cistern room to the living quarters. They're constructed to thwart any attacker, you know, so we'll have to depend on stealth to protect us until we gain the upper floors. Ready?" He looked around at his 'troops.' "Then, let's go."

Braemhor led the way through the entry, where he noted once more that the iron gates securing the room were firmly in place as were those in the chamber which held the cistern. He, Ferguson and Denton crossed the stone floor towards the circular staircase.

Braemhor held his finger to his lips as a last reminder of the need for silent movement. They paused momentarily at the bottom of the stairs.

Then, with a sudden rush, Braemhor charged up the stairs as fast as he could manage the circular pattern. Thoughts of silence and stealth were thrown to the winds. The main effort now was to gain the next level before anyone above became aware of their presence. As his head cleared the stairwell, he looked quickly and ducked just in time to avoid a large rock that had been hurled in his direction. Hoping his assailant did not have a second missile ready to launch, he scampered up the last two stairs and entered the room above in as best a crouch as he could manage, given the very cramped quarters. His assailant did have a second rock, but it was still in his left hand and apparently Ian—for that's who it was—was right-handed and could not launch the second rock with any accuracy. The second rock ricocheted off of the wall beside Braemhor's head and fell harmlessly to the floor.

Braemhor charged across the space from the stairwell to a door in the opposite wall, but he could not reach it before Ian had slammed it shut. Ferguson pounded on the door as he shouted, "Police! Open up!" But to no avail. He looked at Braemhor. "We'll have to break it down," the latter ordered. "Fortunately, it looks more modern than the rest of the tower.

It took more effort than any of the three had anticipated, but the door finally yielded to their combined effort. The room was the small living quarters Sir John had mistakenly exposed to John, Mary and Ron the day before. There was no one there.

"Ah, over here!" John shouted and pointed to another door off the kitchen alcove. They dashed through this second door into a short passage where Ian stood by an open doorway at the other end. This doorway had no door or frame but was only a rectangular opening in an outer wall of the tower.

Looking past Ian, John could see the expanse of Loch Ness below. At this point in the tower they were several hundred feet above the rocks and loch.

Ian stood poised to jump.

"Don't!!" John shouted.

But he did. And with that, the Kenlaine Tower chase was over.

* * * * *

Ferguson's two officers saw Ian Kenlaine fall to his death as they were rounding the loch side of the tower. By the time Braemhor, Ferguson and Sgt. Denton had exited the tower and come around to the Loch Ness side, Ferguson's men had moved him off the rocks where he'd landed, and called for another ambulance to take him to the police morgue in Fort Lochiel.

Ferguson looked at Braemhor and said, "Well, that about wraps it up." He looked relieved.

"Not quite," Braemhor replied. "I want you to call Inverness station and have them pick up Sir John Kenlaine. He's a part of this, you know."

"Way ahead of you." Ferguson beamed. "I called as we were coming down to retrieve Ian Kenlaine's body. They will probably have him in custody before dawn."

"Good." Braemhor admired Ferguson's quick thinking. *Mary's right, he will make a fine DCI someday,* he thought. "You know, both Erlandson and Rhodes identified him as being in the underground dungeon when Ian was bringing them their food."

"Then we shouldn't have much trouble making the case against him. I'll head to Inverness and make sure the local magistrate sets an appropriate bail so we can keep him under lock and key until we can draw up the proper charges and arrange for his eventual trial. Anything else I can do for you before I go?"

"Just one thing. I want to go back into the room where the pipers were held and retrieve their pipes. I promised them I'd bring their instruments to hospital before the day's out."

"Fine. Denton." Ferguson turned to his sergeant. "Go with Mr. Braemhor. And, John, I'll meet you back at the Hotel Nessie after I take care of the Sir John end of this case." With that, he walked to his green and white across the A82 from where they stood and drove off to Inverness.

"Come with me," Braemhor directed Denton as he went back inside to the cistern room where he'd started to pick the lock on the door to the staircase leading to the underground chamber. The sergeant was impressed with the quick work Braemhor made of the lock. Braemhor noted Denton's surprise at the rapidity with which the lock yielded to his work. "Just a matter of practice, Denton." He smiled. "It's a basic skill of the trade."

Inside the room where the men had been held captive, John quickly gathered together the two men's pipes and a few articles of their clothing which were still strewn about. Denton and he then took the items to the pipers in hospital. Then Denton took Braemhor back to the Hotel Nessie. Ferguson was already there, but when he saw John's exhausted appearance, he said, "Maybe I'll stop by and see you later. You look a bit wearied by your night's work."

"Right. It has been a long night. Let's plan on lunch tomorrow, shall we?"

John went immediately up to the room to see Mary, who was dressed and about to come to the restaurant for some breakfast. "Ready for something to eat, John?" was her cheery question.

"I am hungry, but first I think I'd like a long soak in a very hot tub. Can we eat after that?"

"Of course," Mary said as she went into the bath and began drawing a steaming hot bath.

Half an hour later, the two went downstairs and wrapped themselves around a typical Scottish breakfast of baked beans, fried tomatoes, eggs and bacon and the ubiquitous burnt toast. John detailed all of the night's adventures to Mary and calmed her concerns about his safety. "I was never in any degree of danger," he assured her.

"Nonetheless, I think you should take me along on more of these escapades. How will I ever learn to be a proper detective unless I'm in on the conclusions of some of your adventures?" she mockingly pouted.

John smiled. "But, Mary, you played a much more important role."

"How so?"

"You were my backup in case anything really did go wrong. Few people realize how important that is in investigative criminology." Mary smiled and patted his hand from across the table. "Now that I've had a hot soak and a good meal, I think a couple of hours of sleep are in order."

* * * * *

Later, just as John and Mary were sitting down to lunch, Ferguson walked in and sat at the table with them.

"All wrapped up?" Braemhor asked.

"I think so. You know, Mr. Braemhor, I think Sir John is as crazy as Ian. Once we started to interview him, he seemed to become unhinged. Started raving about how the MacDonalds were still trying to invade CraigDhuin. He thinks the pipers were just a part of a broader conspiracy to wrest the castle from his clan. Even though he's the curator, he acted as if he wasn't even aware that the castle is part of the National Heritage and is funded by Historic Scotland. To him, it's still his clan's castle to defend from all comers. And, by the way, he was the one making the threatening calls to the Rosses. He thinks castle tours are just an initial tactic in the battle for control of CraigDhuin.

"It got so bad at one point that he was saying that God himself had anointed him and Ian to protect the castle from usurpers. And you would not believe the things he had to say about me and my officers. To his mind, we murdered his brother and will have to pay for that crime with a life in eternal damnation."

"Sounds like he will need a thorough psychiatric evaluation," Braemhor observed.

"Already underway. The boys in Inverness spotted his instability right away and called in one of the region's psychiatrists to have a look at him. He's now being held in hospital for the criminally insane. My guess is that when this is all over, that's where he will spend the rest of his days," Ferguson concluded.

"What a shame," Mary added. "From my reading, the Kenlaine clan is an old, old clan with a fine reputation. Will they be able to keep any of this side of it out of the press?"

"Doubtful," John observed, "but the clans of Scotland are a resilient breed. All of them have had some dark history through the ages. I'm sure the Kenlaines will survive, as the rest have. But look at the hour." He looked at his watch. "Mary and I have to get back to Daraichburn before the day's out, and we still need to make a stop at Zauberin's shop and pick up a book for Mary's aunt."

The Braemhors bid Ferguson goodbye, put their valises into the Vauxhall's boot and drove to Zauberin's for a quick purchase before going back to Dunmoor Cottage.

Chapter 3

The easterly drive back to Daraichburn was as beautiful as the westerly drive from Daraichburn had been a few days earlier. The undulating foothills of the Grampian Mountains gently lowered the Braemhors to the placid serenity of Loch Lomond with its rippleless surface and slate-grey coloration. Though Americans who had stayed with the Braemhors thought the ambience of Lomond an achromatic dreariness, John and Mary thrived on the cloud-covered sameness of their native Scotland.

"Should we stop at the Thistle Cottage by the loch and see if Mrs. Buchanan is still serving up her famous Scottish cuisine?" John turned to Mary.

Mrs. Buchanan was, indeed, still serving her Scottish delights for the midday meal, and the brief stop was a welcome respite from the drive. The meal, as always, was outstanding, and Mrs. Buchanan's light conversation kept the Braemhors attentive and amused while they ate. They told her, in brief outline, of their adventure at CraigDhuin ruins, while she regaled them with stories of recent night sightings of UFOs over Loch Lomond.

"You should come and investigate the strange lights over the loch. I could reserve my best room for you," Mrs. Buchanan urged.

Before John could assert aloud his interest in yet another unexplained event on Scottish soil, Mary broke in, "That would be lovely, another time perhaps, but for now we need to get back to Dunmoor Cottage. We have two couples coming in tomorrow evening, and we're planning a holiday to the States to visit family."

"Yes," John responded to Mrs. Buchanan, "I have been following the appearance of your strange lights. I read that someone, a Mr. Hayson, I believe, has actually photographed them near the Firth of Tay."

"Oh, yes. It's all the gossip these days." Mrs. Buchanan beamed.

"Well, maybe another time. But Mary is right. We need to get back to Dariachburn for now."

"She's a lovely person," Mary offered as John eased the Vauxhall once again onto the A82.

"Yes, and an excellent cook, too."

It wasn't long before the Braemhors were skirting around Glasgow to the road to Melrose on which Daraichburn was situated. It was early evening when they drove into the small car park in front of Dunmoor Cottage.

While Mary got together a light supper for the two of them, John perused the evening paper. After dinner, Mary phoned her aunt, Rita, at Dunmoor Castle and inquired about her availability to come to Daraichburn to look after Dunmoor Cottage while she and John traveled to the States—"Colonies" John corrected from the sitting room—to visit their son and his family. She also informed her that she and John had gotten a new book on the fairies and another on the Loch Ness monster for her.

"Wonderful!" Rita gushed. "I'll be there on the late train tomorrow! Besides, I'm tired of trying to protect our pheasants from would-be hunters who wouldn't know a pheasant from a grouse. Why, do you know that the other day one American brought me a sparrow to see if it was a pheasant or a grouse!"

"What did you do, Aunt Rita?"

"I told him it was a squirrel, gave him his money back and led him off the estate. The idea! Some people should not be allowed to have a fowling piece, much less shoot one!"

Before Rita could become any more excited, Mary broke in, "John will meet your train in Melrose tomorrow. Plan to stay for a couple of weeks or so."

Mary then quickly called their son, James, and ascertained that the timing for their trip was all right, after which John arranged the flights.

And so it was settled. Day after tomorrow, the Braemhors would fly to America for a holiday with the family. The next day, John drove to Melrose to meet Rita's train from Blanefield.

"Good trip?" John asked as Rita alighted from the train, large valise in hand. Rita Erskine, Mary's maiden aunt, her puckish appearance with her white hair pulled back in a taut bun, wore her omnipresent impish smile which only confirmed her reputation as the eccentric of the family. The only difference between Aunt Rita and the American icon of the "crazy aunt in the attic" was that Rita lived in her own small cottage on the Dunmoor Estate, seat of Mary's family which had lived in Dunmoor Castle since the early days of King Robert Bruce. In fact, the original castle had been a gift of the Bruce family to Mary's ancestors in the 14th century. The original old keep was still maintained as a venue for family festivals and recreation, though a 19th century building now served as the family's living quarters beside the small chapel where family members had sealed their nuptials for centuries.

"It was just delightful." Rita beamed, as she handed her case to John to carry to the car. "You know, you meet the most fascinating people on trains."

"Oh?" John absentmindedly queried.

"Yes, there was this woman in the club car who said that she had actually seen the Loch Ness monster and fed her some biscuits when no one was looking!"

"Really, Rita, Nessie is a mythical creature. She. . .eh, *it* doesn't exist." John found having a sensible conversation with Rita at times very trying.

"Of course she does! The woman even showed me her hand with two fingers missing, because Nessie bit them off with the biscuit. She had them in an icepack, taking them to Glasgow to have them reattached." Rita was incredulous that John did not share the truth of her tale.

"Of course, Rita, and I bet she asked you for some money to help pay for the surgery," John scoffed.

"How did you know, John? Did you meet her, too? Oh, she seemed such a nice lady, but I didn't give any money. Unlike the Americans, we all have National Health!" she proudly stated and then, "I do hope her surgery went well."

"Me too, Rita." As John let the conversation lapse into silence.

Mary greeted the two at the Dunmoor Cottage door with a broad smile and a hug for her aunt, but she read the look on John's face and wondered what had transpired on the trip from Melrose.

"Rita's had another adventure," John whispered.

"Only one? Tell me later," Mary quickly whispered back as Rita took her luggage to her room.

At supper, Rita filled the conversation with bizarre tales of her train ride from Blanefield, which John referred to as her "club car adventures." Besides the woman who had the encounter with Nessie, she also met a wizened old gentleman who claimed he was the uncle of Charlemagne and had guided him in learning to write.

"But I knew that wasn't true, "Aunt Rita proudly announced.

"Because he would have had to be centuries old?" John egged her on.

"Oh, no, John, he looked like he could have been old enough, but I knew he really didn't know Charlemagne because I knew Charlemagne never mastered writing. Imagine! He even wanted me to stop at Glascow to see his collection of photographs of Charlemagne as a small boy! The idea!"

"Well, I'm glad you didn't take up his invitation," Mary interceded as she could sense John about to burst into laughter.

Next morning, John and Mary caught their flights to America, but not before Mary was pulled out of line at the gate and gone over from head to foot with a wand. A detailed search of her purse found a metal fingernail file which the security personnel promptly confiscated.

While this was going on, John not so silently fumed at what he considered to be an absurd exercise and a bureaucratic waste of time. The security guard did not agree and threatened to wand him also if he did not stand back and stop grousing. Then she said, "Please take your shoes off, sir."

"Why?" John rejoined.

"Because an apprehended bomber on an American flight had bomb material in his shoe," was her reply.

"I'm glad he didn't have it in his underwear," John retorted with as straight a face as he could muster.

Finally onboard, Mary, with a faint smile, allowed that: "it was probably because of my grey hair. And that was my favorite nail file, too. I just forgot I had it in my bag."

"Probably was your grey hair. Remember, I always got stopped at the gates when I wore a beard?"

"And then you shaved it off, and they never bothered you again."

"Right. At least I didn't have to take off my underwear this time," John muttered.

"John! What are you talking about?"

"Oh, nothing. It's just a comment on our security system. Same sort of thing." John buckled his seat belt and patted Mary on the hand.

The flight to New Boston passed quickly, with John sleeping for most of the flight and Mary reading Lucretius's *On the Nature of Things*.

Their son, James, met them at the gate. "Good trip?" he asked as he hugged his mother and took the firm grip of his father's hand. Beside James was a very tall, willowy young man.

"Daniel, is that really you?" Mary was shocked, for the boy stood at least six feet, two inches, and was but 14 years of age.

"Yes, Granny, it really is me." The voice was deep, full and firm.

"They certainly grow fast, don't they?" John said to James as he grasped the boy's equally firm grip.

The drive from the New Boston airport to Hiramville where James and Jennifer and the two Braemhor grandchildren lived in an immense, three-story East Lake Victorian, was a pleasant trip as James filled his parents in on the goings-on in the American branch of the Braemhor family. Both grandchildren—11-year-old

Donna, like her brother, was showing signs of eventually being quite tall—were doing well at school and enjoying participating in the area symphony orchestra.

"And what do you think you will like to do when you, eh. . .stop growing?" John asked the younger Braemhor. He hesitated to use the words *grow up.*

"He wants to be an engineer," James broke in, "but it's a little soon to be making a hard and fast decision." James smiled at his son.

"Quite right," Mary agreed, "there is a whole world out there to explore first." The conversation then drifted to the beauty of the American countryside and the sun-filled day that warmed their way to Hiramville, where Jennifer and daughter Donna met the somewhat fatigued travelers on the front porch of their enormous home.

Jennifer already had a sumptuous meal of baked ham and beans on the stove, which restored everyone's energy levels for continued conversation and word games—a favorite of the Braemhor households—until John raised the question he had patiently waited to ask. "What is this about a haunted house?"

"It's right across the street. Here, you can see it from our front window." James rose and led the family into the front parlor, where he pointed at one of the houses across the street from the Braemhor home.

"It looks like a lovely place," Mary observed. "Looks well-kept and freshly painted." The house was three stories, light grey with salmon trim. It was located on a large lot with the driveway going down the left side of the house to a double garage at the rear of the property.

"Nothing very remarkable," James said.

"Except, perhaps, the horseshoe above the double garage doors. It's upside down," John observed.

"How so?" James asked.

"Usually horseshoes are put on buildings—houses, garages, stables—with the opening *up* to retain their good luck essence, so it will not spill out and leave the building unprotected. That one is upside down. The shoe's opening is downward, allowing all of its inherent 'luck' to spill out onto the ground. A true believer in the luck of horseshoes would have known that," John explained.

"Where do you learn these things, John?" Mary, ever impressed with her husband's fund of knowledge, asked.

"I read something about this recently." John smiled. "The protective element of the horseshoe started in the 10th century with a story about Saint Dunstan who supposedly shoed the Devil and extracted a promise from him to avoid houses protected by a horseshoe, nailed, open end up, to the structure."

"Really, John, that's just superstition."

"Of course it is. But you'd be surprised how many people build their life's habits around just such beliefs. In many ways we still live in the 10th century, or worse, regarding beliefs and how they dictate our behavior. But James's neighbors have their superstitions upside down."

"So whoever put the horseshoe up in the first place is in cahoots with the Devil to leave the house unprotected and a safe haven for Satanic invasion," James offered with a slight mischievous smile.

"No wonder the prospective renters think the structure is haunted. It's haunted by the Devil who has free run of the place as long as the horseshoe is upside down," Jennifer added. "All we have to do is to get them to turn the shoe right side up, and the case of the haunted house will be solved."

"Whoa! To use a horsey term." This was grandson Daniel offering his own witty take on the conversation.

"Yes. We need to know why they think the house is haunted, don't we?" Donna asked, completing the inclusion of all the Braemhors in the humorous conversation.

"Quite right, Donna. We don't know yet what makes people think that the house is haunted in the first place." John praised her, pleased at his granddaughter's acumen. *She'll make an astute detective one day*, he thought.

"Oh, I already know that," James answered.

"Oh?" Mary was curious.

"Yes, they hear things in the wall, mainly at night."

"Things? Like what?" John asked.

"Like a small typewriter clacking away."

"Typewriter, in the wall? Really!" Donna was incredulous.

"Yes, it goes clickity, clack, clickity, clack, then it suddenly stops for a short time. Sometimes there is a small thud, followed by a high-pitched screeching, like nails on a chalkboard. Then sometimes there is more typewriting only lower in the wall than at the first."

"That's the same thing Bernie Allen told me," Daniel said. "He said it was really scary, and his sister cried herself to sleep the nights it happened. That was just before the family moved out and tried to rent the house."

"Maybe it is the Devil," James announced laughingly.

"And maybe it's something much more prosaic. We should discuss this more over dessert, don't you think?"

John wanted to bring the conversation back to earth again.

"Good idea. Donna get out the ice cream bars and bring them to the table." Jennifer told her daughter.

For the next hour or so the entire family sat around the large dining room table and speculated on what could cause the strange sounds in the wall, that were preventing the owners from keeping their house let. Finally, Mary signaled to John that it was time for them to retire, and they climbed to the third floor rooms they occupied when visiting.

Before going off to sleep, Mary asked, "Well, John, what do you think?"

"I think, first, that we have a very intelligent and very inquisitive family, and second, we need to talk with the owners of the house tomorrow, if possible."

Mary agreed as she doused the reading light above the headboard.

* * * * *

Next morning, after a filling breakfast of cereal, yogurt and toast, James put in a call to their friends, the Allens, the owners of the "haunted" house and told them of John and Mary's visit and their interest in the sounds that frightened renters.

"They said to come right over. They are just doing some minor indoor repairs, and they would be happy to tell you about the strange goings on," James said as he held his hand over the receiver.

"Tell them we'll be right over," John requested as he went upstairs to get a wrap for himself and Mary.

The Allens greeted John and Mary on the front porch. Both were small, very slender individuals, and except for some worry lines near their eyes and between their eyebrows, seemed to be in good spirits despite their present difficulties. Both sported full heads of blond hair surrounding sunburned faces. Only the white hair of the husband's well-trimmed goatee and at his temples gave away their probable ages—early fifties or so.

The Allens—Richard and Patricia—had moved to Hiramville about six months ago and were very happy with their second home across from the young Braemhors. They had planned to use the house as an income property, but the strange noises began and drove several renters to break their lease, declaring that the house was haunted.

"We had no idea there was a problem," Richard told the Braemhors, "until our first renters, a young couple fresh out of college, said they could not, or would not, stay in the house. It was frightening, they said. They complained of noises like a rapidly worked typewriter in the walls and a high-pitched screeching sound."

"We didn't really believe their conclusion that the house was haunted, but we knew they were unhappy. So we let them out of their lease and rented to another older couple," Patricia added. "All went well for about a week. Then they, too, complained of noises in the walls at night. The woman was the daughter of a well-known mystic who has a fortune-telling shop out on the coast. She was absolutely convinced that the noises were emanating from the unsettled spirits of the previous owners!"

"Yes, both of the previous owners, a man and his wife, died in the house under strange circumstances. We didn't know about it until we looked into the history of the property. Then we discovered that both of the deaths were unattended and are still listed in the official records as unsolved," Richard said.

"But wasn't that information supposed to be disclosed to you when you purchased the property?" John was incredulous.

"Yes! But the previous owners died just after the sale was completed, but before they were to move out. We had a house and no recourse. That's when we decided to rent it to make it pay for itself," Richard explained.

"You see, we came here from the West Coast where it's common knowledge that you must inform a buyer if someone has died in a house before you can complete the sale. We just assumed we would have been told and never thought to ask about it in advance. But apparently, here in the East, the laws are very variable. In some places such information must be passed on before a sale, in others there's no such requirement.

"So we decided to see for ourselves what these reports of strange noises were all about, and Richard stayed one night in the house by himself."

"Why by himself?" Mary asked.

"I had to be away at a professional meeting, and we decided that it would be more efficient if Richard could find out what the problem was while I was away."

"And what did you find?" John directed his question at Richard.

"It was the most frightening experience I've ever had. Everything was deathly quiet. I had settled myself in the parlor with some reading."

"What?" John broke in.

"What?" Richard was thrown off by the abruptness of John's query.

"Yes, what had you chosen to read?"

"Oh, yes. Well, you see, Mr. Braemhor I'm a great fan of H. P. Lovecraft and am working my way through his complete and unabridged fiction. . . . .Well, I was in the middle of reading *The Horror from the Shadows* from *Herbert West Reanimator* when I heard it in the wall. It was like a very rapid typing on an old mechanical typewriter. It seemed to move back and forth along the wall, and then it suddenly stopped and there was silence again. I was just about to attribute the noise to the wind outside when there was a smallish thud followed by the most blood-curdling scream I have ever heard. And then the typing—I don't know what else to call it—began again. I have never been so shaken in my life. I gathered my book and literally ran from the house. I didn't know where I was going, but I was sure that I could not stay in here any longer. I ended up in the all-night coffee shop in town."

"And you see what it's done to him." Patricia pointed at her husband.

Both Mary and John cocked their heads in quizzical angles.

"His hair! For God's sake, his hair! And his beard! There was not even any grey in them when I left. They were both honey blond, but look at them now." Patricia was near hysteria as she recalled that fateful 24 hours.

"Did you notice anything else that night?" John was trying to get as much information as he could before the two Allens descended again into the horror.

"Strange that you should ask." Richard had recovered himself somewhat. "Yes, the clocks. Here let me show you." He led them into the front parlor of the home where two Seth Thomas pendulum clocks clicked away the minutes on the wall over one of the two sofas.

"Look!" He pointed at the clocks. The pendulums of both clocks swayed back and forth in near perfect synchrony. "They've never done that before. They've always moved out-of-sync. When one is going right, the other is going left. Now they go left-right together. Why?" His voice had reached a high-pitched hysteria.

"Ordinarily, the pendulums of two clocks on the same wall swing in the same direction for about 30 minutes, then begin to swing in opposite directions, out of phase. Apparently, it's due to tiny sound waves, created by the two pendulums, traveling through the beams of the wall," John explained.

"But my clocks aren't doing that!"

"That's true, but I'm sure there's a perfectly good reason to explain why your clocks changed their behavior. I'm not exactly sure what it is right now, but I am certain it can all be explained quite logically and naturally. There is nothing supernatural about it," Braemhor pronounced forcefully. "Where are you staying now? I'm sure you and Patricia are not spending nights in the house."

"Certainly not!" Patricia answered. "We have a small apartment in the next village. We leave here before dusk and don't return until after daylight. We just don't know exactly what to do. We can't rent the house or sell it—word has gotten around—and we can't stay in it, Mr. Braemhor." She seemed to have regained some of her composure by this time. "Can you help us? Your son, James, says that you are a private investigator and sometimes help people. Can you help us?" This last request was more of a plea than a question.

"I don't know if we"—John looked at Mary—"can help or not, but perhaps we could look into your problem further. Could we have a key to the house? We might want to stay here a night or two to see for ourselves what has frightened so many people."

"I wouldn't advise that." Richard shuddered.

"Well, you'll just have to trust our instincts as to how best to tackle the problem. A key?" John held out his hand, into which Richard put the key. "In the meantime, I suggest you and Patricia stay in your apartment and try to get your lives together until Mary and I can come up with some logical explanations for what has gone on the past few weeks. You have a phone number where you can be reached if we need to?"

"Of course." Richard wrote the number on a nearby pad and handed it to John. "And, Mr. Braemhor, we really appreciate your willingness to help us." He rose and the Braemhors took their leave and went back to their son's house across the street.

* * * * *

It was noon when John and Mary got back to James's house.

"In the meantime, something to eat?" Mary queried as she surveyed the contents of the refrigerator.

"Good idea; I think my brain needs some extra energy." John set the table in the dining room, as Mary brought in an assortment of cheeses, wursts and breads from the kitchen.

"Maybe some hot tea will warm up the neurons," she added and put the kettle on.

Once settled at the table, Mary looked at John. "Didn't you think it odd that Mr. Allen was reading horror stories while trying to understand what the strange noises in the house were?"

"Maybe he has a masochistic streak." John smiled.

"What did you mean when you told Richard that there was a logical and natural reason for the Allen's clocks' behavior?" Mary asked.

"There is something in the wall that is disrupting the natural movement of the pendulums. I have an idea what it might be, but let's wait until we find the ghosts in the wall."

"You think it's ghosts in the wall?" Mary smiled.

"Something like that." John was non-committal.

"And were you really serious about staying a night or two in the house?"

"Can you think of a better way to find out what's really going on in the 'haunted' house?" John asked as he attacked his sandwich of lettuce, asiago cheese and liverwurst.

Mary thought for a moment. "I think it would help to know more about the deaths of the previous owners. Maybe their ghosts are still rattling around in the walls. Perhaps a chat with the local constabulary might be in order." Despite the sound logic of her and John's approach to stories of ghost-infested houses, she still did not relish a night in the house across the street.

"Good thinking. Let's go to the local station this afternoon and see if they can enlighten us." Thus the afternoon's activity was decided, and after cleaning up from dinner, the two walked the few blocks to the local police station in the center of town.

"How precious," Mary remarked as they approached the small red brick structure with a green convex tile roof.

"It just fits the décor of the surrounding village," John agreed.

Inside, a laminated counter separated them from the police sergeant talking on the phone. "Be with you in a minute," she said, raising her hand in recognition.

On the wall beside the front door was a large bulletin board covered with wanted notices and missing children reports. Mary was particularly struck by the young age of some of the missing children. She was about to say something to John about it when the sergeant hung up and asked, "May I help you?" The voice was deep for a woman's and very businesslike.

John told her that they were visiting family in Hiramville and had been asked by the Allens if they could help them solve the problem they were having with their house.

"The Allens? Oh, yes, the haunted house on Landon." She smiled. "How come you're so interested in it?"

John went on to explain that he was a private investigator and how his son, James, had arranged for them to talk with the Allens about their problem. He wondered if she might answer a few questions about the house and the previous owners.

"Well, private investigator or not, you're obviously not American with that accent. What makes you think I should give you any information at all?" The sergeant became quite testy at this point.

John maintained a cool-headed approach. "Of course, you are quite right. I'm not an American, Scottish actually, but I have on occasion worked with American police agencies."

"Can you prove it?" Skepticism dripped from every word.

"Will this help?" John took two cards out of his wallet: the FBI identification Charlie MacLaine had provided him a few years back when they'd worked together on the case of smuggled Chinese workers in New Boston, and the ID provided by Peter Killmart, the young inspector Braemhor had assisted in the case of the gruesome murders near Hadrian's Wall a year or so prior to his FBI work.

The sergeant perused the IDs carefully, looking first at Braemhor then at the IDs and then back again. "Well, I don't know. . . ." Her skepticism remained.

At that moment, a door behind the sergeant opened and a large, rotund officer, squeezed into a Captain's uniform, strode up to the counter. "What do you have, Sergeant?"

"This guy claims to be a gumshoe from Scotland," she nodded toward John, "asking questions 'bout the Allen house." John winced at the term *gumshoe* but held his tongue. Mary almost laughed at the expression. "Here's what he gave me for an ID." She handed Braemhor's IDs to the captain.

"Hmmm," the captain muttered as he stroked both of his chins and imitated his sergeant by looking back and forth between John and his IDs. "Why don't you come on back here. . " he said as he looked again at John's cards. "Ah, Mr. Braemhor?" He pointed to the office behind him. Looking at Mary, he continued, "and you are?"

John quickly broke in, "This is my wife, Mary. She often assists me with my work. And you are?" He looked directly at the round man before him.

The captain was briefly taken back by the directness of John's query. "Ah, Bramble. . .Bart Bramble. Come into my office, Mr. . .Mrs. Braemhor."

Once in Bramble's office, John gave the captain the same information that he'd given the sergeant about who he and Mary were and how they came to be interested in the problems with the Allen house.

Just as John thought things were beginning to smooth out, Bramble became very formal and asked, "Who do you represent, Braemhor? What's your angle?"

Mary quickly and surreptitiously put her hand on John's arm to keep him from telling Captain Bramble what he thought of his bureaucratic pomposity.

John once again held his tongue. "I don't represent anyone, and I do not have an angle. As I told you, I. . .we. . .are merely trying to help the Allens understand what has been going on in their house."

Sensing the frustration and anger in John's voice, Bramble lightened up somewhat. "I'm sorry, Mr. Braemhor, but these are private matters, and we cannot be giving out information to every willy-nilly that walks through the front door. I don't know how it is in Scotland, but we respect people's privacy here in the United States."

"Perhaps we can start over," John said calmly, ignoring the hostility in Bramble's voice. "I fully understand that there are private matters to consider. We deal with the same matters in Scotland. And we also share information among agencies when we can. So what *can* you tell us about the Allen house and in particular the deaths of the previous owners? Or can you tell us anything?"

Though Bramble seemed to step back from his overly officious demeanor for a moment, the mention of the previous owners of the Allen house quickly re-established Bramble's officiousness. "We, too, like to cooperate with other *legitimate* agencies or individuals. But you have to understand we have to protect ourselves from lawsuits. Officially, I can tell you nothing unless you have been properly vetted and that may take up to three months and many thousands of dollars. I'm sorry, but this is not Scotland, Mr. Braemhor."

Through his frustration, Braemhor tried one more ploy. "Can you tell me anything unofficially?"

"No! I suggest you try the local library. The newspapers covered the deaths of the previous owners extensively. And they've had several stories on the haunted house. Now, if you don't mind I have *important* work to do." He rose to indicate that the interview was at an end.

"My IDs, if you don't mind." Braemhor extended his hand.

"Oh, of course. You see, how do I know that they're not fake IDs?" He got in one last jab.

"You don't, of course. And now you never will." John could not restrain a response.

On the way back to James's house, Mary said, "Well, that was not very helpful."

"On the contrary." John smiled. "I think the good captain is embarrassed. He has a major unsolved case on his hands and is trying to bury it from further public scrutiny, if he can. I think if the head of Interpol walked in, he would get the same run around. This is a petty bureaucrat who's trying to burnish his captain's bars."

"Or it could be worse than that, John."

John raised his eyebrows slightly.

"Really, what if Captain Bramble was involved in the deaths of the—we don't even know their names—two previous owners of the haunted house?"

"He is. He's investigating it."

"No, I mean really involved—say before the investigation."

"You mean as in 'murderer'?"

Now Mary raised her eyebrows.

"And you sometimes accuse me of leaping forward on little or no data!" John chided.

"Just a feeling. There's something about him—I can't really put my finger on it—I really took a dislike to the man and not because of his brusqueness with us. I don't know, but you are probably right, I'm leaping too far. So what do we do next?"

"Let's fill in the gap you just mentioned—the names of the deceased home owners. I'll call the Allens when we get back to the house."

A quick call to the Allens solved one mystery. The names of the previous owners of the Allen's house were Joseph and Helga Smith. "Now to the library," John announced.

The afternoon at Hiramville Public Library—a brick structure with several reading rooms and two floors of collections—was marginally successful. In the main reading room, John and Mary found the newspaper accounts of the sudden and unexplained deaths of the Smiths. Both had been strangled in the afternoon and left in the front parlor. The postman discovered the bodies when he attempted to deliver a package and looked into the front window. The local police chief—Bramble—was the first on the scene, followed by the local fire company with their ambulance. There was no sign of forced entry. Neighbors became aware of something amiss when they noticed the police vehicle in the driveway. They were very distressed by the occasion of violence so close to their own homes.

The Smiths had moved to Hiramville several years ago from New York City. They were Holocaust survivors. He was a retired silversmith and she a homemaker, according to the story. What their income was was unknown to the neighbors although Mr. Smith did sell occasional silver jewelry at the local Saturday morning market. The neighbors found them quiet and unassuming, pleasant but decidedly standoffish. They did not participate in any of the local churches or organizations. Just, the neighbors thought, an elderly couple living out their last years in the quiet of the small town of Hiramville. Their deaths, which occurred about a year ago, just after the Allens had bought the property, were to this day unsolved.

"Not much here," John remarked as he rose to leave the library. "I wonder if any of the neighbors can be of help."

"Let's go see," Mary suggested.

On the porch of the house next to the Allens's, were two pleasant-looking women in their mid-sixties, their rockers providing them with perpetual motion. Mary spoke first, "Hello, we're the Braemhors, James' parents." She pointed across the street to the Braemhor's Victorian.

"Oh, we know James and Jennifer well," Marmy, the younger of the two, answered, "lovely couple and two very lovely children. You must be the proud grandparents from Scotland. Are you enjoying your stay?"

"Very much," John responded, then after a brief pause, "We wondered if we could talk to you about the Allens' house next door."

"The haunted house?" the older woman, who'd been dozing when John and Mary came up the stairs to the porch, asked. "That house is a black mark on the neighborhood, it is. What with ghosts in the walls and that horrible thing that happened to the Smiths." The older woman was a bit more disheveled than the first to greet John and Mary, her white uncombed hair in a tangle around her cherubic face. With that, she launched into a tirade about strange neighbors and ghosts and how the whole affair was frightening her to distraction.

The younger woman broke in, "You'll have to forgive Maud. She's not quite right in her head." She circled her finger around her ear with a knowing look on her face. "Alzheimer's, you know."

"Oh, I'm so sorry." Mary was solicitous.

"Oh, it's all right. It's just that she gets wound up sometimes, and it's hard for her to keep her thoughts ordered. She'll calm down in a moment, and she won't have any memory of the conversation. Now about the Allens. They seem lovely people. Such a shame that ghosts have invaded their house."

"Actually, it was the Smiths who interest us more," John broke in.

"Oh, the Smiths. Very quiet. Hardly knew they were there. Once Mrs. Smith did borrow a cup of sugar in her thick German accent. She was making strudel and ran out, but otherwise we hardly saw them. We did see him in the park on Saturdays selling his silver jewelry, beautiful creations, but otherwise we had no contact with them except an occasional wave as we passed their house."

"They were Holocaust survivors, you know," Maud interrupted. "I saw their tattoos. Right here!" She pointed at her inner forearm.

"Yes, Maud, of course you did." Marmy tired to quiet the older woman. "They were quite old, older than we are." Marmy smiled. "Then one afternoon Chief Bramble showed up in his police car, and he and the postman went in to see what was the matter."

"The police car had been there in the morning, too." Maud suddenly became alert and added to the conversation.

"In the morning before the postman came?" John was curious.

"Oh, you can't pay attention to Maud. She has these little daydreams. Makes up stories, you know." She turned to Maud. "You're just confused, dear. Chief Bramble came after the postman used our phone to call him."

"No! No, I saw him. I was sitting right here on the porch, and I saw him that morning!" Maud was becoming a little agitated. "I did! I did!"

"Of course you did, dear." The younger woman consoled Maud, patting her arm.

"Oh, I guess so." Maud complied.

Marmy turned to John and Mary. "You see how she is."

"It must be hard for you." Mary sympathized with Marmy.

"It's not too bad. I take her to a Memory Center three times a week for a day's outing. Gives me a break and her a change of scenery." After a pause, "I'm sorry we haven't been much help to you."

"No, you've been a wonderful help. But we've taken enough of your time and we'd best get back to James's house to greet the children when they get home from school," John said.

"Yes, perhaps we can stop and talk with you another time," Mary added.

"Oh, we'd like that very much." Maud had seemed to come back into the present by this time.

Back across the street, John and Mary took stock.

"Not much there," John admitted.

"No, and I'm not surprised what with Maud's Alzheimer's. Well, what next?"

"I think we spend tonight in the Allen's house with the ghosts."

Over the objections of James and Jennifer, John and Mary prepared for the evening's escapade. They put together a small package of sodas and biscuits, a couple of torches, and some reading material.

"You'd better take these, too." Donna, their granddaughter, sheepishly offered two small crucifixes, "in case there really are ghosts." Neither Donna, nor the whole family was particularly religious, but Donna had read enough ghost and vampire stories to know what the proper paraphernalia were for ghost chasers.

"Better take some of this, too." Daniel offered a small vial of white powder.

"Garlic?" John smiled as he took the items the children had given him.

"Yes, sprinkle it around your throats."

"That should scare off real people as well as vampires." Mary laughed. "But what about the werewolves?"

"Sorry, we don't have any firearms, much less silver bullets," James added to the light leave taking.

The Braemhors went across the street to meet their new adventure.

* * * * *

"I do hope the family is not too concerned," Mary said as she and John chose two reclining chairs in the front parlor in which to await the evening's events.

"They shouldn't be. I really don't think we will confront ghosts. There has got to be a perfectly logical, natural explanation for what's going on in the walls." John was never one to give much credence to tales of the supernatural. "You know, Mary, I never cease to be amazed at the number of people who live their lives ruled by fears of or hopes in the supernatural. They would be much happier if they would just see the world for what it is and not cloud their intelligence with fantasy. What did you bring to read for the night?"

"I brought a copy of Wilkie Collins's *The Moonstone.*" Mary smiled.

"Very appropriate," John said as he opened his copy of *The Sign of the Four.*

Suddenly there was a bright flash of light that lit up the entire house, followed by a clap of thunder that seemed to come from the very roof itself. The old house trembled.

"Looks like we're in for quite a thunderstorm," Mary noted as a second flash-boom struck the house. It was as if a zipper had been opened in the clouds, and torrents of rain pelted the roof.

"How appropriate for ghost chasing," John said as a third flash-boom struck. I do hope it does not interfere with our hearing the noises in the walls if, in fact, there are any."

But the crashing lightening/thunder did not subside until after one. Then the storm settled down to a steady but very heavy rainfall. Each window looked like a Niagara; the Braemhors could not make out the streetlight in front of the house. And worst of all, the power failed, and the inside of the house became as dark as the storm-ravaged outside.

"Oh, fine," John muttered, "that ends our reading for now."

"We have the torches," Mary suggested.

"I think we'd best save them in case we really need light later. Besides the darkness will let our eyes accommodate better."

Just then it started. A low volume, but high-frequency tick-tack, tick-tack up near the ceiling of the parlor. It continued, tick-tack, tick-tack, moving from the corner where it started toward the center of the wall. Then, just as suddenly, it stopped. Thud. And the most bloodcurdling scream, high-pitched and agonizing, arose from the base of the wall.

Electric shock waves coursed up both John's and Mary's spines and radiated up and over the backs of their skulls. Fright—no!—terror temporarily overwhelmed the two ghost chasers.

"Oh, my God! What is it, John?" Mary's voice trembled, almost hysterically.

"Steady, Mary! Steady! It's real, it's not supernatural!" John almost shouted to hang onto his own composure, though the tremulousness in his own voice denied the calm he was trying to project to Mary. They sat frozen in place not knowing whether to stay put or, as both later admitted thinking, bolt for the door and safety across the street.

Just as suddenly as it had begun the screaming stopped, and the tick-tack, tick-tack began again, but this time at the base of the wall, near where the "thud" had occurred. The sound ran back towards the corner where it had all begun. And then the quiet, the all-enveloping quiet, save for the hard patter of the rain on the roof.

The Braemhors had by then regained their respective composures, but still they sat on anticipatory pins and needles awaiting another onslaught of the sounds that had just encompassed the wall. They sat quietly—waiting, and thinking. Mary looked down at her sweat-covered hands and for the first time realized she had taken a death-like grip on the crucifix Donna had given her.

"I must really have been frightened," she said after she told John of her discovery.

"We both were." He smiled as he raised and waved his crucifix towards her. They both broke out laughing—slightly hysterical sounds attesting to the emotions that had overwhelmed them a few moments ago.

John, now in full command of himself, offered an intellectual comment on what had just transpired. "Isn't it interesting that we two, who profess to face the world with non-emotional logic, descend into an uncontrolled emotional state when suddenly confronted with things for which we do not have a ready, logical explanation. It's the animal in us, built-in to instantly save us from life-threatening events we have not confronted before."

"It's not just instinctual," Mary said. "It's also part of our early upbringing when adults instilled in us the cultural myths and unseen terrors carried in folklore. It is so hard to break with the past."

"That is partially why humans keep making the same mistakes over, and over, and over. But maybe we should assess where we are in this adventure, all right?"

"That's my John. Always the logical, sensible approach."

"Except when he's frightened half out of his wits," John concurred with a broad, relaxing smile. "On reflection though I think I know what we have just encountered." And he told Mary his thoughts on what had just transpired in the wall. No ghost but something very logical. "It was the suddenness of what happened that triggered our animal responses," he concluded.

"I think you're right. Maybe we should go back to James's and get a good rest of the night's sleep. I think we have enough data. We can talk with the Allens again tomorrow," Mary said as she used her torch to gather together her things.

"Good thinking. We both need to unwind after this," John agreed as he led the way out the front door and across the street to James's house.

* * * * *

At breakfast the next morning James observed, "You two were in early last night. Did the ghosts chase you home?"

"No, we just thought we had enough data to solve the puzzle of the ghosts in the wall."

"What did they look like, Granddaddy? Were they white and misty like a cloud? Could you put your hand through them?" That was Donna.

"Of course not," her brother, Daniel, scoffed, "they took one look at Granddaddy and Granny and ran away so frightened that they agreed never to return."

"Were they scary, Granddaddy?" Donna again.

"Yes and no. Mainly they startled us, and that frightened us momentarily. But as I explained, we are pretty sure the noises in the wall were not made by ghosts or any other supernatural beings. Just something in nature that we weren't prepared for. But for now I need to call the Allens so we can set their minds at ease." John went to the telephone in the kitchen.

"The Allens will meet us across the street at ten," John said as he returned to finish his breakfast.

Promptly at ten the Allens pulled their car into the driveway and hurried up the porch stairs to greet the Braemhors who were sitting on the porch swing awaiting the anxious couple.

"Mr. Braemhor, Mrs. Braemhor, what have you found?" Richard Allen came right to the point.

"I think we have solved the problem of the ghosts in the wall." John rose to take Richard's offered, anxiety-moistened hand.

Both Allens visibly relaxed at his words. Patricia Allen even managed a smile and promptly dropped into one of the porch rockers. "That is a relief. We were so worried about the two of you last night. What is it?"

John started to explain, almost pedantically, Mary thought. "A number of years ago Mary and I lived in a rented cottage in Melrose, and one night we were awakened by the scurrying of little feet in the walls and much high-pitched squealing. At first it scared us. . . until we realized that there were mice in the walls, running about and communicating with each other. Then we were able to go back to sleep until the next day when we engaged an exterminator to rid us of the problem. I think you should do the same, though it may mean opening the parlor wall to find the nest."

"And that's all you think it is, mice in the wall? Why didn't I think of that?" Richard chided himself for not thinking of such a simple explanation.

"Because you've never had mice in the walls before," Mary explained.

"But what about the clocks? You," asked Patricia as she looked directly at John, "said the pendulums should have been moving in opposite directions."

"Ordinarily they should have, unless something was interfering with the sound waves moving through the studs. I suspect that you have a nest within the wall that is disrupting the natural pendulum vibrations. Hence they move in near perfect synchronization. Once you get the nest out, your clocks should revert to their natural propensity to swing out of sync," John concluded his brief physics lesson.

"John, I think we'd best get back to the family." She looked at the Allens. "They are taking us to a concert of the Hiramville symphony this afternoon. Our daughter-in-law plays first cello."

"Right," John looked at Richard. "Let us know when the exterminators are coming. I'd like to be here when they open the wall."

"Of course. And Mr. and Mrs. Braemhor, we thank you so much. We really appreciate your help. It's a tremendous load off our minds. If there's anything we can do for you, please don't hesitate to let us know."

"It was our pleasure, Richard. We're just glad it came out so well for you. Be sure to give us a call when the wall is coming down." With that John and Mary crossed the street and prepared for a relaxing afternoon with the family.

Chapter 4

Three days later, John received a call from Richard Allen inviting the Braemhors to come to the house the next morning to watch the exterminators at work.

Mary and John arrived as Richard was explaining the situation to the workmen from Pest-A-Side; they were making plans to open the interior wall in the front parlor. They started along the baseboard carefully removing one panel of sheetrock and exploring the intra-stud spaces for signs of pests. Sure enough, they quickly found a nest of shredded paper and wood chips interlaced with fur and mouse droppings. Before the morning was over they had opened almost the entire wall and discovered three separate nests, each at a different level.

In addition, they found one portion of baseboard that had been sawed to facilitate the removal of a one foot segment of the board without disturbing the rest. John was there watching intently as the workman lifted the segment out and revealed a small chamber that reached back the depth of the studs.

"What's that?" John asked, pointing to a zip-lock plastic bag with something grey in it.

"Beats me," the workman said as he handed the package to John, who unzipped the bag and lifted out a soft grey leather bag. Richard watched, spellbound. "What is it, John?"

"A grey pouch with what feels like pebbles inside." John squeezed the pouch. He then lifted the flap of the pouch, took a quick look and just as quickly closed it again. "Let's go into the kitchen," he said. Richard, Patricia, and Mary followed him into the next room and they sat around the kitchen table.

"I didn't want the workmen to see what we have," John said as he looked at the others. "This is very curious and not very pretty." He closed and locked the door to the parlor.

"Why all of the mystery, John?" Mary was perplexed.

"You'll see."

He opened the flap again and poured the contents of the pouch out onto the table. Out tumbled a couple of pounds of shaped pieces of, apparently, gold!

The three were momentarily stunned. "They look like gold nuggets," Richard stammered. "We've found a hidden treasure!"

"Not quite," was John's sober reply.

"They're teeth, aren't they, John?" Mary observed.

"Exactly." John admired Mary's quick-off-the-mark recognition of what was lying before them. "Human teeth, to be more precise."

"Human teeth! Oh, my God!" Richard was stunned.

Patricia was frozen with her hand to her mouth. "But. . .but. . .what? . .why?" Her voice was barely audible.

John sat silently to let the impact of the find sink in. Then he calmly asked, "Just how much do you know about the former owners, the Smiths?"

"Just what we told you. They moved here a few years back—I don't know from where—and lived a quiet solitary life here in Hiramville. As we said, he made some silver jewelry which he sold at the local Saturday market. We thought it was his hobby, although we did hear that he had been a jeweler before coming here. That's about all."

"Isn't it possible that these teeth did not belong to the Smiths?" Mary wanted to keep everything in perspective.

"Possibly, except that the baseboard panel did not appear to be an old hiding place. No, I think we are dealing with something relatively new."

"But why? Why would the Smiths have hidden gold teeth in the wall? Why would they have hidden them at all? Where would they have gotten them?" Richard was still very perplexed.

"That's what we need to find out. Patricia, Richard, would you trust me to keep these for now so that I can investigate how they happened to be here in this house in Hiramville? As you know, Mary and I will be right across the street with James and Jennifer. I want to see if I can trace where they came from, and more importantly, who the Smiths really were."

Patricia was quite all right with John's suggestion. "Oh my, yes, I don't want them in my house!"

But Richard was hesitant, "Well, I don't know. That's," he pointed to the teeth on the table, "worth quite a bit and. . . we don't know a lot about you, Mr. Braemhor."

"Oh, Richard, they've just helped us out a great deal by finding out what the noises in the wall were. Really, Richard!"

John quickly stepped in to defuse the situation. "How about this? Let me have two or three of the teeth and the grey pouch they came in and you keep the rest here in the house. Then when I finish my investigation, I'll return the pouch and teeth to you. And if I'm the villain you think I may be and run off with the two or three teeth, you won't be out much."

Richard thought for a moment or two and finally grudgingly said, "Well, all right."

"And I'll give you a receipt for what you let me take," John concluded. "All I ask is that you don't do anything with the remainder of the teeth until I finish my work. It shouldn't take more than a week."

"Okay," Richard muttered.

Patricia was clearly embarrassed. "Here, Mr. Braemhor, take what you need, and I'll put the rest in a safe place until you let us know what you find."

"Fair enough." John selected three molar crowns, put them in the grey pouch and motioned to Mary that it was time to go back across the street. As they left the front porch, John smiled and said, "I'll let you know as soon as I have any news."

As John and Mary crossed the street, they heard Patricia, who was speaking not too quietly, "Really, Richard. Whatever possessed you?" John gave Mary a knowing smile and took her hand—the pouch and three crowns securely in his jacket pocket.

"Not very appreciative, was he?" Mary queried as they sat on the front porch swing at James's house.

"No, but he was right not to entrust all of that gold to a stranger, no matter how much of a favor we'd done them. Do you realize, Mary, that I would estimate those teeth to be worth over $25,000. That's a lot of money to entrust to someone you've just met."

"Well, I still think it was very ungrateful of him, and from what we overheard, Patricia thought so too. What I can't figure out is why you insisted on taking the grey pouch as well."

"You didn't see—and neither did the Allens—what was stamped on the inside of the flap."

"No, I didn't."

"An SS Totenkopf—the Death's Head Unit insignia—beneath a swastika!"

"You mean the camps?" Mary asked.

"I think so. I want to get a hold of Charlie MacLaine as soon as possible."

MacLaine was the American private investigator who occasionally worked with the FBI and Interpol. He and John and Mary had teamed up on several investigations in the recent past, and it was he who had supplied John with an official FBI identification.

Over lunch, John and Mary planned out their next moves. First, John called their friend, Charlie, and told him what they'd discovered in Hiramville. Charlie was on the East Coast helping Interpol trace some missing persons.

"John, how do you do it?"

"What do you mean?"

"You always seem to find the most unusual puzzles. I remember once you were chasing Confederate ghosts in Vermont and now this. You should get Mary to play Watson to your Holmes, and she could develop a written record of your exploits. How is Mary, by the way?"

"She's fine. . . and we have too much fun chasing the criminals to spend time with a written record. Can you help?"

"As a matter of fact, I think I might be able to. Can't tell you much about my present assignment over an insecure line, but I think your request will fit in quite well with what I'm doing here on the coast. Give me a few days for some research, and I'll let you know what I find."

"Sounds good. Here's our phone number for the next week or so." John gave James's number to Charlie. "Let us know what you find."

John turned to Mary as he hung up the receiver. "When we were in the town center the other day, I noticed a jeweler's shop. I wonder if the owner would know anything about our Mr. Smith, since he made jewelry for local consumption. And Charlie won't be able to give us anything for a day or two."

"Worth a try. I'll set out some lunch, and we can go right afterwards." Mary started into the kitchen, then turned back to him. "John, I've been thinking. . . ."

"Solved the puzzle of the Smiths?"

"No, but I'm wondering why a couple named Smith in their mid-eighties would have a pouch marked with SS insignia. Don't you think it strange that survivors of the Holocaust—Maud says she saw their tattoos—would have kept such a memento of those horrible years?"

"And Maud has Alzheimer's, remember."

"But she pointed to the right location. How would she have known that, if she hadn't seen the tattoos?" Mary made a point.

"Strange that they would have kept such a memento—yes, perhaps—but remember that individuals who survived the horrors of the Holocaust may not have been thinking quite logically when freedom finally came."

"John, I can maybe understand them keeping the pouch—though I really think that highly unlikely—to remind them of what they'd been through, but the contents? Those were the teeth of their fellow inmates! Isn't that a little gruesome?" Mary pressed her questioning

"Yes and no. Maybe. . .maybe. . .in the chaos at the end of the war with the Allied troops freeing the camps, they stole the pouch from the SS and didn't realize what the contents were until later." John was trying to find logical answers to Mary's questions.

"So you think the Smiths were innocent prison camp internees who were lucky enough to survive and in their weakened conditions stole a pouch containing a gruesome nest egg of their friends' teeth? I don't think that is very likely, do you really? I don't think so, John."

"But the newspaper article told us, and Maud told us, that she'd seen prisoner ID tattoos on their inner forearms. And that's where the Nazis marked their prisoners," John argued back.

"But, John, if you had survived the camps and gotten out with a pouch containing gold, would you have kept a pouch marked with the insignias of your tormentors? I think the pouch argues for the Smiths not being prison inmates."

"Maybe. Maybe."

Mary pressed on and changed tack. "And is their real name Smith? Seems awfully American to me for an elderly couple with heavy Germanic accents, as Marmy told us."

"That's where I'm hoping Charlie can enlighten us. Particularly now that he's working for Interpol. He'll have access to just the type of records we need. Good to see that we, as always, think alike." John patted her hand on the lunch tabletop.

With lunch finished, the two walked to the small jewelry shop on Main Street in the town center. The tinkle of the hanging door bells announced their arrival. A bent old man in his shirt sleeves and a green visor looked up. His dark hair and complexion and his thick Yiddish enunciation announced his Middle Eastern origin. "Help you?" He smiled as he swung his loupe above his glasses.

John introduced himself and Mary to the owner, Mr. Lieberman, and asked if he could give them any information about Mr. Smith, the previous owner of the Allen house.

"Perhaps. A very nice gentleman. We shared a common interest—fine jewelry. Some of his silver pieces were magnificent. And we shared another common interest. We both survived." He pointed to the identification number on his inner left forearm as his face hardened into a pained smile. "It was so terrible what happened to him and Helga."

"Did he ever make any gold jewelry?" Mary asked.

"Not that I know of. His pieces were always fashioned from silver services that he bought in various flea markets hereabouts. I think he had a small kiln in his home. I often wondered why not. I occasionally bought small gold nuggets—very fine quality—from him and fashioned pieces of my own from them. Here. . .here are some I made from his nuggets. Had them for over a year. As you can see from the prices, they don't sell rapidly, but I don't feel I can give away fine pieces."

"Of course not. I wonder if we might see that pendant there?" John asked and pointed to a small golden tulip.

"By all means." Mr. Lieberman glowed as he unlocked his glass display cabinet. "I can make you a special offer on that one." He smiled at Mary.

"It is beautiful." Mary admired the piece.

"And for the price, I'll throw in a gold chain for it." Lieberman beamed at the prospect of a sale.

"We'll take it," John said quietly as he handed Lieberman a credit card. Mary was aghast, but said nothing.

"Were you in the same camp as the Smiths?" John asked as Lieberman wrapped the gold pendant in tissue and put it into one of his gift boxes.

"I don't think so, but it's very hard to tell. There were so many of us."

"Smith was not his real name, was it?" John pressed on.

"I really don't ask such questions, sir. It was enough to know that he was in a camp during that terrible period."

"Of course. Well, we must be on our way," John concluded as he guided Mary towards the door and Main Street.

Outside, Mary confronted John. "John, have you taken leave of your senses?"

"Of course not. I need a sample of the gold Smith was peddling. And besides, wouldn't you like to have a nice memento of our trip?" John smiled.

"Not if it was made from the gold teeth of Holocaust victims in the camps." Mary was adamant.

* * * * *

And now the hard part of the investigation began, the wait for additional data to be supplied by someone else—in this case, Charlie MacLaine. John tried puttering around James's house doing some small house repairs to while away the time. He re-hung a cellar door, tightened two of the loo seats downstairs, and fixed a dripping faucet, but it was to no avail. Between chores he, as always, paced, looked out the window, watched the telephone in anticipation. Each time it rang, he leapt to answer it only to be disappointed that the data he awaited were not forthcoming.

"John, why don't you try reading your book. You can't have finished *The Sign of the Four* yet." But Mary knew it was a lost cause. She'd seen her husband go through the agitated waiting too many times before.

Finally, to Mary's, and John's relief, the call for which he waited arrived.

"John, I think I've got some information for you." The voice on the other end of the line was Charlie's. "I'm only about two hours away from Hiramville. I'll drive over and bring it to you. Maybe we could get some supper somewhere."

"What have you got?" John anxiously asked.

"Rather give it to you. We're not on a secure line, remember. I'll see you and Mary in a little while." Click and he was gone.

"Good news?" Mary asked.

"I think so. We'll see when he gets here."

An hour and a half later, Charlie drove his car into James's driveway. John came off the porch to greet him. "I thought you said two hours?"

"That way I thought I'd get here before you got too agitated waiting for me. Besides, I have a lead foot." He took John's strong grip and looked over John's shoulder. "Hi, Mary, how are things?"

"Very well, Charlie. It's good to see you again." She shook hands with the slender, wiry man with short-cropped blond hair. The last time the three had been together was months ago in Carterville where John was helping the Dean of the College, Stanley Howard, solve a gruesome murder on the campus of Carter University.

"I hope you brought lots of information for John to ponder."

"I think so." Charlie smiled. "Maybe we could find a place to get a meal. I'm starved."

"Care for Italian?" John asked, then suggested, "There is a nice little *trattoria* at the town center. Nice secluded booths that should suit our purpose."

"Sounds great! Only on one condition, I buy. It's not often I get to see my overseas friends."

To Mary's relief, John quietly acquiesced, and she went into the house to tell the family where they were going.

John was right. The three easily found a booth in the back of the main dining area that suited their needs for privacy. After ordering, Charlie took a file folder from his briefcase and laid it on the table.

"Here it is. I checked the agency's files and contacted the Anti-Defamation League Center in the city. Not much there. They are still very active with tracking and exposing hate groups, but the search for missing SS or camp guards from the Hitler era has pretty much wound down. I think they figure they've found about all that are left alive at this point. But then I contacted the Simon Weinheimer Center in Chicago. And bingo.

"The Weinheimer Center still has records naming individuals associated with the Holocaust who disappeared at the end of the war and were never definitely located. I thought that might be worth your while. So, here it is." Charlie was proud of his detective work.

The list, covering a little over a page, named individuals with an accompanying brief paragraph on their last known whereabouts.

"What did you say their names were?" Charlie asked as John quickly perused the sheets of typescript.

"Smith. Joseph and Helga Smith."

"I thought that's what you said. Sorry, no Smiths in the list." Charlie took a bite of his lasagna.

"But then if they were on the run, they would not have kept their own names, would they?" Mary asked as she peered over John's shoulder at the list.

"Ah ha!" John brightened. "Look at this! Here's a Joseph Schmied! He was a guard at Dachau. . . .And a Helga Hasse."

"How appropriate!" Mary added. Charlie was puzzled.

"*Hasse* is German for *hate*, and *Schmied* is German for *Smith*," Mary explained. "Was she at Dachau also, John?"

"Yes! And listen to this." John read from the descriptive paragraphs accompanying each name. "They both disappeared just before the Americans freed the camp. And. . .each was last traced to New York City. This looks very promising."

"Except for one thing." Mary's voice fell.

"What?"

"The identification numbers on their arms. Maud, Marmy and Mr. Leiberman all said they saw the camp's tattoos."

"But think for a minute," John pondered. "If you were a guard at one of the camps and your world was collapsing and you knew you might be captured, what would you do?"

"Try to make myself look like a prisoner not a guard," Charlie chimed in.

"And how would you do it?"

"By having myself tattooed with a prisoner's number," Mary concluded, "and hope to be taken for an inmate, not a guard, when liberation came. The only thing you would have to worry about was the fact that you did not look as emaciated as the real prisoners."

"That could have easily been covered with bulky clothing and hiding your face beneath a hat of some sort." Charlie again added to the deductions.

"I think we have a very good substantive circumstantial case for Joseph and Helga Smith being, in reality, Joseph and Helga Hasse-Schmied of Dachau."

"But how are you going to prove that? And who do you think killed the Smiths?" Charlie asked.

"The first question is the harder one. But I'm pretty sure I already know who killed them, and that will not be easy to prove either," John admitted. "But I think we have taken on enough for one day, and thanks to Charlie here," he looked at their friend and fellow detective, "we have made fine progress."

Then, after an hour's pleasant reminiscing over past cases, Charlie prepared to take his leave to return to his temporary office with Interpol. John stopped him. "One more favor, Charlie. What can you find for me on this name?" He handed Charlie a note.

"I'll see what I can do." Charlie smiled and drove off toward the interstate to New York. John and Mary went back to the third floor apartment at their son's home.

"John, you said you thought you knew who had killed the Smiths." Mary said.

"Yes, and I think your earlier intuition was correct, but let's see what Charlie finds."

* * * * *

Early next day, Charlie called. "I've got your information on the name you gave me."

"That was quick," John said.

"It was easy. He's one of us—law enforcement. Here's what I discovered of his and his family's history: His mother escaped the Nazis when she was about five years old, in the thirties. Family sent her to relatives here in the City. She lived and grew up in a Polish neighborhood, where she met her husband, Georgi Cierń. She had several children, one of whom was the one you asked about. All of her family in Europe was killed in the camps over the course of the Holocaust. She was the sole survivor.

"Her son's history is even more interesting. He grew up in the City, went into law enforcement as a young man and served on several forces before moving to Hiramville. Apparently his mother never let her children forget what the Nazis had done to the family."

"How do we know that?" John was incredulous at the detail of what Charlie had found.

"Wherever the son went in his different positions, he never ceased to talk about the Holocaust and what it had cost his family. He became known as the 'Nazi hater' among his fellow officers. By the time he reached Hiramville, his hatred had generalized from Nazis to German people in general. He could not tolerate working with anyone of German descent, hence the many moves in his career. Many of his fellow officers thought him very odd personally, even a bit crazy, with little or no control over his emotions. Finally, when he came to his present position he seemed to settle down and lose much of his previous blatant anger. He's done well in Hiramville, though still very quick to anger. I'm pretty sure this is your man, so, John, I would be careful not to rile him too much in your investigation. He could still be a dangerous character. I hope this is of some help."

"Immense. One last question, then I'll let you get back to your Interpol work. What is the name of your contact at the Weinheimer Center?" John asked.

"Oh, sure. That was . . .let me see . . .I've got it written down somewhere here. . .ah, here it is, Marcia Freedman. And here is her private number."

"Charlie, I don't know how to thank you. I think you may have wrapped up this case for me."

"Always happy to help a friend, John." Charlie smiled through the phone, as the conversation ended.

"Well, John?"

"Give me a moment. I want to look up something on the internet." He went into James's computer room.

Then, when he returned, "Now we're getting somewhere!" John turned to Mary and summarized Charlie's information for her. "Even the mother's name fits."

"What do you mean, John?"

"Cierń. His mother's name was Cierń!" John beamed.

"Yes?"

"Don't you see? Cierń is Polish for Bramble! Brad Bramble was born 'something' Cierń, a man with an inordinate, and well-deserved, hatred of the Nazis, particularly those who ran the camps. They had murdered his entire European ancestry. No wonder he killed the Smiths!"

"We don't know that, John. We're leaping ahead of our facts again."

"Don't you remember what Maud told us? She saw Bramble's police cruiser at the Smith's house the morning *before* he returned in the afternoon when the postman called."

"And don't you remember that Maud has severe Alzheimer's? No court would believe her word over a trusted public servant like the police chief."

"You're right." John was crestfallen.

"Unless we can find another neighbor who saw what Maud claims she saw." Mary tried to save John's hypothesis.

"Then let's survey the neighborhood. But first let's have breakfast with the family—they are really why we're here, remember?" John put a lighter touch on the conversation.

At breakfast most of the conversation centered on John and Mary's investigation and the presence the previous evening of a real FBI agent right here in the small town of Hiramville. John mentioned the perplexing problem of trying to verify what Maud had told them.

"Oh, she's right," Jennifer said. "I was in the kitchen—it was a Saturday—and Daniel called me to ask why there was a police car across the street at the Smiths. I didn't know, so Daniel, Donna and I watched Chief Bramble go in the house and then come out and drive off about fifteen minutes later."

"Where were you?" John directed his question at James.

"I had gone to the grocery store, I think."

"Hmmm." John pondered. "So the three of you saw the Chief that morning?"

"Oh, yes," Jennifer continued, "but what was odd was that he returned in the early afternoon. We didn't know what was going on, but then later, we found out. Terrible tragedy."

"You may not realize how much of a tragedy it really was," John counseled, "but right now I have to call Chicago." He went into the front parlor for privacy.

"Oh, how exciting! We're seeing Granddaddy solve a mystery!" Donna exclaimed.

John dialed the number Charlie had given him. "This is the Weinheimer Center. I'm Marcia Freedman. How can I help you?"

"This is John Braemhor, Charlie MacLaine's colleague. He talked with you a couple days ago."

"Oh, yes. I faxed him a list of those Holocaust guards we've never been able to locate. Was it of some help?"

"Very much so." And then John told Mrs. Freedman what he knew and what he suspected.

There was a slight pause on the other end of the line. Marcia Freedman made a quick decision. "I can have an investigative team there by tomorrow afternoon. Will that be all right?"

Braemhor was delighted, gave her the address of James's house, and went back into the dining room to tell Mary and the family what had transpired.

Later, as John and Mary took a stroll about the village, John smiled and said, "I think it's time to turn this investigation over to the real professionals in Nazi hunting."

"I'm glad to hear you say that, John. For some reason I have found this case particularly depressing."

"I'm not surprised. The Holocaust was a gruesome and depressing period in the history of the world. I still have difficulty imagining what it must have been like to be a Jew, or any minority, living in Europe at that time. Can you imagine, Mary, millions of people exterminated from the face of the earth, and for what?" He sighed. "Well, as I said, let's leave the wrap-up to the real professionals."

The next afternoon, Marcia Freedman and her team appeared at James's front door. After introductions, John pointed out the Allen house and Maud and Marmy's home as well. The team split up, two going to the Allen's, two to Maud and Marmy's, and two to the local police station.

By the next afternoon, they had called in the state authorities to follow up the story Maud had told, and that Jennifer and the children had corroborated, about Chief Bramble.

Still later that afternoon, the local fire siren screamed its call for volunteers, and the volunteer ambulance service raced through the village to Chief Bramble's office.

"I wonder what that's all about?" Jennifer asked. But then she realized that John and Mary were already on their way to the center of town.

State police had cordoned off a few blocks, but John was able, with a show of his FBI identification, to pass the barrier and move quickly to the center of activity— the local police station. There he found Mrs. Freedman and two of her team.

"What happened?"

"I think your case is wrapped up—as you suspected." Freedman was somber. "Seems your suspicions about the chief, Bramble or Cierń, were correct. Not long after our interview with him, he ended his life with his service pistol. Fortunately, he left us a note of regret and confession. Saved the police authorities a lot of work. I don't think they could have convicted him on the testimony of an Alzheimer's patient." John did not trouble her with what Jennifer and the children saw the morning of the Smith's deaths.

"Poor man. He was so eaten up with hate and anger. And then our call made him realize that he, by killing the Schmieds, had become one of them. He could no longer hold his head high as a victim and so he ended his life to preserve what little self-respect he had left. Poor man." She dabbed away the tears that wetted her cheek. "You see, Mr. Braemhor, ours is not a happy occupation, even if we do take pride in promoting justice. Forgive me. You see, tragedy touches us all, and I am not always as objective and detached as I pretend to be." She managed a faint smile.

When John got back to Mary on the other side of the police ribbon, she looked at him and asked, "John, what's wrong? You look like you've been crying."

"Maybe I have. Maybe I have. Just something that Mrs. Freedman said." He blew his nose and wiped his eyes.

* * * * *

Just before the Braemhors were to leave for the train station to continue their holiday in the northern reaches of New York State, John went to the Allens to return the three gold crowns and the grey camp pouch he'd borrowed for his investigation.

"I want to return these," he said to Patricia Allen when she came to the door.

"Thank you, Mr. Braemhor. And thank you again for all of your help. I just want to let you know, too, that Richard has given the teeth that you found in the wall to the Weinheimer Center. They'll know better what to do with them.

"I think that is a very wise choice, Mrs. Allen. Goodbye for now. Perhaps we will see you and your husband next time we visit James and Jennifer and the grandchildren."

As John was returning to James's house, the small, bent and wizened figure of Mr. Lieberman hobbled down the sidewalk.

"Mr. Braemhor. . .Mr. Braemhor! May I have a word?"

"Of course, Mr. Lieberman, of course. How are you today?"

"Not very well, not very well. Mrs. Freedman from the Weinheimer Center came by to see me yesterday. I am so saddened. She told me who the Smiths really were. I was shocked. To think that I bought gold from that man! Gold stolen from the mouths of my people! Oh, my! Oh, my! It is just terrible, terrible! I feel like I have betrayed my own people. I feel responsible that those people could hide so well in our midst. I should have recognized that they were not what they seemed to be." The tears flowed down his cheeks from his red-rimmed eyes."

"Not at all, Mr. Lieberman, not at all." John embraced him and held him to his chest as loud sobs wracked the old man. "You didn't know. You didn't know. None of us did. The Smiths were very clever in their disguise, but in the end a certain justice played out, and you should not hold yourself in any way responsible."

"And then I heard what happened to Chief Bramble." Lieberman sobbed again.

"In a way I think he thought he was righting the wrongs of Dachau," Braemhor consoled Lieberman, "but the anguish from the past blinded him to what he was doing and so he crossed a basic tenet of civilization and fell into the same dark reaches of what the Holocaust promoted. So he did not avenge the millions of victims but added one more life—his own—to the lost souls that came out of that era of our history. Life is, at times, a sad business, Mr. Lieberman, which you know better than most, but the cure for our sadness," John took Lieberman by the elbows, pressed him back and directly met his eyes, "is to keep progressing and doing the best we can to be part of the good people of the world. You're a good person, Mr. Lieberman, and don't you ever forget that."

Lieberman stood quietly before Braemhor staring down at his shoe tops. Then slowly, he raised his head. "Mr. Braemhor, I have something for you." He handed John a slip of paper. John took it and looked down at it. It was a credit slip for the cost of the pendant he had bought in Mr. Lieberman's shop. John frowned.

"I cannot take your money for that pendant, made from the sadness of my people. It would not be fair to you; it would not be fair to my beliefs."

"Nor can I keep the pendant," Braemhor said as he handed Lieberman the small package. "Send it to the Weinheimer Center, if you want. Maybe it can help fund their good works, and that way give back a little to your people for all they suffered in those horrible years."

Lieberman took the package, reached up and patted John's cheek with his hand, then turned and shuffled back to the village center and his shop.

Chapter 5

The train trip north along the Hudson River and then
west along the Mohawk was the same scenic beauty it
had been last winter, but without the snow and blustery
winds. It was a good several hours in which both John
and Mary could relax from their sad adventures of the
past few days.

"Oh, look, John, there's West Point." Mary pointed
to the military college across the river, the training
ground for the officer corps of the U. S. Army.

"Beautiful location," John remarked as he scanned
the scene on the west side of the river. "We should stop
and see it sometime. In fact, there are a number of
historic sites along this stretch of the Hudson. Very
historic area.

At Albany their route turned west. Along the river
stood factory sites of the nineteenth century. Finally,
their train rolled into the huge old station of the city just
north of Carterville, home of Carter University and
Dean Stanley Howard and his wife, Jane. As before, a
student driver met them as they stepped onto the
platform, announcing that she was instructed by Dean
Howard to bring them to their usual lodgings at The
Retreat, an austere building secluded in a small forest of
90-foot Norway spruces with guest rooms and a quiet,
multi-religious library especially reserved for visiting
dignitaries of both academic and non-academic stripes.

Mrs. Parker, who managed The Retreat and prepared
all of the meals for visitors, met them at the door

between the living quarters and the small airy chapel that glowed golden in the afternoon sunlight which was filtered by massive golden glass panels.

"I've reserved your same room for you." She smiled. "Dean Howard said he will pick you up at 6:30 for supper at his house." She led the Braemhors down the open stairwell to the guest room level and handed John the room key.

"I'm beginning to feel like this is a second home," Mary said as they entered the plain, austere room that was to be their lodgings for the next few days. She looked out of the picture window. "Not quite as pretty as it was last winter in the silent whiteness," she observed.

"But beautiful in its green clothing this season," John said, as he unpacked their bags.

At half six, there was a light tapping on their door. Mary opened the door to Stanley Howard, the blondish-haired, flushed-face Dean in his early sixties. "Stanley, it's so good to see you again." She took his hand as John appeared behind her at the door.

"Greetings once again, Mary, John, welcome again to Carter University. He beamed as he took both their hands. Stanley Howard had taught for twenty years before assuming the position of Dean of the College. Always cheerful and one to look on the bright side of each academic issue confronting the college, his philosophy was that every change was an opportunity. As Dean he'd helped several faculty members initiate innovative academic programs, and under his guidance the college had become known nationwide as one of the most innovative liberal arts colleges in the country.

"Your campus is beautiful in the spring as well as the winter," Mary noted as they drove through the hilly campus to the Howard's home in the village. Theirs was a large two-story Federalist structure. The furnishings and décor were a mix of 19th century Victorian and modern Indian, highlighted by Isfahan and Bokhara floor coverings. Many of the Indian pieces came from the year the Howards had spent in Madras while Stanley was on sabbatical leave.

Jane was the perfect model of a Dean's wife. She was delighted to host a variety of faculty soirees throughout the academic year. Often she engaged the University string quartet to entertain while the guests gorged themselves on her gourmet dinners. The Howards were an excellent fit for the deanship.

Jane greeted the Braemhors at the door, announcing that she had prepared a special curry accented meal for their "homecoming."

"Let's hope that this visit will be less tumultuous than the last two." John smiled as he took her hand.

"Things have been very quiet on the crime front," Stanley said as he led them into the dining room. "We hope your presence will keep it that way."

"No crime? No stolen computers? No vandal signs chalked on the sidewalk? Your campus security must be very good," John remarked between bites.

"Stanley exaggerates," Jane said. "We do have one problem."

"Oh?" Mary looked at Jane.

"We've had a reported rape on campus," Jane went on. "I could not believe it! What are present-day young people thinking about? Our students are supposed to be the cream of the crop, and now we have one accusing another of the worst of behavior! It's disgraceful!"

"Jane, let's not bother John and Mary with that. It's all being kept very quiet right here on campus." Stanley did not want the conversation to drift into campus problems.

"Rape. Kept quiet on campus? I thought that was a felony crime here in the Colon. . .States," John said.

"Well, technically, I suppose it is, but we have formed a special committee to deal with these things." Stanley was still trying to defuse the conversation.

"A committee?! That's certainly a novel approach to crime." The more John heard, the less he understood the thinking behind what was going on. "Explain that to me. What is this committee? And who sits on the committee?" John continued to press the issue.

"Well, you see our colleges here in the States are very closed communities. We prefer to deal with our internal problems ourselves. . . ."

"Without airing our dirty linen in public," Jane broke in.

"Yes, for example, one fall several minority members of our football team complained that they were not being treated fairly," Stanley continued. "They said that they were denied first team positions because of their race and that the coaches were unduly harsh with them."

"They even called them hate crimes," Jane broke in again.

"Yes," Stanley continued, "so the President of the University appointed a committee of three faculty members to investigate the allegations, even though hate crimes are considered punishable crimes by federal authorities. It consisted of two black faculty members and one white. In fact, one of the black committee members dubbed it the 'Oreo Committee.' The President was not pleased, though many of the minority faculty thought it quite witty and clever. At any rate, the committee investigated the complaints, wrote an extensive report, and the matter was quietly taken care of without involving non-campus authorities."

"But isn't there a difference between a complaint of unfair treatment and a felony?" Mary joined the discussion. "Who were the members of the committee to deal with the rape allegations?"

"There were three faculty—one each from Psychology, Sociology and Political Science, three administrators and two students."

"And they all had training and experience in law and crime detection?" John drove to the central issue.

"Well, no, but they were very good people, all very interested in protecting the rights of all involved. And, in fact, one of the administrators was a University counsel." Stanley seemed to become a little embarrassed by John's questioning."

"Well, you certainly do things differently here in the United States," Mary observed as she touched John's knee under the table to signal for him to terminate the direction of his questioning.

John, catching the meaning of Mary's touch, said, "That's certainly true. You know, Stanley, Jane, I always learn something new when we visit your illustrious campus."

The conversation then drifted into more prosaic topics, such as a lecture at the University observatory the next night on the aurora borealis, including a video of the phenomena.

"The observatory is a small space, so I reserved seats for the four of us." Stanley smiled.

"That will be delightful," Mary said with genuine enthusiasm. "I saw the aurora once in Sutors Cove. The lights are something to behold. What time is the lecture?"

"It starts about nine. We'll pick you up a little before. The observatory is on the same hill as the President's home."

"That will be fine. One thing we would like to do on this trip is look up Bill Edwards. We heard him lecture last year in Edinburgh and told him we would try to see him next time we visited the campus. Is he on campus this term?"

"I believe he is, but I can check in the morning. Call my secretary. She'll have the information for you."

With that, the evening ended and Stanley took the Braemhors back to The Retreat.

Later in their room, Mary said, "I do hope we did not offend the Howards."

"About what?"

"The rape committee."

"Oh, I don't think so, though Stanley did seem to get a bit defensive about it," John answered, "but you have to admit that it is an unusual way to deal with such a major crime. I'm surprised the local and state authorities haven't had something to say about the way universities handle it."

"Me, too. But I understand that's the way a lot of American universities handle such accusations. You know, John, if I were the parent of the accuser, I would have gone right to the police authorities."

"I agree, but haven't I told you before, the Colonies do things differently than we do in Scotland?"

* * * * *

Next morning, Mrs. Parker gave the Braemhors a brief message at breakfast.

"What does it say, John?" Mary asked as she tapped the shell on her soft-boiled.

"It's from Stanley. Says Bill Edwards has office hours from ten until noon in Matheson Hall. We can probably see him there and renew our acquaintance this morning."

"Fine. That should give us time to see the new exhibit at the library," Mary said.

"What exhibit?" John was unaware of what Mary was talking about.

"I saw it in the local campus newssheet just before we went to the Howard's last evening. They have a display on an American abolitionist from the 1830s who has just been inducted into the American Anti-Slavery Hall of Fame in a nearby village. Seems Bill Edwards and his wife Eleanor were instrumental in his being inducted into the Hall of Fame. We should ask Bill about that when we see him. Maybe we could see the Hall of Fame while we're here. Should be historically interesting," Mary suggested.

"Good idea. I'm sure Bill can tell us more about it when we see him."

After a brief stop at their room to get their light jackets, John and Mary walked down the hill past two dormitories and a student dining hall to the library which was nestled on the next lower plateau in the hillside. As they descended the long outdoor stairs, the entire valley spread before them—the front campus with its willow surrounded lake, the village of Carterville beyond that, and farms investing the valley still farther on. Even the small rural airdrome, where a number of faculty and staff took flying lessons from a local farmer turned pilot, could be seen farther down the valley. Marvin Tarbuck had turned one of his farm fields into a landing strip years ago and his enterprise had expanded into a full-fledged airfield with a hard-surfaced runway capable of handling Lear jets. Some faculty members had gone into flying in a big way, buying and refurbishing WWII vintage aircraft for their Sunday recreational flying. Carterville airport now sported one Spitfire, one Corsair and one Mustang, all in tip-top flying condition and on display weekends, to the delight of the children of the area.

"There's another place we might visit this trip." John pointed to the thin landing strip barely visible in the distance.

In the library, a smallish abolition display told the story in pictures, old letters, and pamphlets of a young minister who sacrificed his life in the cause of the abolition of slavery before the American Civil War. "Isn't it amazing," John commented, "even in the smallest, most rural of areas there are dedicated people who give their all for others? Gives you some hope for the future of our civilization."

Around ten, the two Braemhors walked the strenuous uphill paths to the academic buildings and Matheson Hall to find Bill Edwards's office. It was on the third floor, no elevator. As they reached Edwards's office door, Mary, between deep inhalations, observed, "Now I understand what I've been seeing all morning."

"Oh?"

"So many of the female students seem to have unusually well-developed calf muscles. I thought at first that we had run into the gymnastic team, but no, it's all of the walking up and down the campus hills that has developed their legs."

"The advantages of higher education," John snickered. "Shall we see if Bill is in?"

"John, Mary! So good to see you again. What brings you to Carter this time?" Bill Edwards greeted the Braemhors at the door, his brown hair still cascading over his left eye. *I don't think I've ever seen a more boyish looking professor in my life,* Mary thought as she took his hand.

"Come in. Come in to my small castle." Edwards swept inward with his hand as he stood aside to let them enter. It was a typical professor's office, walls lined with overfilled bookshelves, a large wooden desk looking out the window at the rear of the room which offered an expansive view of the campus. Edwards set up two folding chairs in front of his desk and motioned to them to have a seat.

"Is this a vacation or are you two here on criminal business?" Edwards asked.

"Just a short holiday to see old friends and acquaintances, but we understand that you do have an ongoing problem with student relationships on campus," John answered.

"Oh, the alleged rape case. Yes, not all is well at Carter. And I've had the misfortunate to be chosen to be one of the three faculty members on the committee investigating the allegations." He screwed up his face.

"How did you manage that?" Mary asked.

"I don't know. I think the administration drew the names out of a hat. But I will say it's an interesting process."

"Do you have any background in criminal investigation or witness questioning?" John was interested in what expertise members of the committee might have.

"None whatsoever. It makes no sense at all to me. Rape is a crime and should be investigated by properly trained authorities. But this is a university, and we seem to think we are an enclave totally separate from society at large. This is part of the reason some of the society hold us in contempt as elitist stuffed shirts. To me it is a case of 'she said, he said,' and I don't for the life of me know how you decide who's really telling the truth. I'm just pleased I'm in the profession I'm in and not law. But enough about the trials and tribulations of a professor in an elite undergraduate college. What is new in your lives?"

John quickly told Edwards about the Loch Ness adventure and the case of the haunted house and then mentioned that they were going to hear a lecture on the aurora borealis this evening.

"Ah, yes, Professor Manchester. He's been studying the northern lights for over 25 years now. I might be there myself."

"Coming back to your committee work, you said the case is one of 'she said, he said,' and it's hard to tell which one is telling the truth. Would hypnosis be of any value in the investigation?" John changed the subject.

"I think it might be, but I'm not sure the university would allow it. Some of the staff still view the technique from a Svengali/Trilby perspective. All mystical and supernatural, you know. I haven't even raised the question. But I think it could be of value in trying to understand what actually happened that night. You see, the victim, if I can use such a term, has no recollection of the event. All she reports is that she was drinking heavily at a party. According to her, one thing led to another with the accused, a well-known student athlete, and the next thing she knew, she awakened in a bedroom upstairs feeling she had been violated."

It was as if John's question had opened a floodgate, and without thinking Edwards was pouring out the details of the case.

"She called some of her friends and they took her home. It wasn't until the next morning that she said anything about it to anyone in authority, and then it was only a dorm monitor. By the time she was seen by anyone at the Student Clinic, three days had passed and she had begun her monthly menstruation, so any physical evidence was no longer available. We—the committee members—weren't even sure she had been assaulted sexually. Then she identified the young man, but he claims he was not at the party, that he was in his room studying for an examination the following Monday. You see what I mean—'she said, he said'."

"Does the accused have legal representation?"

"Yes and no. The committee appointed a staff member to act in that capacity."

"A staff member?! Does he or she have legal training?"

"Not that I'm aware of, but there was a university lawyer sitting with the committee to protect the university's interests."

"Good heavens! What a mess!" John shook his head in disbelief. "What about motives?"

"Motives are so complex in these cases," Mary observed.

"Yes," Edwards went on, "she could have claimed to have been molested to cover up her active part in what happened, or she may have had some sort of grudge against the young man, or any number of strange motives. And he, by the same token, could be claiming not to have been there for obvious reasons. It's unbelievably complex, and as I said before, I do not think it's something that should be adjudicated by an academic committee. We don't have the training or skills to do a proper job."

"I certainly agree with you there," John said as he looked at his watch, "but I see we have to leave. We are to meet Dean Howard at the faculty club for lunch."

"Will you be there?" Mary asked.

"Not today. Our committee is having a luncheon meeting that will probably go on throughout the afternoon. But please stop in before you go back to Scotland. It's been fun talking with you two again."

Chapter 6

Stanley Howard met John and Mary at the front door of the Faculty Club, housed in an enormous Victorian on the lower campus. It had once been the President's home until an alumnus donated money for a new structure which was built on a hill overlooking the campus.

Inside, the rooms were spacious. The original living room, dining room and library were set with tables for lunch. In the dining room, where Dean Howard had his table, was a crayon wall drawing around the entire room depicting the early history of the college. He noticed Mary admiring it.

"Nice? Hmmmm? Drawn by an artistic alumnus around the turn of the 20th century. Quite valuable now as a piece of art. It's one of the things I particularly like about Carter. There are any number of valuable artifacts distributed about the campus. Ah, here is Professor Manchester now." He rose and waved to the tall, slightly rotund gentlemen with a large head of white hair, who was entering the room. He came to the table and Stanley introduced him to John and Mary.

"We look forward to your lecture tonight," Mary greeted him.

"I'm glad you'll be able to be there. I'll try to give some background on the physics of the aurora before we see the video." Through lunch, Manchester gave John and Mary some of the history about how he became interested in the northern lights.

As they were about to leave the Faculty Club, Stanley told John and Mary that he would pick them up a little before nine that evening for the lecture. Stanley went back to his office, and John and Mary returned to the library to view the Special Collections, particularly the collection of first edition books by George Bernard Shaw.

As they browsed the Shaw letters, manuscripts and first editions, they were delighted to see similar collections of Joseph Conrad, T. S. Eliot and James Joyce. As they were about to return to The Retreat for one of Mrs. Parker's delicious suppers, Mary spied another collection of note. "Oh, look, John. They have a collection of 17th century English pamphlets. We must come back tomorrow and see those," Mary said as she pointed to the glass display case. John nodded his agreement.

After supper, the Braemhors browsed The Retreat's small library. In addition to over 5000 religious books, there were art works such as a three-century-old Natarajan, a page of Kufic calligraphy from a 9th century Qur'an and original drawings by Rembrandt, Picasso and Kandinsky. "You could spend a lifetime in this one room," Mary noted as Stanley and Jane appeared at the library entrance.

"All set?" Stanley asked.

"It's a fascinating collection, isn't it?" Jane joined in.

"Most decidedly, most decidedly," John agreed, and they went in Stanley's car for the short ride to the observatory on the other side of the small, three-hole golf course, modeled after the Carter family's private course in England.

The lecture room in the observatory was small, seating only about 30. The room was full—except for their four reserved seats on the front row—when they arrived. Dr. Manchester started his lecture promptly and delivered a thirty minute explanation of what is known about the origins of the aurora. Manchester kept the talk as non-technical as he could. "The beautiful display of colored lights we are to see tonight is mainly a display of electrons and protons disturbed from the magnetosphere by solar winds. The magnetosphere is the magnetic field surrounding objects in space and controlling charged particles, which are ionized and lose energy as they are disturbed by such as the solar wind. As they lose their energy and ionize they emit the multiple colored lights that you will see tonight."

At his last statement a rumble of excitement engulfed the room. "Yes, folks," Professor Manchester continued, "we are very fortunate. The lights are in the sky and the sky is moonless and cloudless. Perfect for viewing. So we will dispense with the video and go outside and see the aurora in all its glory." With that, he led the group outside to view the northern lights.

It was as spectacular as he'd said. The aurora fell like a green veil over the upper reaches of the northern sky. Around its edges sparkled colors from the red end of the visual spectrum. The *oohs* and *aahs* of the group spread across the upper campus as they admired the display. Then suddenly in the midst of the emerald cloud, there appeared a semicircle of oval white lights. The semicircle moved across the sky, maintaining its arc through its range. Then, just as suddenly, it raced across the sky at enormous speed towards the horizon and was gone.

"What was that?' Mary turned to John.

"Not sure. Looked like a battery of spotlights. In fact, it looked very much like the picture Robert Hayson took in Perthshire last month. Strange," John said as he took out a small pad and noted the date and time.

The rest of the group also saw the lights and asked their lecturer about them. Manchester had no explanation. "Maybe it was a UFO," he quipped, but offered no more serious interpretation.

"Fascinating lecture and display," Mary commented as the four friends motored back to The Retreat.

"And we even arranged a UFO display as well for our guests," Jane offered in an uncharacteristic attempt at humor.

"The icing on the cake." Stanley smiled as he pulled the car to a halt at the walkway to The Retreat entrance. "Shall we meet again at the Faculty Club tomorrow?"

"That would be fine. Around noon?" John responded.

Next morning, there was an unusual amount of activity on the library floor of The Retreat. Many feet traversing back and forth in the library and entry hallway. John went upstairs to investigate.

The first person he encountered as he emerged from the stairs was Harry Phillips, Chief of the Carterville Police Department. Beside him was the head of campus security, Joe Burke.

"Harry, what are you doing here?" John queried.

"John, good to see you again, except that every time you show up in Carterville, I have a major crime on my hands." He smiled as he extended his hand.

"Not another murder, I hope."

"No, thank heavens, just stolen artwork, we think."

"Tell me about it." John was on the scent again.

"Mrs. Parker called me about ten minutes ago. She was cleaning the library when she noticed that the small painting by Picasso was not in its usual place. She searched the whole library and couldn't find it." Mrs. Parker appeared as he spoke.

"Oh, Mr. Braemhor, this is terrible. We've never had a theft at The Retreat before. I feel just awful!" Mrs. Parker looked on the verge of tears.

"Was there any sign of a break-in?" John asked.

"Nothing like that," the chief answered quickly. "The Retreat is always open. General policy. Always open to anyone who wants to do research in the library."

"Or to use the chapel for meditation," Mrs. Parker added. "Only the guest rooms have locks, for visitors' privacy."

"So it could have been anybody? Student? Faculty? Staff? Local people? Anyone?" John was startled by the possibilities.

"It doesn't make finding the thief very easy, not to say recovering the stolen item," Phillips sounded almost downcast, "and it doesn't make my job very easy. I've told the university time and time again that, even though we're rural and don't have many robberies, locking your doors is always a good policy. But they won't listen. Something to do with academic freedom or some such nonsense." A note of disgust had entered Phillips's tone.

"How does the insurance company—I assume the university carries insurance—feel about that?" Braemhor was a bit incredulous concerning what he was hearing.

"Oh, they're not happy about such a policy. I think they charge the university exorbitant rates, or so I hear."

"Not surprising!" Phillips again.

"How will you proceed?" John turned to Phillips.

"The usual. Contact heads of various organizations and groups and see if we can pick up any scuttlebutt that will lead us somewhere. But usually that's a dead end. Of course, we'll dust the area where the picture was and see if we can get a match, but that's not very fruitful. My guess is the insurance company will pay up, tell the university to lock their doors and raise their rates again. We've been through this before," the chief replied.

"Can I offer a different approach this time?" Braemhor had visibly brightened now that he was on the chase again.

"Of course, John. You've been a big help before. What do you have in mind?"

"First, who knows about the theft right now?"

"Just the four of us. I haven't called in a general alarm yet."

"Good." John turned to Mrs. Parker. "Do you have any more valuable paintings or drawings?"

"Yes, we have a Kandinsky and even a Rembrandt." Mrs. Parker looked puzzled. "Why?"

"Because the thief is apparently interested in paintings, particularly modern art, if this theft is any indication. Now, can you, Mrs. Parker, get the university to put a simple notice of the theft in the local papers?"

"I think so, but I'll have to clear it with the Office of Communications."

"Not good. Too many people getting involved." John was thinking out loud. "Can Dean Howard help? We need to keep the notice of this crime as quiet as possible, and yet advertise it in the papers. The fewer people involved, the better. Get Dean Howard on the phone for me, will you?"

Two minutes later, Stanley Howard was on the phone. Braemhor quickly explained to him what had happened and what his suggestion was for the immediate handling of the situation. Stanley said he could arrange it, as soon as Braemhor told him what the news release should say, but he would have to bring the head of Communications in on the plan. Braemhor agreed and dictated a statement for the university to release. Howard took care of that part of the plan.

Turning back to Phillips, Mrs. Parker, and Burke, "Now here is what I propose." Braemhor had taken over leadership by now. "Howard will put out a news release describing the theft, but including a statement that the university was very relieved that two other valuable paintings, a Kandinsky and a Rembrandt, both still in The Retreat, were not taken.

"You two," he looked at Joe Burke and Harry Phillips, "will need to have The Retreat, particularly the library where the paintings are, staked out around the clock for the rest of the week. Then we'll wait to see if the thief is greedy and wants another valuable painting to add to his collection."

"I like it," Phillips said. "Always easier to have the criminal come to us rather than have to go out and find him." The burly chief smiled.

"I have a suggestion." This was Burke.

"Yes?" John looked at the youngish man with the close-cropped hair.

"Let's make sure the student newspaper runs the story. They come out tomorrow, and I'm sure they would cooperate. Might even put it on the front page."

"Excellent!" John agreed. "Would you see to that?"

"Glad to. I'll get right on it." With that, he left The Retreat and headed back to his office.

"Anything else?" John looked at Phillips and Mrs. Parker. "Okay, then, let's put it into action and hope we get lucky. Harry, which vigil will you be taking?"

"I thought tomorrow night."

"Fine, care if I join you?"

"Glad to have you. And, John, thanks."

"Don't thank me until we see if my idea works." John smiled as Phillips went out to his cruiser and Mrs. Parker went back into the kitchen to fix breakfast for John and Mary.

At breakfast, John told Mary about the morning's happenings. "Looks like we'll be here for a few days," he concluded.

Supper at the Howards was the usual delicious, Indian curry-laced fare, but the whole evening was somber. Stanley apologized for being unable to lighten the evening with humorous repartee.

"I'm not surprised. Considering what has happened, we really appreciated your having us to dinner. You have enough worry on your hands and are most gracious to even consider dinner guests under the circumstances. I don't imagine it's every day the university has a priceless painting stolen." Mary tried to console the Howards, particularly Stanley, who as Dean felt the weight of responsibility.

"That's most considerate of you, but I just cannot get the situation out of my head. It keeps rumbling and rumbling around. I should have listened to the insurance agent the last time we had a theft and locked more doors. But that is so un-academic. The very nature of a university is to be open with all of its facilities available to anyone who wants to learn. It flies in the face of what we are and what we should be."

"It's just that the world is not what we would like it to be, or what it should be," John added, "but let's not give up hope yet. If the thief is greedy, and most of them are, we may yet recover the Picasso. At least it's not a human life we're talking about this time."

Stanley emitted a faint smile. "Thank you for that. Thank you for seeing the positive side of the situation. No, no, you're right. It is only a painting."

"Only a painting! Really, Stanley! It's a Picasso!!" Jane exploded.

"I know. I know. But in perspective it's not as bad as it could be. And who knows, with John's help we may yet recover the painting and live to smile another day." Stanley brightened some. "John, when does your plan start to take effect?"

"Tomorrow. By then the newspapers will have carried the story—even the student paper. Harry will have a plainclothes officer in The Retreat's library tomorrow all day. Then he and I will spend tomorrow night there. That's in addition to officers on the grounds. Harry is even setting up a portable TV monitoring device to keep an eye on the other two paintings. As I said, if the thief is greedy I expect he or she to come for the Kandinsky or the Rembrandt or both within the next day or so. Try to stop worrying so much. All we can do now is wait for events to unfold." Braemhor sounded calm about the sequence of events to come, but Mary knew that this was the hardest part of any investigation for John, the waiting for things to happen.

"Well, I do feel a little bit more serene knowing that you are here. You seem to have taken over the investigation from Chief Phillips," Stanley observed

"John's like that," Mary explained. "Once in, he likes to run the operation even if there are others involved."

"Just like to make certain that everything runs smoothly." John stared down at his food as he tried to clarify Mary's explanation. He quickly changed the subject. "I see the Carter University's football team is doing quite well this year." He looked at Stanley.

"Football? Football? Their season this year was a disaster. Only managed two wins. What are you. . . . Oh, oh, *football*. You mean soccer. That's what we call it over here. Soccer. Yes, yes they did quite well. Won their league championship." Stanley let his school pride show through a broad grin.

And so the conversation continued and ended on lighter notes than when it had begun, so that by the end of the evening Stanley appeared to be able to put aside some of his worry—if only for the time being.

Around nine, Stanley drove the Braemhors back to the quiet of The Retreat.

Agitated waiting gripped Braemhor all the next day, though Mary tried to distract him by having Stanley Howard arrange a university car to take them to the local airdrome to see the WWII vintage planes in one of the hangers and to the Anti-Slavery Hall of Fame in a nearby village.

By suppertime, John was experiencing his usual adrenaline high and found eating a full meal off-putting. But eat he did, especially when Mary reminded him that the night's vigil would likely be a long one.

Finally, about nine, Phillips arrived, and Mary went down to their room with a book she'd found in the library.

"Let me show you what I had installed today." Phillips motioned John into the library. He had hidden a small closed-circuit TV camera near the ceiling, pointing down at the two paintings side-by-side on the wall opposite the door. The wire from the camera to the monitor was concealed under the acoustic tiles of the ceiling, passing over the entry foyer, and exiting in the kitchen on the other side of the building.

"This way we can sit in the kitchen and watch all that goes on in the library. Anyone entering or leaving will appear on the surveillance monitor, and we can grab them as they leave the library. I've also got a man hidden on the grounds outside in case we should slip up and miss the culprit. Satisfactory?" He looked to John for approval.

"Excellent!" John responded. "Now let's go into the kitchen, get some comfortable—but not too comfortable—chairs and see if Mrs. Parker has left us any snacks and coffee."

"Fine with me. I find stakeouts rouse my appetite." Both of Phillips's chins smiled in their agreement with John's idea.

And so the waiting began. For awhile they chatted about various new criminology techniques, drank coffee and munched the snacks. Then they took hourly turns closing their eyes and resting. John had brought a book of short stories by one of the faculty members who'd been honored with a national award.

About 2:00 a.m., the short story John was reading about a family's burden caring for a child with cerebral palsy was interrupted when the monitor revealed a diminutive figure dressed all in black quietly approaching the wall on which hung the two paintings.

Braemhor quickly placed his hand over Phillips's mouth and gently shook him. Phillips's eyes opened as he muttered "Harrumph" into John's hand. John pointed to the monitor screen. They watched as the individual lifted the Kandinsky off its hook. Phillips alerted his man outside to stand ready by the front door. Quickly, Phillips and Braemhor moved out of the kitchen and down the short hall to the foyer where they waited for the thief to exit the library. A few seconds later a person carrying the Kandinsky came out of the library and headed to the front exit. At that point, Phillips's man outside blocked the way, and Phillips grabbed the individual from behind, pinning her—it was a female—arms behind her as Braemhor lifted the Kandinsky from her grasp.

Phillips put her wrists in handcuffs, told her her rights, and took her to the police cruiser that another of his men had brought up to the entranceway. "I'll be going to the county seat, have her arraigned, and put her into a nice quiet cell. I'll call you later."

"And I'll put the Kandinsky back on the wall and let Dean Howard know we were lucky," Braemhor said. "It's been a good night's work." John was pleased.

He replaced the painting and then went to the phone in the foyer and placed a call to Stanley Howard.

After five rings a muffled, groggy voice came through the line. "Hello."

"Stanley, it's me, John Braemhor."

"John, do you realize it's three in the morning? What do you want?" Howard was clearly not pleased.

"Just thought you'd like to know, we got lucky. We got the culprit trying to walk off with the Kandinsky. Phillips has taken her to jail at the county seat, and I've put the painting back on the wall where it belongs. Just thought you ought to know."

"Of course, John, of course. Sorry if I was short with you, but I'm not used to phone calls at this time of night."

"Right, I'll let you get back to sleep and tell you more about it tomorrow." The two hung up and John rushed downstairs to tell Mary of the night's events. He was still on a high from the fruits of the investigation. An hour later, he was finally able to settle down to sleep, having told Mary to rouse him as soon as Phillips called.

It wasn't until almost three in the afternoon that Mrs. Parker came to the Braemhor's room to say that Chief Phillips was on the phone.

"Braemhor here." John picked up the receiver.

"John. . . Harry. . .I can pick you up in about ten minutes and bring you up-to-date. Okay?"

"Fine. I'll be outside looking for you."

Phillips's timing was as good as he had estimated, and ten minutes later he parked his cruiser in the car park across the road from The Retreat and strode into the foyer. "Where should we talk?" He looked around.

"Come into the music room. Mrs. Parker just offered to cook up some scones and tea. I'll call Mary."

The three sat down at a table in the music room, and Phillips began to recount the events since the arrest. "Well, I got the young lady—she's one of the students here at the college—arraigned and safe in a cell. She used her one phone call to call her father in Chicago. Seems he's a big-time lawyer or some such. At any rate, by eight this morning he had arranged bail and she was free to go. I've had nothing but flack from him and his representative all morning. Then the university legal staff got on my case by noon, claiming I was putting the university in jeopardy for not going through campus security and their internal judicial committee system first. That I really don't understand, but. . . .

"Anyway, she's claiming all kinds of psychological damage because she was put into a jail cell. Imagine! The family has already been in touch with some high-up mucky muck in the state legislature, would you believe. Sometimes, John, I don't know why I stay in this business."

"Because you believe in law and order no matter what level of society the criminal comes from," John interceded. "What's next?"

"Well, it will be up to the university as to whether or not they bring charges. I just arrest 'em," Phillips said with a sigh, "and another thing, her lawyers are saying we can't charge her with breaking and entering, because the doors weren't locked."

"That's probably true, but she was carrying out a painting that did not belong to her." John thought that this one fact would make the case.

"Yeah, John, but we nabbed her *before* she actually got over the threshold on her way out! And she's claiming that she was only moving the painting to the window to see it in better light!"

"At two in the morning! You're kidding me!"

"I wish I were." Phillips was beginning to sound and act despondent.

"So what's going to happen now?"

"My guess is that the university will fold and not press charges—this is a rich, influential family, you understand—and the case will be dropped. I've done all I can. I filed my report of criminally attempted robbery and it's up to the plaintiffs to take it from there. Unless we can find the Picasso and tie its theft to her, this may be as far as this case goes. Joe Burke and I have searched her room and locker at the gym to no avail. No Picasso."

"I hate to see this case get away from you," Braemhor commiserated.

"You and me both, but there you are. I think I'll retire." He ended in mock disgruntlement. Then, after a pause, "Oh, yes, one other thing, she's the same student who's involved in the rape case on campus."

"The one who claimed that she was raped at a party, and it's being investigated by a university committee?" John was even more incredulous.

"The very same," Phillips offered a sardonic smile.

After another pause while Braemhor assimilated all Phillips had been telling him, he said, "Well, first things first. We need to find the Picasso. You say you've already searched her room and her other campus venues?"

"Every place we could think of."

At this point, Mary joined in, "John, if you want to find a tree, where do you look?"

"In a forest, of course," John answered absentmindedly.

"Of course." Mary looked at Phillips. "Does she have any pictures on the walls of her room?"

"Couple of posters, yes. Oh, I see! Of course!"

"Shall we go see?" Braemhor rose.

Ten minutes later, the three entered the student's dorm room. It was disheveled from the morning's searches. On the wall were three large framed posters, one advertising a student production of *An American in Paris,* another of a new Broadway show, *Something Rotten,* and a third touting the 1899 production of William Gillette's *Sherlock Holmes.*

"If we're right, does anyone want to take bets on which poster?" John framed the question in everyone's mind.

"Oh, John, this is like something out of a poorly written novel," Mary summed up as she lifted the Sherlock Holmes poster off the wall.

"Harry, you're the official here. You open the back, but carefully." John handed Phillips a small penknife to work with.

Five minutes of carefully stripping the paper backing off the poster revealed, at last, the missing Picasso. All three broke out into broad congratulatory smiles. "Now, I think you have the evidence you need to prod the university into legal action." John looked at Phillips.

"John, Mary, what would I do without the two of you?"

"Probably retire," Mary joked.

That night, the Braemhors had another grand supper with the Howards, but this time with a much relieved Stanley and Jane.

"Again, I don't know how to thank the two of you," Stanley gushed.

"Really, Stanley, it was our pleasure to help friends out," John assured him.

"Maybe we shouldn't visit so often. It seems we carry a dark cloud with us every time we come to your delightful college town," Mary added.

"Oh, no, no. You must come back so we can share some more adventures together." Stanley was a gracious host.

"Are you sure you can take it?" John chuckled.

"For friends like you two, certainly."

"Well, we wish we could stay longer, but we really do have to get back to Daraichburn. We still run a B&B there, you know," Mary said.

"And you will be leaving when?" Jane asked.

"We thought we would catch the 11:00 a.m. train to West Point, and then from there, the next day to New Boston.

And so the evening ended on a happy note all-around.

Chapter 7

After a brief stop to see the U. S. Military Academy at West Point, the Braemhors settled in for a weekend with James, Jennifer and the two grandchildren before flying back to Scotland.

Rita was there to greet them at the door of Dunmoor Cottage when they arrived back home.

She giggled her pleasure at having them home again. "Did you have a good visit with the family?" she asked as she hugged Mary and John.

"Very good. And how have things been here at the Cottage? Any problems?"

"All quiet, except for one American who wanted to know where the UFOs were. I sent him to Loch Lomond and told him they were really fairy airships built to carry fairies from one galaxy to another. Do you know, I don't think he believed me, but that's what it said in the fairy book you bought me."

"Zauberin strikes again," John whispered to Mary, who just smiled and tried to keep him from laughing aloud.

A few days later, while John was tending his apple trees and Mary and Rita were getting the Cottage ready for new guests, Mary heard the postman put some letters through the front door slot.

"John, there's a letter from Bill Edwards," Mary called as she picked up the post from the front hall floor where it had dropped.

Dear Mary and John,

It was so nice to see you again and you were very accommodating to let me unburden myself regarding my new committee assignment. There is some news on that front. The co-ed who made the accusation has recanted. Says she was never assaulted. Her friends say she was just angry because the young man wouldn't give her a tumble and take her to the round of spring parties. So the case is considered closed, the committee disbanded, and I don't have to worry anymore about proper protocol determining guilt and innocence. I can't tell you how relieved I am. Now I can get back to my hypnosis research.

The other curious thing about the whole affair is that she has now dropped out of college amidst unconfirmed rumors that she was having some sort of problem with the local authorities. I don't know what that is all about, but I'll let you know if I find out.

Meantime, it was good seeing you two again and maybe the next time I take a study group to Edinburgh, I can make a side trip to Daraichburn and stay in your B&B.

Best regards,
Bill

"I'm pleased for him. He's such a nice young man," Mary said as she handed the brief note to John.

"Me too, and I'm sure he's relieved to be out of that committee. I still don't understand why the university would try to handle such a serious accusation within the college's committee structure. I guess I will never fathom the way they do things in the Colonies," John concurred.

"Imagine what their politics must be like." Mary smiled.

"Anything for me?" Rita asked expectantly.

"No, Aunt Rita. Who are you expecting a letter from?" Mary was curious.

"Sir Arthur Conan Doyle, of course." Rita gave her signature impish smile, wrinkling her nose in the process.

"Rita!" John jumped into the conversation. "Doyle has been dead since 1930! What are you talking about?"

"That just shows how much you know, John. Sir Arthur was a spiritualist, and his website gives an address where you can reach him." Rita was indignant and a little feisty. "I've been trying to correspond with him ever since you went to Fort Ewen and brought me back the first book on the fairies. But I don't think he cares." A note of disappointment entered her voice.

"You haven't been sending his website money, have you?" Mary was horrified.

"Of course not, Mary. I won't send a cent until I know he'll answer my letters."

"That's a plus." John joined in again as the telephone rang.

Mary answered. She covered the receiver as she handed it to John. "John, it's long distance from Manchester."

"Braemhor here."

"Hold for Mr. Street, Mr. Nigel Street," a female voice intoned.

Nigel Street, hmm, that's interesting, John thought as he waited.

"Mr. Braemhor, Nigel Street here, from Manchester. I need to talk with you."

"I'm listening." Braemhor was intrigued that MI6 would be contacting him after the run-in he'd had with them while working on the Gorman suicide case a year or so ago, and on the mystery of the hum more recently.

"Not on the phone, I'm afraid. When can you be in Manchester?"

"Tomorrow, if need be, but can you tell me anything?"

"Not really, but I have something you might be interested in." Street continued to be coy.

"Are you hiring me?" John smiled to himself. *This is quite a turnaround.*

"We can discuss that when you get here. Tomorrow then, shall we say about two?"

"I'll see you then," John said as Street hung up.

"Nigel Street wants to see me." John turned to Mary.

"From MI6?"

"The very same. Something he won't discuss on the phone. Even implied he might hire me! He's certainly mellowed since we last talked."

"Finally recognizing your value."

"Well, we'll see. I'm going to Manchester tomorrow for an afternoon meeting."

* * * * *

At 1:55 p.m. Braemhor entered the large, grey stone structure in Manchester that housed MI6 and a number of other governmental agencies. The receptionist at the ground floor entrance recognized him from his last trip.

"Ah, Mr. Braemhor, for Mr. Street, right?"

John just smiled and nodded as two burly men, obviously some sort of agents, approached him from either side and, gently this time, took him by the arms and led him to an awaiting elevator. A quick ride up and they deposited him in front of a door marked: "N. Street." He knocked. Street greeted him at the door.

"Come in. Come in." Street's smile appeared forced, but he did smile. "My, my, we are prompt, aren't we? Here, have a seat," he said as he pointed to a cushioned chair in front of the overly large executive desk on the back wall.

"We got off on the wrong foot last time we met. I hope we can do better this time."

"I don't see why not." Braemhor met Street's accommodating tone with an agreeable approach.

"Fine. Then let us begin. Your findings in the Gorman case, which you shared with the agency, were most helpful, though, as you know, I did not approve of your methods of interfering with official government business. And the data you uncovered on the 'hum' and how by disrupting signals, it caused submarines to have near-accidents in the Una area were, I must say, of value to our investigations." Each sentence of praise for Braemhor's skills as an investigator seemed to get more and more difficult for Street to utter. Street was just not one to offer praise for another's investigative skills, but he did understand and live by rules of a certain graciousness in interpersonal interactions.

"Now we have another situation, near Sutors Cove on the Moray Firth, where the services of someone not directly associated with the agency might be of value. The population in that area is thin so that any new people come under unusual scrutiny by the locals. And it's more difficult to pass off our agents as traveling tourists on holiday. It occurred to me that someone like yourself, who has seasoned investigative skills, might more easily pass as a tourist and gather information without arousing as much attention. You with your wife—I understand she sometimes assists you in your investigations—would make a more plausible 'tourists on holiday' appearance."

"We have occasionally spent some holidays at the Seaview Hotel in Sutors Cove. They know us there," Braemhor informed him.

"Excellent. That is just the sort of scenario I had in mind. The fact that you and your wife are already known as occasional tourists would fit perfectly." Street's rigidity showed the first signs of melting into cordiality.

"What are we looking for?" John interjected.

"We think that there is some sort of clandestine activity going on along the coast. Rather large trawlers are seen from time to time off Sutors Cove, but their cargo and purpose are unknown. Mostly they are flying flags of Baltic nations, occasionally of Russia. They anchor in international waters, stay a day or two and then move on, usually to a Scandinavian port, Sweden most often. That much we have traced. Most of their cargo centers on radio and telephone communications, though furniture and crude petroleum products are also part of their manifest. But the question is: why do they go out of their way and make a stop in the Moray Firth? Are they dropping something off in Scotland or picking up some cargo on their way? No one on either end seems to know, and we have not been able to discover the answers we want."

"Let me understand. Trawlers from the Baltic area are stopping in international waters along the Sutors Cove coast on a diverted path to Scandinavia for a few days and then continuing their voyage. You think something illegal might be going on, but you have no idea what and no solid evidence of any criminal activity?" Braemhor asked.

"That is correct."

"Have you intercepted any of their craft or personnel?"

"No, they stay in international waters, you see. We have been in contact with some of the ships' companies in the Baltic area, but they vehemently deny that their ships are stopping in Scotland before going on their way, obviously a fabrication. You are right, Mr. Braemhor, we don't know whether or not any criminal activity is taking place, but you must admit that it's odd for a trawler to spend several days off of our shore without some purpose. We need to know why they stop instead of going directly to their ultimate destination."

"Interesting," Braemhor thought aloud.

"Will you agree to assist the agency?" Street got directly to the point. "I can offer you a reasonable per diem plus expenses for you and your wife, but I will need you to begin immediately."

Braemhor thought for a moment, then said, "Yes, I will, but we will not be able to go to Sutors Cove until day after tomorrow. Agreed?"

"That will be acceptable." Street pushed a button on his desk console. "Ross, come in, will you?"

Ross was a young man in his middle thirties with a shock of red hair that made him look more like an Irishman than a Scot. "Sir?"

"Mr. Braemhor is going to be working for the agency for a few weeks. Make out the usual paperwork. He'll pick it up on his way out."

"Sir." Ross nodded and exited.

Street continued, "You understand, Mr. Braemhor, that none of these data are to leave this room. Nor are you to talk to anyone—your wife excepted—about why you are on holiday in Sutors Cove. See what you can find, and let me know as soon as you have anything of value. Now I have other business to attend to. See Ross on your way out for the appropriate papers." Street abruptly ended the interview.

Braemhor completed the proper papers in Ross's office and returned to Daraichburn, arriving just before Mary was setting out supper for herself and Aunt Rita. She added another plate at the table.

"Rita, can you stay on for another fortnight?" John asked after he was seated.

"Oh, I'd like that," was Rita's reply as she attacked her portion of the chicken in the heather casserole.

"What was that all about—Rita staying for another fortnight?" Mary asked when she and John had reached the privacy of their bedroom later that night.

John quickly told her of Street's proposal and of their need to have Rita look after the Cottage for a while longer.

"So we're going to Sutors Cove as 'tourists' to discover an unknown crime for which there is no evidence, and that one of the largest and best spy agencies in the world doesn't even know if it has been committed. Should be challenging." Mary was somewhat incredulous.

"Challenging, indeed," John agreed, as he turned off the lamp on the nightstand.

* * * * *

Two days later, John and Mary took up Street's challenge. They drove their usual northern route bordering Loch Ness to Inverness, where the A9 led them to the A832 to the Ebony Isle and the picturesque seaside village of Sutors Cove. Long a naturally protected, active seaport of the war years off the North Sea, its economy was still supported by the North Sea oil fields, though the size of the village itself had never outgrown its past, still housing less than 1,000 villagers.

On their earlier visits both John and Mary had found it to be the near-perfect, restful holiday venue.

As before, the Braemhors booked a room at the Seaview Hotel located on the coast overlooking the Moray Firth. From the balcony of their room they could watch the small waves of the Firth lap the beach that afforded the local children a sandy playground this time of year until about 11:30 p.m. when darkness finally engulfed their view and the cold waters of the harbor.

"Ah, Mr. and Mrs. Braemhor, so good to see you again. Your usual room on the front?" Ian Ross's salt-and-pepper hair cascaded over his left eye, which sparkled with its usual twinkle.

"That will be very nice, Mr. Ross," Mary answered.

"Things quiet up here in the Highlands?" John asked.

"Oh, yes, sir. Our usual quiet, restful village, except for occasional visits from UK spy agencies."

"Spy agencies?" John was intrigued.

"Oh, you know, spy types, dark suits, wires hanging from their ears, bulges under their jackets. They think we locals don't notice. It all started shortly after the ships began spending a few days anchored off our coast."

"Ships off the coast?" John wanted to keep the conversation going as long as he could.

"Oh, yes, Mr. Braemhor. Started a month or so ago. First they were smallish trawlers then some larger freighters. Don't know what they are doing. They drop anchor for a day or so, then weigh up and off they go again. Strange, but they don't seem to be bothering anyone. In a way it's nice. Gives our few tourists something different to see and talk about. One just left yesterday, but I suspect one will be here in a day or two. Maybe you'll get to see our new tourist attraction." Ross smiled.

"Oh, I hope so. That will be interesting." Mary played her role as tourist.

In their room unpacking their valises, Mary raised her eyebrows.

"We've come to the right place," John concluded. "Too bad MI6 couldn't do a better job of fading into the background. . . . But yet it affords us a paid holiday. I think I'll have a longer talk with Mr. Ross, see what else I can discover. My guess is that the locals know more about what's going on than Street's boys have been able to discover." He went back downstairs to reception while Mary reclined in the chaise lounge on their balcony and enjoyed the sea view the hotel was famous for.

An hour later, John returned with a lighter bounce in his step.

"Find something, John?" Mary came in from the balcony.

"Not much, but I think our best informants will be the locals. Seems the ships come in between 11:00 p.m. and midnight, drop anchor and sit just off the coast for no more than 48 hours, during which time—particularly in the dark hours, three or four in the morning—a lot of static breaks up the radio stations on shore. Problem is not many people are listening to their radios at that time in the morning, but a few are and I've got the name of one who may be of some help—the local lighthouse keeper. He tends the lighthouse at night so plays his radio in the wee hours." John told Mary what he had learned.

"Signals of some sort?" Mary asked.

"Very possibly. But they're not visual signals, if they are."

"Infrared?" Mary offered.

"Mary, you're wonderful. We think so much alike. Infrared frequencies have been used in open air communications, and it's something we will have to keep in mind. The ships are not sending any visual signals that anyone has noticed—and MI6 would have noticed that—but locals have experienced some interference with radio transmission, so infrared may be a distinct possibility.

John continued, "the ships sit in the firth for a day or two and then move on. No one has seen any crew come ashore night or day, and all of their small craft stay onboard. If they are bringing something, or somebody, to our shores, they are either not depositing it on shore or are being devilishly clever about how they are unloading it. There are only two possibilities. The contraband is coming ashore by air or under the surface of the sea."

"There are other possibilities, John."

"Oh?"

"Maybe they are bringing information."

"And they signal it ashore and then go on their way?"

"Possibly. . . . Or maybe there's another possibility."

John was intrigued with Mary's reasoning. "Yes?"

"Maybe they aren't bringing or picking up anything."

John had to laugh at that idea. "You mean they're just harassing our MI6 agents. Sort of an international signal game to see how good, or how gullible, our counter espionage is?"

"Information gathering," Mary summed up.

"Well, we shall see. We shall see. But for now let's go have some supper and then go to the lighthouse. It's just a short walk."

The lighthouse was just a short distance from the hotel on the point of the Ebony Isle that extends into the firth. A small light on the ground level of the structure showed the Braemhors that the keep was indeed on duty. As they approached the front door, they heard the sounds of mechanical grinding followed by a loud metallic "whoosh," that accompanied the periodic rotation of the main light, telling all those at sea that here was a jut of land to be avoided.

John waited until the whoosh had transpired then knocked loudly on the oak door of the keeper's lodging. The huge light continued its 360° rotation as John and Mary awaited a response from within. In the midst of the next whoosh, it came. The small, wizened man who opened the door had white and grey stubble running from his temples to the point of his chin. The hair on his head—what there was of it—was also white and grey, highlighting his grey eyes and wind and sea ravaged face.

"I wonder if we could have a word with you about the ships that have recently been anchoring off the point?" John started.

"Aye. You from the gov'ment, too?"

"No, no, we're from Daraichburn near Glasgow, on holiday. But since we arrived, the ships are all we've heard about. It's all the local gossip and it aroused our curiosity. When we've been here before, it has always been so peaceful and quiet. Mr. Ross at the Seaview said you probably know more about them than anyone."

"Did he, eh? Well, he's right. I've probably seen more of 'em and heard more of 'em than anyone around. Come in. Come in. I've just heated up some tea. Maybe you'd like some?"

"That would be nice, Mr. . . ." Mary entered, followed by John.

"Wren, Achilles Wren, and you are?"

John came forward. "I'm John Braemhor and this is my wife, Mary."

"On holiday, you say?"

"That's right."

"And what do you do?" Mr. Wren was quite inquisitive.

"Oh, I'm retired," John said reluctantly.

"We run a B&B in Daraichburn," Mary quickly interjected. "Have you been a lighthouse keeper long?"

"All me life. Runs in the family. I'm the fourth generation."

"Doesn't it get lonely?" Mary persisted.

"Not at all. I have me books and me radio, except when the ship's signals interfere. Think I might try a telly next year."

"How do you think the ships interfere with your radio?" John was quick to jump on an opening.

"Don't know, but it's gotta be the ships. Me radio goes down—static just wipes out the programs—only when they're out there and always in the early morning. Used to have the same problem during the war years when part of the UK fleet was hiding up here. But then you could always see them signaling to one another. International Morse, you know, but not now. Everything's as quiet as a graveyard, but lots of static. Can't hear me programs."

"Maybe it's just storms," John offered.

"Only when the ships are there and only between three and four in the morning? I don't think so. It's the ships, all right."

"But what do you think they're doing?" Mary asked between sips of tea. "Do their crews ever come ashore?"

"Don't think so. They just anchor out there." He pointed out toward the firth. "And then they leave after a day or two. But the gov'ment boys sure are interested. Been here several times, asking all kinds of questions. Almost like the war years."

"What were the war years like?"

"Oh, busy. Not like now. The fleet was always flashing signals to one another then, like a bunch of fireflies. But not now."

"You don't see any signals from the ships now?

"Aye, that's the puzzle. Not like the war years when I'd sit upstairs and read the flashing lights between ships. All dark now, but something's going on. Just the bloody—oops, sorry ma'am—static."

"Oh, that's all right, Mr. Wren, I've heard a lot worse in my lifetime." Mary smiled.

"And the static is only in the early hours of the morning?" John asked.

"That's right. Like they turn up their static machine for an hour and then turn it off."

"Never in the daytime?"

"Don't think so. 'Course I sleep a lot in the daytime. Mine's a night job, you see."

"Of course, of course. Well, Mr. Wren, we've bothered you enough and interfered with your reading and radio long enough. Thank you for sharing what you know about the ships with us. It certainly seems to be quite a mystery for such a holiday village. But we need to get back to the hotel now. Maybe we'll stop by another evening and learn more about life on the Ebony Isle, if you don't mind."

"Not at all. Can always do with a little company once in a while. Specially when I can't listen to me radio. Hope to see you again, then." Wren rose and offered his gnarled hand to John and Mary in turn.

As the Braemhors walked along the shore to the Seaview Mary summed up, "Not much there, John."

"Maybe not, but I think our Mr. Wren might be a good source in the future. Maybe tomorrow we'll walk the village and take in some of the sights. Play our role as tourists until another ship shows up," John finished as they entered the Seaview.

* * * * *

Next morning, following breakfast, John and Mary visited a number of merchants' houses along Church Street, and bought two books by a local author for Rita. Farther down the street was St. Dinsden's Kirk, still in use from the 1580's.

As they were viewing the interior of the kirk and its laird's loft, a high-pitched feminine-sounding voice accosted them from one of the side pews. "I know who you are! But you don't know who I am!"

John turned and faced the slender, almost emaciated young man dressed in what appeared to be a centuries old brown tunic. "And who are we? And who are you? And how do you know who we are?"

"Oh dear, oh dear, oh dear. So many questions. And all at once. I can't cope. Go away you, strange, strangers." With that, the individual ducked behind one of the fluted columns, peering around the structure with one exaggerated exophthalmic eye.

"Of course, you can," John assured him. "Just take them one at a time. First, who are we?"

"Don't you know?! I would have thought of all of us here, you would certainly know who you are. But, alas, you are without an identity. I sometimes feel that way, too. When my other self is in charge. But then I come back."

John decided to question their newfound "friend" with, "Who are we? What do you call us?"

"There you go again! Too many questions all at once. I'll take the first one first," he said as he stepped out from behind the column. "You are the Braemhors. Ah ha, you see, I know more about you than you know about me."

"Quite so. Quite so." John continued the rather disjointed conversation. "How do you know we are the Braemhors?"

"Me uncle told me."

"Your uncle?" Mary entered the conversation.

"Yes! He of the gigantic rotating eye."

"He means Mr. Wren, I believe," John whispered to Mary.

The young man astonished the Braemhors with, "That's right. . .Mr. Wren."

The acoustics in here are nothing short of amazing, John thought to himself.

"And who are you?" Mary asked.

"I'm Jeremy—Jeremy of the ancient kirk."

"And you live here?" John stated.

"How did you know?" Jeremy became noticeably wary. "Are you a wizard?"

"No, just a lucky guess." John smiled to reassure the now skittish young man. "You have a beautiful home. Have you lived here long?"

"Longer than you know." An impish smile darted across Jeremy's face. "You're here because of the green ships."

"Green ships?"

"In the Firth. I see them at night with my special eyes. And sometimes they spit green daggers."

At that point, another voice—a deep bass sound—entered the conversation, "Jeremy! What have I told you about disturbing our guests?"

Jeremy was obviously cowed by the figure of the priest in his long, black vestment and white starched collar. "These are my new friends, Father, I was only talking with them. I have so few friends, you know."

"Quite so, Jeremy. Now run along and I'll talk with you later." Jeremy scurried away like a frightened mouse.

"You'll have to forgive Jeremy. He lives here in the kirk, and we try to look after him as best we can. It's the only home he knows, you see."

"Nothing to forgive, Father. We were just looking at your lovely kirk when Jeremy engaged us in an interesting conversation." Mary spoke first. "We're here on holiday and came to see your kirk. Such a beautiful building and in such an outstanding location."

John entered the conversation. "Why does Jeremy live here at the kirk?"

"It's a long story." The priest smiled. "You see, Jeremy comes from a very poor family here in Sutors Cove and when it was realized that he was—how shall I put it?—mentally challenged, the family had no choice but to look for institutional housing for him. I thought that would be a family and personal tragedy, so I arranged for him to stay here with us. We constructed a small apartment for him in the attic where he spends most of his time. He shares our table and in return does many odd jobs, cleaning and the like, for us. It has turned out to be a blessing because he is here near his family and contributes to the well-being of the kirk.

"That's wonderful," Mary observed.

"It's what the church is supposed to be about, you know. Caring for others, and particularly those who cannot care for themselves." The priest seemed pleased to be able to teach a lesson in Christianity to these visitors. "And Jeremy seems to be very happy with us."

"Why does he refer to the ships in the firth as the 'green' ships?" John asked.

"Oh that. Well, as you have no doubt discovered, the ships that have been coming and going for the past month or so are the talk of the village. Everybody talks about them and now they are even beginning to attract tourists, like yourselves. Jeremy watches the ships, mainly at night, and I thought perhaps he might like some inexpensive night-vision goggles to see them better. It was a simple thing, but it did seem to please him very much—and keeps him entertained for hours on end."

"He seems to be very happy here," Mary observed.

"Oh, we hope so. Sometimes when he thinks I am displeased with him, he gets very upset, but by and large we have a very good relationship." The priest was obviously proud of his own good works toward Jeremy.

"Well, thank you very much for sharing your kirk with us but we'd best not take any more of your time." John was ready to leave.

"Quite all right. Please come back most anytime. I can show you some of the ancient session records, if you like. They date back to the beginning of the kirk."

"Perhaps we will come back. We're here in Sutors Cove for a week or so." John led Mary outside.

Just as the Braemhors left, they heard a distinctive "pssst," from around the corner of the kirk. It was Jeremy beckoning them.

"What do you want, Jeremy?" Mary asked gently.

"A green ship is coming tonight." He was beaming with enthusiasm.

"And will it send green daggers, Jeremy?" John asked in earnest.

"I hope so. They are so much fun to watch."

"And are some of the daggers little, short daggers and others long daggers?"

"How did you know? I knew it. I knew it. You are a wizard! Oh, I have my very own wizard! Yes, some are short and some are long."

"Do they sometimes send short, short, short, long, long, long, short, short, short?"

"No, they've never done that." Jeremy seemed appalled that Braemhor would ask about a pattern of lights he had never seen.

"That's good, Jeremy. Because if they ever send that string of daggers it would mean they were in trouble. So your green ships are safe from harm," John assured him.

Jeremy was visibly pleased to know that his green ships were all right.

"You say they are coming back tonight?"

"Yes, Mr. Wizard, but you knew that all along, didn't you? Wizards know everything."

"Will you do something for me?"

"Oh, yes, yes." Jeremy was delighted to be asked to do something for his personal "wizard."

"When the daggers start coming, write down if they are short or long for as long as they keep coming. Can you do that for me?" John was enlisting Jeremy's assistance. "Can you spell those words—*long* and *short*?"

Jeremy was crestfallen and hung his head in apparent shame.

John put his hand on Jeremy's shoulder. "It's all right. Just put down a dot, like this, for the short daggers and a dash, like this, for the long daggers. Can you do that?" John had taken out a small pad and pencil and was illustrating what he was asking Jeremy to do.

"Oh yes, yes, Mr. Wizard. A dot for short daggers, and a dash for long ones." Jeremy was happy again.

"And put them down just as they come. All of them. Right?"

"Oh yes, yes, Mr. Wizard. This will be so much fun."

"This will be our own secret code just between you and me. Don't tell anyone else, not even the good Father. I will come tomorrow to see what you've written down. All right?"

"Oh yes, sir. Yes, sir, tomorrow." With that, Jeremy disappeared around the kirk and the Braemhors walked back to the hotel.

Mary was slightly perplexed. "What was that all about, John?"

"First, the reason the ships look green to Jeremy is because they emit heat as infrared waves, and seen through night-vision goggles they will appear greenish. The goggles convert the invisible infrared into visible light, but only at the green end of the spectrum. And Jeremy's green daggers are, I'll wager, bursts of infrared carrying information, just as you originally supposed. Your infrared idea was right on the mark, Mary. I think the ships are using International Morse Code to convey their messages, and so Jeremy's short daggers are dots and the long ones, dashes."

"And the 'dot, dot, dot, dash, dash, dash, dot, dot, dot' you asked him about?"

"That's Morse for SOS, the universal distress signal and assuming none of the ships have conveyed such a signal, it was an easy way to find out how really attentive our Jeremy is. I think he will be an excellent information gatherer, mentally challenged or not."

"Very clever, Mr. Holmes." Mary smiled.

"Thank you, Mrs. Watson." John answered as they entered the Seaview.

Chapter 8

The sun sparkled on the placid surface of Moray Firth the next morning as Mary awoke to find John up, dressed, and on the balcony with his binoculars.

"Come, look at what the new day has brought us," he called.

Mary came to the balcony door, looked out over the waters and observed, "Just as Jeremy predicted. How did he do it?"

"Lucky guess. He knew it had been several days since the last ship appeared. But there she is. We'll have to go see Jeremy again and see if he picked up any signals in the early morning."

Following a breakfast of smoked herring, baked beans, burnt toast, and coffee, the Braemhors walked down Church Street again to St. Dinsden's where they found Jeremy sweeping the long walkway to the front of the kirk.

"Ah, Mr. Wizard. I did just what you wanted and wrote down all of the daggers from the green ship. I'll get them." He ran back into the kirk and reappeared minutes later clutching a crumpled paper in his hand. His face was beaming with delight. "Here, our secret code." He stood bouncing from one foot to the other with excitement. "I did a good job, didn't I?"

"You certainly did. This is excellent. Excellent." John patted Jeremy's shoulder as he spoke.

"What does it mean? What does it mean?" Jeremy could hardly contain himself.

"It tells us where something exciting is going to happen. Now, tell us about last night."

"Is she a wizard, too?" Jeremy pointed at Mary.

"Oh, yes, she is Mrs. Wizard," John answered with a straight face as Mary listened to this odd conversation, "so tell us about last night."

"All right. I was sitting in my room waiting for the green ship when I heard it coming up the firth. And then with a great clank and a huge splash it dropped its anchor. I watched it very carefully with my special eyes, for a long time. But nothing happened until much later. Then the green daggers started, first with a short, short, short, short, short. Then it stopped for a moment and started again with long, long, short, short, short. I wrote them all down. See?" He pointed to the paper in Braemhor's hand.

"I see. That's very good," John praised Jeremy.

"I did good, didn't I?" Jeremy's need for praise was evident.

"You certainly did, Jeremy, but now Mrs. Wizard and I have to go back to our room at the hotel and study this paper with your writing. Now, I want you to do the same thing tonight. And remember, don't tell anyone else. Just me and Mrs. Wizard. All right?"

"Yes, Mr. Wizard. All very secret." Jeremy was obviously pleased to be a part of Braemhor's—Mr. Wizard's—secret mission.

"Where to now, John?" Mary asked.

"First, I think we will go back to the Seaview and translate this." He held the paper up. "I think it's code for a location somewhere here in the highlands. If so, then I will want to go to Inverness and get myself a set of night-vision goggles. It'll be important for us to verify Jeremy's observations."

Back in their room at the Seaview, the Braemhors sat at a small table on their balcony while John applied International Morse to the series of dots and dashes on Jeremy's paper. "There!" John showed Mary the translation of the message on the paper: "57 39 37 and 3 36 53"

"What is it, John?"

Latitude and Longitude, if I'm not mistaken. Let me check the internet and see where it is." He got their small laptop computer from the valise and entered the figures as coordinates. "Ah, ha. Just as I thought. These are the coordinates of a marina across the firth from us. Care for a short drive this afternoon?"

An hour later, the two arrived at the marina in a small coastal village located on an inlet three quarters of the way north up the eastern coast of Moray Firth. The Braemhors walked idly around among the skiffs and small power boats anchored in the safety of the natural cove.

"Can I help ye?" The voice was as cracked as the face. "Need to let a skiff? Do a little fishin?"

"No, thank you. We're just on holiday. Staying over in Sutors Cove and thought we'd see this side of the firth. Mind if we just wander around a bit?" John put on his best cordiality.

"Help yourselves. Not much to look at. We're a small marina. There are some bigger ones farther north." The old man was friendly. He went back to smoking his pipe.

"Not many visitors, eh?" John probed.

"Not many, 'cept for you two and our regular gentleman."

"Regular gentleman?" John's antennae were alerted.

"Oh, yes. Comes over from Sutors Cove, I think. Every week or so. Spends some time walking 'round the docks then takes a stroll on the dunes 'cross the way." He pointed east. "Says it's good for his health. Strange person. Seems kinda cultured like."

"Cultured?" Mary asked.

"Yeah. Uses big words, you know. Like maybe he reads a lot. Strange, but nice enough."

Suddenly John said, "Maybe we'll look at the dunes too. They sound unusual. All right to leave our car here?"

"Help yourselves. I'll be here most of the afternoon."

The Braemhors crossed the road that had brought them to the marina and walked out onto the extensive dunes covering the landscape for as far as the eye could see. Mary took her shoes off to make the walking easier.

"This is beautiful, John."

"Certainly is and barren and desolate. Once you leave the road no one would know you were here. Let's go deeper in." And so they strode eastward until it was like they had walked off of the edge of the earth. All they could see around them were sand hills without definition or recognizable features."

"John, I don't like this." Mary had become concerned. "Are. . .are we lost? I don't want to have to wait until dusk to find our way back west."

"Not to worry," John said as he held up his key fob which also held a small compass.

"Thank heavens you plan ahead." Mary was clearly relieved. "But where do we go from here?"

"I think we can start to circle back. . . . But wait! What's that?"

In the middle of the next dune to the east something smallish and grey protruded from beneath the sand. John went to investigate.

"Careful, John," Mary called as he approached the item.

"You stay there," he ordered and proceeded up the dune to the unknown object. He pushed away the sand that partially covered it. What he saw took him by surprise. He quickly examined it, opening a rectangular box on the underside. The inside of the box was quite clean except for traces of a white powdery dust. Just as quickly, he put some of the powder on a piece of paper torn from Jeremy's note, carefully folded it and put it into his jacket pocket. Then he pressed the rest on the webbing of flesh between the thumb and forefinger of his left hand. *Hmm, I think we've struck gold,* he thought.

Then he carefully re-covered the object and rearranged the sand around where it was hidden. He did the same to the sand around his footprints as he retraced his steps back to Mary. Concern was written all over her face. Her eyes asked the question.

"It's a small commercial drone," he answered her unspoken question, "and its cargo compartment contained traces of a white powdery substance."

"Cocaine?" Mary asked.

"Very possibly because it made the skin on the back of my hand numb. But it could also be heroin. Whatever it is, I need to contact Street right away and tell Jeremy to stop spying on the green ships, at least for now. I don't want to put him into any more danger than he may already be in."

John and Mary re-arranged their footsteps in the sand all the way back to the coast road.

"Have a good walk?" the marina manager asked as John unlocked the Vauxhall.

"Quite. It certainly is beautiful," John replied.

"And desolate," Mary added.

"That's what the other gentleman always says. He likes the solitude."

As soon as the Braemhors reached a lay-by just south of the marina, John pulled in and dialed Street's private number.

"What have you got for me, Braemhor?"

"More than I can say over an insecure line."

"How far are you from Inverness?" Street's clipped voice asked.

"About half an hour."

"Then go to our office there." He gave Braemhor the address. "Call me from there. I'll smooth the path in the meantime." Click and he was gone.

Twenty-five minutes later, John parked in a "Reserved for Agency" slot in front of the reddish brown building that Street had directed him to. Inside, the receptionist immediately recognized his name and ushered him into a small soundproofed chamber with a red phone on a mahogany desk. He picked up the receiver and in a moment Street said, "Now, tell me."

Braemhor kept it simple and straightforward. "The ships are using infrared to communicate with the shore. They send GPS information, indicating, I think, where the next drop-off is to be. The merchandize is carried ashore in small commercial drones directly from the ship."

"Who receives the message ashore?" Street interrupted.

"I don't know for sure, but I think it's the lighthouse keep in Sutors Cove. My guess is that he then calls a pickup who finds the drone—they're landing on the dunes just east of the Faraway Marina on the east side of the firth—relieves it of its contraband and takes it back to the Sutors Cove area. Most of this last part is by deduction. Mary and I found a drone with traces of either heroin or cocaine onboard in the dunes. I think there will be another drop tonight, or rather tomorrow morning between three and four, so I think it will be prudent to tap the lighthouse keep's landline to find out who he calls after he gets the ship's signal."

"And you want me to take action based on your deductions?"

"Yes," was John's brief and decisive response.

There was a long pause, then Street continued reluctantly, "All right, Braemhor, but your deductions better be sound."

Why? The agency hasn't come up with this much information in several months of trying. Braemhor was put off by Street's condescending and patronizing tone, but held his tongue.

"Anything else?"

"Not now." Braemhor hung up. When he returned to the car and Mary, she could see he was not pleased.

"What's wrong, John?"

"Nothing, really. Just Street's pomposity. But I should expect that from a bureaucrat. He's going to put a tap on Wren's telephone and watch the dunes tomorrow morning."

"Wren? Why Wren?"

John smiled. "Sorry, Mary. I just think he's the most likely individual to be receiving the ship's signals ashore. He says he watches the ships and as a mariner living on the firth—particularly during the war years— he would be likely to know Morse. And he is up during the hours of usual transmission."

"But he's not likely to be the 'cultured gentleman' the marina manager spoke of."

"No, clearly not, so he contacted someone else to pick up the contraband. My reason for suggesting to

Street that he tap Wren's phone line. We need to know where the powder goes after it comes ashore. For now, I want to get a pair of night-vision goggles since we're here in Inverness, then we need to get back to Sutors Cove and see Jeremy."

* * * * *

Jeremy was doing outdoor chores again when the Braemhors returned to the St. Dinsden's Kirk. He brightened when he saw the couple. "Ah, Mr. and Mrs. Wizard! I'm all ready for tonight! I sharpened my pencil and have a new notepad! I like watching the green ship!"

"He certainly does." The voice was that of the kirk's priest from behind a hedge-row near where Jeremy was working. "I have never seen him so enthusiastic about watching the green ships."

"Did he say why?" John was concerned that Jeremy could not contain his excitement and had told the priest of his chore for "Mr. Wizard."

"No, only that it was very important that he watch the ships very carefully. Sometimes Jeremy takes a notion into his head that none of us really understand, but if he is happy that's all that matters. Are you still enjoying your holiday?"

"Very much," Mary answered. "We went into Inverness for some shopping today. Certainly is a thriving metropolis."

"Well, those of us who've known London would hardly call Inverness a metropolis, but yes, it's a fine small community." The priest smiled. "Well, you'll have to excuse me; I have to prepare for this evening's vespers. Do come back again, won't you?"

"We'd be delighted," Mary agreed as John moved closer to Jeremy to see what chore he was attending to.

"Jeremy. You did such a good job writing down the daggers that tonight I just want you to write down if the daggers appear or not. If they appear, write down a 'Y', like this." He illustrated on his pad. "And 'N' if they do not appear. Is that clear? Nothing more tonight. All right?"

"Oh, yes, Mr. Wizard! This is so much fun. A different game each night. What will tomorrow night be?"

"Well, we'll just have to wait and see, won't we? And remember, don't tell anyone about our secret code." John hoped that the anticipation of what he would be asked to do the next night would keep Jeremy quiet for one more day.

John and Mary took their leave, and left their happy accomplice weeding the beds around the base of the kirk.

During supper in the near empty dining room, John, in hushed tones, outlined what he planned for the next 24 hours: "We'll take an early bedtime and then get up about a little before three and watch the 'green ship' with our new goggles."

"And then what?" Mary asked.

"We'll see what transpires between three and four and make plans accordingly." John smiled.

"Oh, John, there's no need to be secretive with me. I'm not Jeremy, you know." And she struck his shin under the table with her shoe.

"Ouch!" was his response.

* * * * *

Promptly at 2:45 a.m., their alarm called them both out of a deep slumber. John was up immediately and got their heavy jackets while Mary dozed for a few extra moments. By three they were dressed and seated on their balcony, John wearing the night-vision goggles focused on the ship anchored off of the lighthouse point. The heavy jackets were a welcome addition to ward off the early morning chill.

At 3:15 a.m., Jeremy's "daggers" started. John quietly spoke, "short," "long," as they came while Mary jotted down dots and dashes as he identified them. Every fifteen minutes, a series of invisible daggers flashed unseen from the ship, and John spoke and Mary wrote. During the third series they reversed roles, and she vocalized the dots and dashes as John wrote down the sequence. At 4:00 a.m., the transmissions abruptly stopped and all was quiet again.

John quickly translated the dots and dashes and discovered that the same coordinates as the night before were repeated over and over and over. "We're in luck. They're headed to the same rendezvous. Let's go! Back to the dunes."

By 4:20 a.m., John pulled the Vauxhall into the Faraway Marina car park among several other cars. "That way our Vauxhall won't be so noticeable. Mary, you stay here. I'm going to the dunes to find today's drone."

"John, I don't like this. What if something happens?"

"I've got my mobile and you have yours. If there's trouble, I'll call. If I say 'All is well here,' you are to immediately call Street, give him our location, and tell him to send help right away. If, however, I say, 'The dunes are beautiful at night,' you'll know everything is all right and that I will be back shortly. Now set your mobile on vibrate only. Okay?"

"Okay. But I still don't have to like it. Please be careful, John."

"Not to worry," John said as he surreptitiously—he thought—put a box of baking soda in his jacket pocket.

"What's that for?" Mary was always a keen observer.

"Hope to make a quick substitution for the real contraband, if I'm lucky and find the drone before the 'cultured gentleman' gets to it. Maybe we can sew a little dissention among the smugglers. Better they're at each other's throats than after ours." He kissed her on the forehead and jogged across the road toward the dunes. Using his fob compass, he tried to shoot straight east to where he and Mary had found the drone the day before. Five or 600 yards into the dunes, he came across it, half-buried in the sand of one of the larger dunes. *That was lucky,* he thought as he looked all around to make certain that he was still alone. He was.

Quickly, he pulled the drone free and opened the cargo container in which he found a rectangular package wrapped tightly in white plastic. A quick swipe of his pocketknife opened the container. He poured the white powder into a plastic bag he'd brought with him and sealed it with a twisty. Then he poured the baking soda into the plastic container, resealed it and placed it back into the cargo container. As he was partially re-covering the drone with sand, he caught the slight movement of the top of a dark cap in his peripheral vision.

He dropped flat onto the dune behind the re-hidden drone and squirmed his way over and down the other side of the dune, hoping all the while that the individual in the dark cap had not seen him. Once down the back side of the dune, he wiggled himself into a position that was perpendicular to the path by which he'd entered the dunes and also 20 yards or so from the drone. Then he covered himself with as much sand as he could and waited.

From where he lay he could barely make out the top of a dark, navy blue driving cap. When the cap reached the approximate area of the drone, it disappeared momentarily. *He's bending over the drone,* was Braemhor's thought. *Good.* Then the person in the dark cap stood up, looked around and turned back down the marina side of the dune. Braemhor breathed a relieved sigh and relaxed.

As soon as he was assured that there was enough distance between himself and his adversary, he dialed Mary. "The dunes are beautiful at night," he whispered into his mobile, and then, "Where are you?"

"I'm on the back floor of our car, under our car robe. Can you come soon? I have news. I saw the man who followed you out onto the dunes. He parked just a few spaces from us." Mary also whispered although there was no need for her to do so.

"Excellent! Let me know as soon as he leaves. I'll start working my way back to the marina, but I'll come a roundabout route."

"Right." Mary finished the conversation.

Fifteen minutes later, Mary signaled, "He's driven off."

Another half hour and John was still not back. Mary began again to worry, but just as she was about to ring him, he came walking down the coast road from the north.

"About time!" she chided.

"Just wanted to be sure we were clear." John got into the car. "You drive. To Street's office in Inverness, first. Hurry! But not too fast." John's orders were like a general deploying his troops.

"Do you have the contraband?" was Mary's first question. John patted his inner jacket pocket. Then she said, "I got pictures of our 'cultured gentleman' and of his car, including the plate."

"Fine. We can give those to MI6 also. I think Street will be satisfied." John was beginning to relax from the tension of the morning.

At the MI6 office, the receptionist again ushered Braemhor into the small cubicle with the red phone.

"Braemhor here. Did you trace the call Wren made after the ship's signal? Find out who was receiving the contraband?"

Street's voice was, surprisingly, a bit contrite. "No, we did not."

"What?! Why not!!?"

"Mr. Braemhor, you have to realize that I cannot tap anyone's line based on the deductive guesses of one of my agents. I need a more substantial reason for compromising a citizen's privacy. Maybe you do that sort of thing in Scotland, but we are a little more civilized than that down here in England."

"Have you totally lost perspective?! I think we have our arms around a major, international drug smuggling operation and you don't want to compromise a citizen who may be a major link to bringing the whole thing to a close!!"

"Calm yourself, Braemhor, calm yourself. I realize that you are unfamiliar with our ways and that you in the private sector are freer to ignore the rules. But the rules are the rules. Now do you have any more information for me, because I'm a busy man and have other investigations on my plate."

Braemhor bit his lip and proceeded, "All right, Street, I have removed the contraband that came on today's drone and substituted a neutral substance in its place. That should create turmoil in the smugglers' ranks. Also I have a picture of the individual who picked up the drone and of his motor car, including the plate, quite visible. Do you want these items?"

Street was clearly annoyed, but he agreed to receive the items. "Yes, I suppose. Mr. Henderson is in charge of our station there in Inverness. Give the materials to him and he will properly receipt you. Now is there anything else?"

"Yes, I think you will need to identify the man in our photo images and take him into custody as soon as possible. As soon as it's discovered that the contraband has gone missing, his life will not be worth much, and he could be a valuable source of information about the whole operation and who the other individuals involved are. Don't you think?"

"Yes, I suppose so. Give what you have to Henderson, and he can take it from there. I'll talk with Henderson before you see him so he understands what is going on." Then he hung up.

Braemhor exited the safe room and went to the receptionist. "Mr. Street wants me to talk with Mr. Henderson."

"Of course, sir; he's on another phone with him now. It should only be a minute or two."

Ten minutes later, a tall, slender, physically fit young man in his late twenties entered reception. "Mr. Braemhor?" He strode to where John sat on a side bench. "Come in here, please." He led the way into his office.

"Have a seat." He motioned to a chair in front of the desk. "This shouldn't take too long. Mr. Street tells me you've had quite a day, so far. He briefly told me about you working temporarily for the agency and how far you've gotten in your investigation. He also said that you have some items for us."

"That's right."

"You know, Mr. Braemhor, we've been working on this Sutors Cove item for almost two months, and I must say, between you and me, you've gotten farther in two days than we have in two months. But that's between you and me, you understand." He smiled.

"Of course." Braemhor took an instant liking to the young station master. He then gave Henderson a detailed accounting of the last two days' investigation, indicating also, perhaps more than he should have, his displeasure with Street's attitude and tone.

"I understand exactly what you're saying, but, of course, I can't comment on your views of Mr. Street." A wry smile flashed across his face.

"Quite. But I do think it's very important to move quickly on the individual who met the drone in the dunes this morning. He could be an excellent source, but he won't last long once it's discovered that the contraband is missing."

"I understand completely. Let me have someone extract the images from your mobile while we talk and we can get right on that. And you'd better let me have the contraband also, so we can properly secure it." Braemhor gave both to Henderson, who had a clerk draw up a receipt for the contraband."

"If that turns out to be what I think it is—cocaine or heroin—will you be boarding the ship in the firth?" John asked out of curiosity.

"I don't know. You see, we may not be able to do that without raising an international ruckus. That I will have to leave to Mr. Street and people further up the chain than I. But I hear your concerns. Ah, here is your receipt and your phone. I think that probably wraps it up for now, Mr. Braemhor. Maybe you can get back to Sutors Cove and let us take it from here. And, Mr. Braemhor, try not to be too hard on some of us. We just work under a different set of rules than the private sector. We are really all working towards the same end." Henderson smiled as he offered John his hand.

John slipped in behind the wheel of the Vauxhall. "We need to get back to Sutors Cove. I want to see that Jeremy's all right." He then told Mary what had transpired in the MI6 office.

"Do you think this area chief—What was his name, Henderson?—will follow-up or is he another bureaucrat like Street?" Mary was incensed at the way her husband had been treated.

"I think he'll do everything he can. He's not like Street."

Half hour later as John entered Sutors Cove, he headed directly to St. Dinsden's where they found Jeremy tending the roses near the entrance to the kirk.

Jeremy met them with a huge grin. "Mr. and Mrs. Wizard!"

"Things quiet here, Jeremy?' John asked.

"Oh, yes, sir, yes, sir. All very quiet. And I did just what you told me."

"And what was that, Jeremy?" John was apprehensive.

"Nothing. I watched the green ship, but I did not write down the daggers when they started. Just like you told me."

"Good lad, Jeremy. You did everything just right." John was relieved at Jeremy's answer.

Just then there was the most terrible, the most discordant scream John and Mary had ever heard.

"What is that?" Jeremy was literally trembling from head to foot.

The priest, who'd just rounded the corner of the kirk shouted the same question as he ran toward the Braemhors and Jeremy.

Across the street in the graveyard stood the housekeeper of the kirk, a thickly set woman in her fifties. She was flailing the sky with her hands and emitting the most awful screeching sounds which quickly devolved into: "They're dead! They're dead! Oh, saints save us! Saints save us!"

Braemhor sprang into action. "Mary, you stay here with Jeremy! Father, come with me!" he ordered as he ran toward the graveyard.

"Father, take care of her!" He pointed to the screaming woman.

Just beyond where the woman stood, shrieking, trembling and burying her face in her hands, were the bodies of two men, their throats slit and upper chests mutilated by what John supposed to be a 12-bore shotgun. "Take her back to the kirk, and tell Mary to take Jeremy back there, too. I'll call the police," he shouted to the priest.

After he called the local police, John inspected the bodies more closely. One, he recognized. It was Mr. Wren from the lighthouse, Jeremy's uncle. The other, he did not. *But my guess is this is the cultured gentleman who picked up the drone earlier,* John thought as he heard the wail of the police siren approaching.

Then he placed a quick call to Henderson. "You're too late. They got to Wren and another man who I suspect is the one I saw on the dunes early today. They're in the graveyard near the kirk here in Sutors Cove. Better get some agents here quickly if you want to be in on the investigation. The local police are about to arrive."

"Right, Mr. Braemhor, we'll take it from there. . .and thanks."

For what? Braemhor thought as the local constabulary drove up and got out of their green and white.

"Oh, my God!" the younger of the two constables said as he saw the bodies. The older one turned to Braemhor. "You find 'em? Mr. . . ."

"Braemhor, John Braemhor. No they were found by the housekeeper from the kirk. She's in the kirk with the priest and my wife. We're tourists from Daraichburn, staying at the Seaview."

"If you don't mind, sir, stay around until we can get this sorted out."

"Of course. I'll be in the kirk with my wife and the others." John walked across the road and into the kirk.

Inside, Mary and the priest had managed to calm the housekeeper somewhat. Jeremy was highly agitated, literally jumping from one foot to the other, wanting to know what was happening. John took Mary outside.

"Who are they, John?" Mary asked as soon as they were out of earshot of the others.

"Give me your mobile. I want to see the picture of the gentleman you took at the marina."

"As I thought," he spoke in subdued tones to Mary, "one is Mr. Wren and the other is the gentleman you encountered earlier at the marina."

"Oh, Mr. Wren, Jeremy's uncle?"

"I'm afraid so. As I suspected, he was part of the operation. I think he was the spotter of the messages from the ships. Then, my guess is, he passed on the information."

Mary interrupted and pointed out to the firth. "Look, John!"

Jeremy's green ship was gone.

"They didn't waste any time, did they?" John smiled. "Well, Mr. Street and his boys will have a devilish time rounding all of them up."

About that time, the sound of a helicopter drowned out all conversation as it landed in the graveyard. Henderson and three agents alighted. The local officers greeted the newcomers and after a brief conference crossed the street to the kirk.

"Mr. Braemhor, Mrs. Braemhor, you're free to go back to your hotel, but I would still appreciate your being available for the next day or so. In case we need to clarify anything. I must say, you certainly have friends in high places, Mr. Braemhor." The officer shook his head. "MI6, yet," he muttered to himself as he turned back to take charge of local matters.

Inside the kirk again, John and Mary spent some time helping Jeremy regain his equilibrium and promised to see him again the next day before they returned home. He seemed much more calm knowing that Mr. and Mrs. Wizard were to be his friends forever.

The next day, as John was putting their valises into the boot, a call came from Henderson. "Just thought you ought to know, Mr. Braemhor, we did stop the ship on its way into the North Sea. Loaded with illegal drugs and a couple of the locals from Sutors Cove. We also found over 50 pounds of cocaine in the lighthouse on Ebony Isle so it looks like the keep was, indeed, the local receiver of the ship's messages—which were, in fact, sent by infrared. The other body was that of a smuggler well-known to Interpol, so your idea of creating havoc in the ranks of the smugglers may have reduced our workload, at least by one. Believe it or not, I think Mr. Street will be pleased, though don't expect boisterous accolades." Braemhor could discern a smile in Henderson's voice. "Send us your expenses and we'll see that they are promptly dealt with."

"Right." John smiled back. "Glad to be of some help."

He finished loading the Vauxhall, then he and Mary started the beautiful route home to Daraichburn and the quiet of their B&B and Aunt Rita.

Chapter 9

Aunt Rita met John and Mary at the door with homecoming hugs. She was bubbling over with news.

"Since you went to Sutors Cove I've been reading up on dark matter," she gushed, "and I've found a website that's willing to sell boxes of dark matter to interested readers!"

"Dark matter?" Mary queried.

"Yes. It makes up to 75% of our universe. It's all around us!"

"And what does it look like?" was John's cagy question.

"That's the problem," Rita answered. "You can't see it. So I said to myself: 'How will I know if they really sent any dark matter, if I can't see it'?"

"That's right. Dark matter is a hypothetical construct invented to explain certain gravitational phenomena in our universe. It can't be directly seen or measured," John instructed.

"Good thinking, Aunt Rita," Mary agreed. "How much did they want for it?"

"Oh, it was very inexpensive. Only a pound for a pound, but still, I thought I'd ask you two what you thought before I ordered some."

"I think it's a scam, Aunt Rita. Don't order it."

"I agree," John said. "Give me the name of the website and I'll look into it."

Rita was crestfallen, but she did defer to the Braemhors' advice, particularly after they assuaged her disappointment by giving her the books they'd gotten for her in Sutors Cove.

After John sent the expenses for his work at Sutors Cove to Henderson, the next few days were spent preparing the Cottage for guests and taking Rita to Melrose for the train back to Blanefield. After that, the next few weeks were very quiet except for evening discussions with American guests about the upcoming elections in the States and the strange ways Americans choose their elected officials. One couple thought it would be a good thing if the next president had no government experience or training at all.

"Would you let an individual with no experience and no training in auto repair fix your car's brakes?" John could not pass up the opening.

"That's different." The American husband bristled.

"How so?" John continued.

"It takes skill, experience and training to repair an auto," was the reply.

Mary's unseen squeeze of John's hand tempered his response to a bland, "I see." Later, in their room, Mary said, "You have to remember, John, these people are our guests."

"Then I fear for our world," John quietly muttered and opened his bedtime reading.

Next day, Mary called to John as she looked through the post which had just been thrust through the front door.

"John, a letter from Henderson in Inverness." It was a check for his expenses, an official letter of thanks for his work, and a brief personal note from the young MI6 station master thanking him for his work which allowed MI6 to bring their Sutors Cove investigation to a close.

"Henderson is a credit to MI6," John reflected as he read Henderson's personal note. "He should go far, if the bureaucracy doesn't get him down. It's good to know that there are young people in our world who still adhere to the common interpersonal courtesies of our generation. Gives you faith in the future."

"I wonder what our elders thought of us a generation ago," Mary wondered aloud.

"Times never really change, Mary," John concurred, as the telephone rang.

"Dunmoor Cottage, Mary Braemhor here," Mary answered the call.

"Mrs. Braemhor, could I speak with Mr. Braemhor, please? This is Basil MacErich."

"A Basil MacErich for you." Mary handed the receiver to John.

He answered, "John Braemhor here. How may I help you?"

"I hope that you may. Would it be too inconvenient for me to stop by Dunmoor Cottage this evening and discuss a problem with you?" The high-pitched, tenor voice on the other end of the phone asked.

"I think that would be all right. Let me check my calendar." Mary handed John the Cottage registry.

A moment later, "That would be satisfactory, Sir Basil. I assume I'm speaking with Sir Basil MacErich?"

"That is correct," came back the reply.

"And what seems to be the problem?"

"Briefly, the problem is we seem to have misplaced my brother, Donald."

"Misplaced him?" Braemhor thought it a peculiar turn of phrase.

"Well, yes, but I think I can better explain the circumstances to you in person. Shall we say seven?"

"That will be fine. We will expect you then."

John looked at Mary as he replaced the receiver. "Seems that Sir Basil has misplaced his brother, Donald."

"Misplaced him!?" Mary laughed.

"Interesting way to put it, don't you think? Well, we will see what this evening brings."

* * * * *

Promptly at seven the doorbell of the Cottage announced the arrival of Sir Basil, a tall, slender man in his early fifties, with an outdoor complexion and hazel eyes. "I very much appreciate your agreeing to see me on such short notice, but we are very much distraught over a recent turn of events."

"Sit down." Braemhor motioned to one of the settees in front of the fireplace in the sitting room of Dunmoor Cottage. "Now, tell us—this is my wife, Mary—what has happened."

Sir Basil began, in his pronounced tenor voice. "It all started about a week ago at the family dinner—we eat together once a week at the castle. My brother, Donald, his twin sister, Julia, my wife and I were there. It started with a family disagreement about how best to keep the estate afloat in the present economy. I proposed renting presently unused portions of the castle to tourists who wanted the experience of living, briefly, in a medieval castle. It was a silly thing, really, but as the head of the family I felt bound to consider all possibilities for the good of the family and the family name. To my shock, Donald took extreme umbrage at the idea and accused me of trying to destroy family traditions, and before I realized it, we were into a discussion of the Scottish independence movement, in particular, some of the fringe movements associated with independence—not legitimate organizations like Yes, Scotland or the SNP. We have long had opposing views on this issue. I don't think many younger people realize the difficulties of smoothly running an independent nation. No matter how hard I tried to convince Donald of the sensibleness of staying within the UK, he just became increasingly distraught and verbally abusive. I lost my composure, as well and we ended in a shouting match that did no honor to either of us. Donald is in his mid-twenties, but still living in the rebellious years. In many ways he has just never matured. He stomped out and went back to his cottage.

"And Donald lives?" John interrupted.

"He has an apartment in the castle, but he also keeps a small place on the loch."

"Loch Lomond?"

"That is correct. It is a smallish Victorian structure. Only 12 rooms plus servants' quarters and a coach house. Well, following our discussion," Sir Basil continued, "he stormed out of the castle and, I presumed, went back to his cottage. I thought little of it at the time and put it off to our family temperament. We are, you see, a rather hotheaded family quick to anger. I guess that's what carried our ancestors through Culloden in earlier times. But we have also always been just as quick to forgive. And so the next morning, I called his cottage to make amends and apologize for my part in the argument.

"His man informed me that Donald had not spent the night at his cottage, and, in fact, had not been seen by the staff since he'd left to come to the castle for dinner the night before. I thought that very strange, but did not, at that time, become alarmed. Donald, you see, is a very independent spirit and often disappears for days at a time only to reappear, having taken very impetuously an unannounced trip, like to the highlands, or London or just an extended fishing excursion on the loch.

"However, more than a week passed and we heard nothing from him, which is most unusual. Finally, I called his cottage again and was told that Donald had not been home since I first called. At this point, I did become rather alarmed because his impulsivity has never lasted this long, no matter how strident our disagreements in the past.

"I immediately had the staff at his cottage search the building and premises. Even had them walk the extensive shoreline of the loch that is part of our overall estate. Nothing! By now I was quite worried, but I did not want to contact the local authorities. We don't need a family scandal, you see. For that reason I contacted you in the hopes that you could, very discretely, help us find him." He paused and looked pleadingly at John and Mary.

"First, I can assure you that whatever inquiries we make will be carried out with the utmost discretion. But I need to know more about Donald's general routines, where does he go frequently, what does he do, who are his friends and acquaintances? Also I would like to see his cottage on Loch Lomond and his apartment in the castle. Can that be arranged?"

"By all means. Just let me know."

"Can you arrange for us to have access to his cottage tomorrow morning, say about ten?" John was anxious to begin as soon as possible.

"Yes, I will let the staff know in the morning that you and Mrs. Braemhor will be coming by. For now, I need to return to the estate." Sir Basil rose to leave. "Let me know as soon as you find anything or need anything." He took Mary's and John's hands in turn and exited the Cottage.

"Interesting story," Mary observed as Sir Basil drove away.

"Yes, and I think Donald's staff may be the most valuable informants. We'll see tomorrow," John agreed as he extinguished the front lights on the Cottage.

* * * * *

Next morning the Braemhors drove to Donald MacErich's cottage on Loch Lomond. The house was a large stone structure seated on a high promontory with an exceptional view of the loch. Sounding the bell to the left of the oaken double door brought Donald's man, Ernest, to the entrance.

"Mr. and Mrs. Braemhor?" John nodded. "Please come in. Sir Basil telephoned us earlier. This way, please." Donald's man, Ernest, was unbelievably thin almost skeletal. On first encounter Mary thought, *cadaverous*. His eyes were sunken into his face above two protruding cheek bones, two dark orbs from which peered the blackest of irises. And his skin, his skin looked like whitewashed parchment.

Mary felt like she was crossing the river Styx into Satan's lair of Death. She visibly shuddered as Ernest led her and John up the narrow stairs from the small entry hall to the next level which opened into a large library/living room. It was usually warmed by a massive fireplace, but this morning was cold as a tomb. Behind this room was a lavish dining room, behind which were the kitchen and the staff quarters.

"Welcome to Linlith. Will you have some tea?" Ernest rasped as he rang for the kitchen maid.

"That would be nice." Mary spoke first, while John perused the volumes on the shelves on either side of the fireplace.

"Mr. MacErich seems to be of two minds," John observed.

"Sir?" Ernest was taken slightly off-balance.

"An interest in mystery and in hunting and fishing," John explained.

"Oh, yes, sir, I see what you mean. The Ernest Bramah and Conan Doyle collections and the Theodore Roosevelt collection. Yes, sir. Young Donald is an avid reader in both those genre. And he is a passionate outdoorsman also." He pointed to several stuffed trophies on the wall opposite the books. Then he added, "The collections are all first editions, you know, quite valuable, and a pride of the house." He managed a smile which appeared more like a grimace.

"How does Mr. MacErich spend his time, besides reading and sporting?" John wanted to know more.

"It used to be mostly with the gaiety of his young friends. Linlith was always graced with the laughter and conversation of young people."

"You speak of Linlith?"

"Oh, yes, sir, the cottage is named for one of the old haunts of the very early MacErichs, an isle on the coast."

"I see. And where does Mr. MacErich do most of his hunting and fishing?"

"North America, mostly. He has a favorite private hunting preserve he frequents at least twice a year in Texas. He fishes off the coast of New Jersey also. Many boats are for hire in Cape May for deep-sea fishing. Sometimes though, when he's feeling especially despondent, he will fish the loch," Ernest answered.

"Does he get despondent often?" John jumped at the opening.

"About once or twice a year. Other times he's a bundle of energy. Happy. Active. The life of any social gathering. All of the staff loves the warm, friendly atmosphere he cultivates most of the time. But when his mood turns dark, we all worry about him. It seems like he's always searching for something, never quite happy with life as it was. Ah, here is your tea." The kitchen maid had entered with a silver service.

The arrival of the tea broke the trend of the conversation briefly, until Mary asked, "Do you have a picture of him that we might see?"

"Yes, ma'am." Ernest reached among a group of photographs on a side table by the fireplace. "Here is young Donald with a number of his friends." He handed the picture in its gold frame to Mary. John and Mary studied the photo, in which a short, slight individual with blond hair smiled out from the center of a social gathering.

"He appears to be rather short of stature," John observed.

"Yes, sir, that was one thing he always felt badly about. His height. He was always slight of frame from the day he took his first steps. If you don't mind my saying so, I think that's why he took so strongly to hunting, fishing and other outdoor sports. He was making up for being the smallest of his group of friends." Ernest seemed embarrassed to share his views on his young master.

"You've been with the family a long time?" Mary asked.

"Oh, yes, ma'am. I came into service with the MacErichs two years before young Donald was born."

"You helped raise him?" Mary continued her questioning.

"Like he was my own," Ernest said with a mixture of pride and embarrassment. "All of the staff is terribly distraught by his disappearance. It's just not like him.

There were times before when he would absent himself from Linlith and the family—quietly hunting or fishing by himself, but never for this long. Sir Basil said he had hired you two to help find young Donald. If I or the staff can do anything to help, please let us know what we can do."

"We will do that," John assured the very shaken and very concerned servant, "but for now we would like to just take a brief walk around Linlith and see the grounds." Picking up the name Ernest used for Donald MacErich, John then asked, "Are there places on the loch that young Donald especially liked to seclude himself?"

"I can show you, if we walk the grounds together, if you like." Ernest was eager to help.

"That might be helpful, but first the chambers of Linlith."

It did not take long for the Braemhors to see the remaining rooms of the so-called 'cottage,' all but a few were closed off and empty. Mary still felt that it was like walking through the rooms of a mausoleum and was relieved when they went outside to walk the shore of the loch.

From one point on the shore they could see a smallish isle, Innis Braam, on the other side of the loch. "He did a lot of his fishing off that island." Ernest pointed west across the loch.

"Where did he keep his sporting equipment?" John suddenly asked.

"In a ground floor storage room off of the billiard room. This way." Ernest led the Braemhors back into Linlith's ground floor. "His long guns were kept here." Ernest pointed to a glass-fronted cabinet containing two Holland and Holland 12-bores. "His rods and nets are he. . . ." Ernest stopped in midsentence.

"What's wrong?" John was quick to ask.

"His. . .his favorite rods and net are. . .aren't here," Ernest stammered. "They're gone!"

"Is it possible that he quietly returned to Linlith that night, got his fishing equipment and has taken himself off on an extended fishing holiday?" John was a bit irritated that he and Mary may have been called out unnecessarily.

"I. . . I. . .I really don't think so, sir. I'm. . .I'm sure he did not spend that night with us. Oh dear, maybe the young master has gone off on one of his dark adventures and he's not really missing." The last was said with a mixture of perplexity and hope. "But how could that be? His skiff was still moored at our landing the next morning."

"He has friends who share his interest in fishing?" Mary asked.

"Yes, yes, he does. But. . .but. . ." Ernest was profoundly confused.

"I think we need to explore more before we draw any conclusions. But let's start at Linlith's landing." John brought the conversation back down to earth.

"Yes, sir, yes, sir. This way, please." Ernest, again energized, walked off towards the loch's shore with John and Mary close behind.

John whispered to Mary, "Let's not get any closer to the water than a couple of yards." To Mary's quizzical look, he went on, "I want to see if there are any tracks along the shore."

But just as they reached the shore and the Linlith landing, Ernest stopped short and a look of horror passed over his face. "It's gone, sir! It's gone! The master's skiff is gone! But. . .but I'm sure it was there the morning after we first started looking for him! I'm sure!"

"Then he, or someone else, took it later. Why?" John was thinking aloud. Then suddenly, "Ernest, I think you have shown us quite enough for now. You may go back to the cottage."

Ernest was surprised by John's abruptness. "As you wish, sir." And he walked up the shore rise to Linlith Cottage, shaking his head in perplexity.

"Let's walk the shoreline." John turned to Mary.

"Fine, but why did you dismiss Ernest so brusquely?"

"At this point in our inquiry, we don't know who to trust. While Ernest certainly presents a picture of loyalty and genuine concern for Donald MacErich, there is something about him. . . ." John could not quite express what he was feeling.

"His specter-like appearance?" Mary smiled.

"That, too." John returned the smile.

About a quarter of a mile northward John spied what he'd been looking for. "Stop!" he commanded. "Look here." He pointed to multiple footprints in soft earth at the shoreline. He got down on one knee to inspect them more closely.

"At least four different sets of prints—two large, one smallish that could be a woman's, and another of medium size. And look here." He pointed to where the footprints ended—at a deep v-shaped indentation in the shoreline right at the water's very edge.

"What do you think, John?" Mary asked, "Abduction?"

"Possibly. Possibly. But maybe just a small group of young people, probably in their cups, off on a fishing lark in the middle of the night. And yet. . .from the depth of that indentation, I'd say that a small boat's prow had been pressed into the earth, like a heavy weight was suddenly taken aboard."

"Like a body?" Mary opined.

"Yes and no. Could be anything being dragged. Look at the marks in the ground."

"Maybe one of them was too drunk to walk on their own."

"Let's hope no one will disturb these prints until we can get more data."

"Our mobiles can take pictures, John." Mary said quietly.

"Of course. Of course. Why can't I think in modern terms? Mary, shoot some images of these prints and the indentation from the boat prow, will you please?"

As Mary took the pictures, she asked, "Does this mean that young Donald has been kidnapped?"

"Not necessarily, but the evidence is mounting. Even if the medium-size prints are his, all we know is that it looks like he and three others came down to the shore and boarded a small boat of some sort. Whether they were going fishing or something else. . . . Well, I think we've found enough for now. Let's go back to the car."

"I'll tell Ernest that we have enough information for now and then we can be off," John said when they reached Linlith. After John spoke briefly to Ernest, they drove off in the Vauxhall.

* * * * *

"Where to now?" Mary asked.

"I thought we'd go to the west shore, see Mrs. Buchanan, book a room and get another of her fine dinners."

"John! Don't play games. What are you thinking?" Mary was a little irritated.

"All right. There's a small harbor just across the road from her Thistle Cottage where, I hope, we may be able to let a skiff and explore Innis Braam island. It was Donald's favorite fishing site on the loch. We need to know more about him, his habits, his haunts."

Mary thought for a moment. "But what about Donald's skiff? Why would it disappear after he did?"

"Either he returned to get it, or someone else did. If he did, then we may just have another of his solitary, black cloud fishing excursions. If someone else did, then the scenario may be more ominous. We'll just have to wait and see."

"But what about his fishing gear? Ernest also told us that was missing." Mary could not let go of the puzzle.

"The fishing gear could lead us to a happier ending. Ah, here's Thistle Cottage."

Mrs. Buchanan did not disappoint, and it wasn't until after the delicious baked brown trout dinner that John inquired about boats to let at the small harbor across the street.

"Oh, yes, Mr. Braemhor. See Captain Strong, Dan Strong, and tell him I sent you. He has skiffs you can let, or if he's not busy, he'll take you on the loch in his motor launch."

Dan Strong was a bull of a man. Short and barrel-chested, with skin to match his hours in the sun—brown, defined by lines and spots of sun damage. "Where you want to go?"

"We'd like to see Innis Braam," John responded.

"Fishin'?"

"No, just thought we'd walk around the island."

"That's interesting," Strong commented.

"What is?" John asked.

"You're the second person in the last week wanting to walk around Innis Braam. Gentleman here from Edinburgh said the same thing. Just wanted to walk around the island. Strange. Besides that, Innis Braam is a hard island to walk on. All heather and brambles. Not much to see, if you ask me. Why is everybody so interested?" Captain Strong asked.

"Just the same, we'd like to see it."

"Suit yourselves, but it would cost you less if I just let you that skiff over there and you could row yourselves over. Wouldn't take long." He pointed. "If I have to take you out and then wait 'til you're ready to leave, it'll cost you a lot more."

John paid Strong the rental and started rowing to the island. "So we're not the only ones interested in Innis Braam."

It took about ten minutes. "Good exercise," John commented as he beached the small skiff. Except for the tiny beach where the Braemhors went ashore, Innis Braam was indeed a heather and bramble-covered waste. "Good thing we brought our walking boots," John remarked as they strode off into the heather.

Innis Braam was small, and it did not take the Braemhors more than an hour to cover the entire landscape. One of the first things they found was another secluded boat landing cove. "Ah, ha," John exclaimed as he pointed to the footprints where the earth met the water. A quick examination of the find revealed the same pattern they'd found on the Linlith side of the loch, including a v-shaped impression in the shoreline, the shape and size of a boat prow. "My guess is that this is where they landed. Let's keep looking."

This second landing spot yielded more than Braemhor had hoped—just off the shore was a skiff, half-sunken barely below the water surface. John quickly removed his boots, stockings and trousers and waded out to the boat. He found a large hole in the keel which accounted for its sinking. But it was resting on an earthen shelf extending from the island into the loch.

"I wonder if this is Donald's skiff that Ernest said was missing." John spoke as he returned from his wading expedition.

"But why is it in such shallow water?" Mary asked.

"It could be that someone deliberately sank the skiff but did not realize it was still over a shallow shelf. Ernest told us that the skiff was still there the next morning. But since then, someone—or perhaps Donald himself—returned for the skiff and brought it here to Innis Braam. Maybe it was at night, and they could barely make out that the skiff sank after it was damaged. Perhaps they didn't realize that it caught on a shelf and barely sank below the surface. Now, if the sinking was deliberate, why would anyone sink Donald's skiff?"

"So you think that whoever came over to the island was involved with Donald's disappearance and returned to get his skiff. You remember that Ernest said the skiff was still at Linlith landing earlier, but missing when we got to the landing. And then this person or persons sank the skiff to create the appearance of a water accident." Mary was fully into John's speculations.

"Right. To make it appear that Donald had come toward the island and drowned while fishing, in some sort of freak accident. There was a rod and hand net still in the bottom of the skiff. But my guess is that Donald, for all of his lone fishing sorties, was an accomplished boatman and probably a good swimmer. We can verify that later from Sir Basil."

"Aren't we going a bit beyond the data, John?" Mary was trying to keep their scenario fact-based.

"Quite. I admit it. We will still have to verify these speculations with more data. But let's keep this idea in mind. Of course, if my assumptions are correct, it was a pretty clumsy attempt to mislead whoever might investigate Donald's disappearance."

"Or Donald himself," Mary went on.

"What?" John was not quite following Mary's thoughts.

"Maybe this is not an abduction but a planned disappearance by Donald, himself. He did have psychological problems, you'll recall."

"Ah, yes. Well, let's keep all of these threads in mind. Let's keep exploring. We'll follow this smaller path." He pointed. The path ended in an overwhelming entanglement of brambles and heather. Mary almost fell into a bush that had been uprooted and laid carefully across an opening into yet another smaller pathway heading east.

The brambles tore at their clothing impeding every step as they pushed their way forward on the side path. "Look here, Mary." John pointed down. There was a clear indication that something had been dragged down this secondary path to a slab of stone about three feet high. Scrapings on the ground showed that the stone had been moved recently. John examined the stone carefully and found that if he put pressure against the right side, it yielded, revealing an opening into the larger rock face behind. "It's an entrance to a cave, I believe." He turned to Mary, taking an LED torch from his jacket pocket.

John was right. The entrance was a little over four feet high, and by bending down, he and Mary were able to enter the open space behind. Once in, they could straighten and walk upright into a large room.

"And what do we have here?" John cast the light of his torch about the cave.

"Looks like the remains of several meals, and. . .look here, John, another fishing rod." Stacked against a side wall was a lone rod and a scaling board with dried fish scales on it. "Donald's?" Mary asked.

"Very possibly. Let's take them back with us and ask Sir Basil. And what else do we have here?" In a secluded corner of the cave was a stationer's pad of high rag content foolscap, several crumpled pieces of paper and some ballpoint pens. John tore off the top three sheets of paper and slipped them carefully into a plastic bag from his jacket pocket along with one of the pens.

"Put this in with those, John." Mary handed him a small silver barrette she had discovered near the food remains.

Taking one last look around the cave, John said, "I think we've got enough for now. It's time we go back to Thistle Cottage, get some supper and review what this day has revealed."

In their room, after a light supper, the Braemhors sat at the oval table in the sitting area. "Mary, let me see the barrette you found."

It was a bow-shaped sterling silver barrette inscribed with the letters, *J. M.* "Interesting, those are the initials of Donald's sister, Julia. Maybe she made the small imprints we found by the water, but why?" John thought aloud.

"If his sister was one of the group, that would argue against an abduction, wouldn't it?"

"Probably, yes, but possibly, no. Families can be deeply divided. We'll hold that hypothesis."

"Well, for now I think we should use your favorite investigative tool."

"Which is?" John was mildly perplexed.

"The sleeping brain. For now, let's let our brains work on what we know, while we sleep."

"It has been a long day."

Chapter 10

The orange arc of the morning sun was just cresting the isles of the loch, its golden rays reaching out like fingers of life announcing the birth of a new day, as John stood on the front porch of Thistle Cottage admiring the beauty of his native Scotland. The morning vapor enshrouded the water leaving the tops of the many islands to peek above the mist's mantle as if they were the heads of so many mythical monsters just bestirring in the morning's awakening. *This is the way people were meant to live, in the full sunlight of life, not in the dark, dank hovels of despair,* he thought. *Why? Why can't we create this beauty and this fullness for all of us?* He shook his head slightly, as Mary's arm encompassed his waist and she said, "I'd give a penny for your thoughts."

"They're worth at least a pound." John smiled and put his arm around her shoulders. "But we've got more important things to do than use this beautiful morning in sentimental reverie. Let's just remember how fortunate we are and get back to the task of Donald MacErich." They went inside to the breakfast nook.

"Now, let's review what we have so far. Donald MacErich disappeared a couple of weeks ago after a set-to with his brother, Sir Basil, over family matters and the Scottish independence movement. His man, Ernest, informed us he's not been seen since, but along the shore of the loch were prints possibly indicating that several people boarded a boat. We have explored an island near which Donald was known to fish. A sunken skiff, possibly his, was near the island caught on a shallow shelf in the loch. And in a cave on the island we found the remains of food but no indication of bedding, and a silver barrette initialed, *J. M.*, possibly belonging to his twin sister. Is that it?" John turned to Mary.

"Don't' forget the gentleman from Edinburgh Captain Strong told us about," Mary reminded him.

"There is one other place I'd like to look at."

"What?"

"Linlith boathouse. It's the one MacErich structure we haven't seen. I'll check out with Mrs. Buchanan while you pack our valise." John rose and went to the door of the breakfast area to get Mrs. Buchanan's attention.

Half an hour later, John parked in the Linlith Cottage car park. "Mary, you go see Ernest while I go to the boathouse. Don't tell him where I've gone and engage him as long as you can. Tell him I'm just walking the loch shore again. Find out if Donald was a skilled boater and swimmer." John walked toward the landing, and Mary went to the front door of the cottage.

The boathouse was a two-story affair, the slips on the ground level and some modest living quarters on the upper floor. Braemhor quietly slipped through the unlatched door onto the ground level where a medium-sized motor launch was moored. He quickly and quietly bounded up the open staircase to the upper level.

My, my, what do we have here? he thought. He had entered a small kitchen off of which a door led to a sleeping area. It was evident that the kitchen had been used recently—probably that very morning—as half-eaten pieces of burnt toast still lay on the countertop and fresh coffee was still in the urn.

He went into the sleeping/sitting room and found an unmade bed which also appeared to have been recently used. He felt the bed. *Still faintly warm,* flashed through his mind. *Whoever used it is not far ahead of me.* Just as quickly, Braemhor looked at the computer—still warm—and papers fresh out of the printer. They were print-outs of pages from Black Heart, a well-known terrorist site in the highlands. A quick perusal verified that the pages contained instructions for making various destructive devices, including bombs from ordinary household and farm chemicals.

This does not look good, he thought. Then suddenly he heard the door downstairs open. *Where to hide,* wiped out all other considerations. The best he could manage was under the bed. From his hiding place, he could barely make out the individual who'd entered and climbed up the stairs to where Braemhor was trapped. Fortunately, the person stopped in the kitchen, poured himself additional coffee and put it into the microwave. It was then that Braemhor, peering out from behind the sheet which he had draped over the edge of the bed and down to the floor, was able to get a clear view of the coffee drinker. *If I'm not mistaken, we have found young Donald!*

Braemhor was hardly daring to breath, wondering what he would do if Donald MacErich were to come into the sleeping area. But Braemhor's luck held. Once his coffee was reheated, the mystery man took it and descended the stairway to the slip level. Shortly the motor in the launch leapt into action, and Donald MacErich—if that's who it was—backed out and into the loch. Once out, he powered up and headed toward the western side of the loch. Much relieved, Braemhor went downstairs and inspected the ground level of the boathouse before leaving.

And what else do we have? he exclaimed to himself as he pulled back a black plastic tarpaulin in the back of the slip area. There lay over 20 50-pound packages of fertilizer, the type used for crop production on an ordinary farm. But this was no ordinary farm. *That does it for this morning,* he thought as he eased his way out the door, and walked briskly down the shoreline so that if Ernest saw him, he would appear to be coming back from his stroll.

Well that he did, because just as John reversed course and walked back towards the main house, Mary, with Ernest in tow, came out and began walking toward the loch.

Ernest greeted Braemhor with a smile and "Good morning, Mr. Braemhor, did you have a nice stroll?"

"Lovely, thank you. The estate certainly sits in a beautiful location. Mary, I think we'd better be on our way. We have several errands to attend to before we go back to Daraichburn."

Just as they approached the main house to retrieve their Vauxhall, an older man dressed in the coveralls of a gardener came around the corner of the building. John quickly engaged him. "You must be the head gardener?"

"Yes, sir, Hiram Fraser, sir." He tipped his cap that had covered most of his sun-worn face.

"You have beautiful grounds here. Must take a lot of work." John made small talk.

"Oh, not too bad, sir, but it's a fulltime job." He smiled.

"You must use a lot of fertilizer to keep it looking so nice and lush."

"Oh, not so much, not so much as a working farm. Maybe a hundred pounds or two a season. Have to use it sparingly or you'll burn all of your plantings."

"Well, you obviously do a good job."

"Thank you, sir." Fraser tipped his cap again and went back to his work.

John turned to Ernest, who asked, "Any luck with your search, Mr. Braemhor?"

"Not yet, but don't say anything to Sir Basil. I don't want to discourage him."

"Right you are, sir. Have a pleasant trip back to Daraichburn." He waved slightly as John backed the Vauxhall out of the car park.

At the first lay-by on the A811, John pulled off and turned to Mary. "What did you find out?"

"You were right. Donald MacErich is an expert helmsman and swimmer. Lead long-distance swimmer on his college's swim team. I don't think he drowned in the loch."

"I know he didn't. I believe I just saw him in the boathouse at Linlith," John told her.

"Good, then we can report the good news to Sir Basil." Mary was happy to have wrapped up the case of the disappearance of Donald MacErich so quickly.

"Not quite so fast." John smiled. "I also found over 20 bags of fertilizer in the boathouse, hidden under a black tarpaulin. As Fraser told us, you do not need that much fertilizer for a non-farming estate."

"I wondered why you mentioned fertilizer to Fraser."

"I just hope I was obtuse enough that my query did not ring any bells with Ernest."

"Those bags of fertilizer really trouble me. Fertilizer can be a basic component of homemade bombs. Remember the Oklahoma City bombing in the Colonies a few years back? Ordinary fertilizer was the major component of the explosives that took over 150 lives.

"And there are some fringe groups that would not hesitate to use violence to separate Scotland from the UK. Remember the days of Bruce. And the Irish troubles certainly showed us what extremes some will go to."

"Surely, John, you don't think young Donald is involved in something that drastic." Mary was taken aback by the idea.

"I certainly hope not, but remember for now we still have to keep our hypotheses open. I need to talk to Nigel Street. Let's get to the next roadhouse and get on a landline. Besides, it's time for dinner anyway."

The roadhouse, a few miles further on the A811 toward Sterling, was a rustic half-timbered structure. After ordering dinner, John asked for access to a landline and dialed Street's private number.

"Nigel Street here, who is this?" was the rather bored demand on the other end of the line.

"Braemhor here, John Braemhor."

"What do you want this time, Braemhor?" Street emitted another bored sigh. "Didn't I tell you that this number is for official and *important* messages? And what are you doing in a roadhouse on the Sterling highway? Not meddling in government affairs again, I hope."

"I needed a landline," John explained the reason for his location and then proceeded to tell Street about being hired by Sir Basil MacErich to find his brother.

"And what has that got to do with me and MI6? I'm really not interested in your private investigations, you know." Street's voice dripped sarcasm.

"I think you might be," and then Braemhor told Street of his and Mary's findings so far and how they might, just might, fit into something far more important than a missing heir to one of the larger estates in the highlands.

"Still at it eh, Braemhor?" However, Street's voice took on a different tone and made clear his interest. John had gotten his attention. There was a brief pause, then, "I think you need to be talking to MI5. This sounds like it could be more domestic." He took charge and began to sound like the professional he was. "Here is the private number of James Smyth. He's MI5's number one at the Sterling office. I'll let him know that you'll be calling him. Give me five minutes, then call him. Tell him what you just told me. I think he'll be interested. Anything else, Braemhor?"

"I think that will do for now. Thank you."

"Not at all, and, Braemhor, let me know how it comes out. Just professional interest, you understand."

"Of course, bye." John went back to the table with Mary.

"Have to wait about five minutes, then I'll call MI5. Street thinks, and so do I, that this is probably a domestic rather than international matter." He went back to the landline.

"James Smyth here," was the gruff voice on the other end.

"Braemhor, John Braemhor here."

"Ah, yes, Mr. Braemhor. Nigel Street said you would be calling. He thinks quite highly of you as an investigator."

That's news, John thought.

"How may I help you?'

John went into a detailed account of his search for Donald MacErich and the things he had found along the way. "What concerns me most is the unusual quantity of fertilizer being stored on the estate, while the gardener informs me that he does not use but 20 per cent of that amount each year. Do you have pictures of the leaders of the Black Heart organization?" Braemhor seemed to be changing the subject.

"Yes, we have those. We've been following that group for several years now. Why do you ask?"

"Because I want to identify the gentleman that I told you about who also visited Innis Braam recently. Could I pick up copies of those images today?" Braemhor wanted to move things along as rapidly as possible.

"Of course, I understand the possible connection," Smyth said. "You're at the Dryloch roadhouse now. I'll have them ready for you at reception. Meanwhile I'll put a quiet watch on the MacErich estate until you can confirm your suspicions. And, Mr. Braemhor, we do appreciate a private citizen's input. I'll talk with you later."

Three-quarters of an hour later, John parked in front of the brick office building containing the MI5 branch offices. Inside he identified himself to the receptionist who smiled and said, "Oh, yes, Mr. Smyth said you'd be coming. Here is your package." She handed him a sealed 5x7 manila envelope. Back in the Vauxhall, he quickly inspected the contents and showed the three glossy photographs to Mary.

"Looks like a rogue's gallery of terror," was her comment.

"Right. Now we need to get back to Captain Strong and see if any one of these shows the gentleman he said visited Innis Braam recently. For Sir Basil's sake, I almost hope not." He turned the car again onto the A811 but headed west this time.

An hour later, the Braemhors pulled up in front of Captain Strong's loch side shack with the red and white sign that read: *Fishing supplies. Boats, Tackle, Bait.*

"Ah, ha, you're back again, Mr. . . .Mrs. Braemhor. Want another skiff today?" The pound signs showed in his eyes.

"Not today, Captain, but I'd like you to look at these pictures and tell me if you recognize any of the men in them."

A puzzled look came over the face of the barrel-chested dock owner as he took the images from Braemhor. He shook his head quickly at the first two he looked at. "Not these," he concluded. But the minute he looked at the third, his face brightened. "This one. This is the one who was here a few days ago. Sour sort, you know. All business. Just wanted a quick rental, nothing else. No small talk. Just 'how much? I'll take it,' and he was off to the island."

"Thank you, very much, Captain Strong. You have been a great help."

The Captain was puzzled. "What do you mean? What's this all about? You some kind of copper? Or what?"

"No, no. Just trying to locate an old friend who's gone missing. And now at least I've found him as far as your boat dock. That's all." Braemhor hoped his hastily developed explanation would defuse the Captain's curiosity.

"If you say so, sir. Glad I could help." And he turned back to the net he was mending at the time that John and Mary arrived.

"Let's go over to Thistle Cottage. I need another landline." John was bristling with unspoken excitement. "Besides, there's something else we can do at the cottage."

Mary raised her eyebrows.

"I must really be slipping with age, Mary. In all the excitement of searching Innis Braam, we never evaluated the sheets of foolscap we found in the island cave."

Inside Thistle Cottage, Mrs. Buchanan was delighted to see them again. John told her of his need for a landline and a small table. She sat them in the breakfast area and brought an extension to the table. Braemhor took the top sheet of foolscap and began buffing it with the broadside of a soft pencil. Sure enough, parts of words that had been impressed on an original sheet from above became faintly visible.

"Look at this, Mary!" The words *time to act* and a date were clearly discernible.

"You don't suppose?!"

"Yes, I do, and that date is tomorrow!" he said as he rapidly dialed Smyth's number.

"Smyth!" John exploded as soon as Smyth picked up. "One of the three images you gave me was the man who went to Innis Braam last week—Mike Blackston."

"Not good news, Braemhor. He's Black Heart's bomb expert!"

"Also, I've got some sheets from a pad of foolscap that was left in the cave. Two things are clear on the paper, 'time to act' and tomorrow's date. John could hear Smyth's reaction on the phone.

"Well, they haven't moved the fertilizer from the boathouse so far. My boys have been keeping a close watch on the place. My guess," he was now thinking on the fly, "is, if they are planning what we think, they'll move it tonight, under cover of darkness. I'll double my surveillance. What I want to do is let them move it out tonight so that we can follow them to their main headquarters—we don't know where that is at present—and kill two birds in one operation."

"Thwart a bombing and find out where they hide," Braemhor concluded.

"Precisely. Mr. Braemhor, if all goes well by noon tomorrow we may be able to put a major dent in the operations of Black Heart. Call me tomorrow, and I'll let you know how successful we were. Anything else?"

"Not at the moment. I'll talk with you tomorrow." Braemhor hung up with a broad smile encompassing his face.

"Good news?" Mary responded to the relaxation that she saw coming over her husband.

"We should know by this time tomorrow, but for now let's spend a relaxing night in Mrs. Buchanan's fine establishment after we enjoy another example of her delicious cuisine;

* * * * *

Shortly after noon the next day after a pleasant evening at Thistle Cottage and a relaxing drive back to Daraichburn, Braemhor rang up Smyth again.

"Good news, Mr. Braemhor. Just as I suspected, Blackston, the MacErich boy, and two muscle men from Black Heart picked up over half of the fertilizer at Linlith Cottage and started transporting it eastward toward Edinburgh. You'll never guess who the driver of the lorry was."

"Donald's man, Ernest," Braemhor answered flatly.

"Yes! How did you know th. . . . Well, never mind. We almost lost them near Falkirk but our agents were able to track them to a modern suburb of the city. The house was one of their major hiding places, and we picked up Blackston, MacErich, and four other members of the organization.

"They were, in fact, planning a major action against the parliament building to coincide with the EU vote. This is a major coup for us, Mr. Braemhor, thanks to you."

"No thanks to me, Smyth, I was just trying to find a lost family member for Sir Basil and stumbled on what was going on." John demurred.

"But the important thing is that you recognized what was going on for what it was, a major domestic terror plot. Most citizens aren't tuned to recognize dangerous signs, if they fall over them. As you know, it takes a trained investigator to put all of the pieces together. And we in the agency thank you for doing the major portion of our legwork in this case." Smyth was most praiseworthy of Braemhor's skills.

"Have you informed Sir Basil, yet?"

"I was about to do that when you called. Would you like to inform him of his brother's activities?" Braemhor could pick up the sardonic smile even through the phone wire.

"I think not." John himself smiled. "I will have quite enough to tell him about finding his lost brother. I don't know how he will take the information that because of my investigation into his brother's disappearance, young Donald now may face charges for domestic terrorism. No, I'm much more comfortable with you telling him that part of the story. I'll give it about an hour for the devastation to sink in before I see him with my report. What about the sister?"

"Nothing we can hold her for, though I have a decided opinion that she was as involved as Donald. Unfortunately, all we have is the barrette you found in the cave. Unless I can pressure a member of the Black

Heart to implicate her, that's a dead end. However, I will put her on a silent watch list for the foreseeable future, just in case." After a slight pause, "Well, Mr. Braemhor, again I thank you for your assistance on this one. I'll pass the word on to Street. He sometimes has difficulty seeing the value of citizen input in keeping our country safe."

"Don't thank me. I'm just glad that it all ended without violence."

John went into the kitchen to Mary and told her what he'd just heard from Smyth. "Care for a drive to the MacErich estate to talk with Sir Basil?"

"No, but I'll come because I know how difficult this will be."

* * * * *

The Braemhors arrived at the MacErich estate about three. The woman who answered the door was a new face to them since Ernest was in gaol with the rest of the Black Heart organization.

"We are the Braemhors," John told her. "We need to see Sir Basil."

The maid nodded and led them up the stairs to the library. "Sir Basil will be with you in a moment." She left the room.

A moment later, Sir Basil appeared. His countenance reflected the misery he was enduring since Smyth's phone call. His usual robustness had faded, and he appeared tired, haggard and very depressed.

John spoke first, "Sir Basil, I am so sorry that finding your brother could not have ended better."

"I understand, Mr. Braemhor, when you discovered what you did you had no choice but to go to the proper authorities. I just so wish Donald had come to me and talked with me about what he was doing, the people he had fallen in with." He shook his lowered head, and tears began to escape his red-rimmed eyes. Embarrassed by this display of emotion, he continued, "You will have to forgive me. This is a very difficult time for me, for the family. But we must," he said as he straightened up slightly, "manage to move on and find a way to help young Donald, as best we can.

"Mr. Smyth has told me of the evidence you discovered and turned over to him, but when did you first suspect that Donald's disappearance was as horrific as it was?"

"My first suspicions were aroused on Innis Braam. Things just were not adding up to an abduction or an angry brother running away from the family estate. The real confirmation of what I had hoped not to find was the inordinate amount of fertilizer stored in the Linlith Cottage boathouse and finding that he'd apparently been living there all the while. That also confirmed my suspicions that Ernest was involved. He is so utterly devoted to young Donald, and I did not believe that Donald could have planned and carried out the plot without help from inside the estate. But it was MI5 that confirmed everything in the chase to Edinburgh." John paused to allow Sir Basil to gather himself together.

"Well, Mr. Braemhor, despite how it has turned out, I do know that I was right to engage you and your wife." Sir Basil looked at Mary. "Perhaps someday we can see one another under happier circumstances." He rose. "But I really have to get back to the family. They, too, are devastated. You understand." He offered his hand to both of the Braemhors and finished with, "Send your statement."

"I don't think so, Sir Basil. Under the circumstances I would rather forego any payment for services." John shook his head.

"Mr. Braemhor, I made a contract with you, and I do not intend to renege on my part of the obligation. The MacErichs, and I in particular, take pride in our family's standards. I hired you to do a service, and you performed it very well. I cannot allow you to go unrewarded." Sir Basil had become quite adamant despite his personal sorrow.

"Perhaps a simple donation to, say, *Medecins sans Frontieres* or a similar organization, will bring our business transaction to a satisfactory conclusion," John suggested.

"Excellent compromise, Mr. Braemhor. Thank you again." With that Sir Basil turned and left the room, and John and Mary descended the stairs to the outside.

Chapter 11

The early fall rain had been enveloping Dunmoor Cottage for almost a week without a break, making a muddy swamp of the car park in front of the Braemhor's B&B. The grey overcast enhanced the ground fogs that reduced visibility to no more than a car's length and made even shopping for daily nutrition a task of enormous perseverance. One late afternoon the fog was so thick that John had to walk in front of the Vauxhall holding out a large white handkerchief to help Mary navigate the road from the green grocer's to home. It was a slow process and, John thought, a bit dangerous as well. Both John and Mary relaxed some as he sloshed his way to the spot where they kept their automobile, and she cautiously applied the brakes to avoid the wintery-looking remains of their rose bushes surrounding their car park.

"Well, that was an experience," Mary said as she emerged from the car and immediately put her right foot into a puddle two inches over her shoe tops. "Ouch. That's cold," she stated, as John retrieved the fruits of their shopping from the boot.

"Let's just hope this weather clears somewhat by tomorrow," John said as both doffed their soggy shoes in the entry and carried the food into the kitchen.

"Why by tomorrow, John?" Mary asked.

"I have to get Rita from the train station in Melrose at 3:00 p.m. Did you forget?"

"Oh, John, I did. My poor brain just can't keep up anymore. And we have two couples coming this evening for the weekend. I do hope they will be able to find us all right. They're both American, and I'm sure they're not accustomed to our wet fog."

"Well, it will just make their holiday all the more exciting." John smiled as he brought a scuttle full of peat turves into the sitting room. "At least a peat fire will warm their sodden clothing and dispositions."

Both couples did arrive wet and soggy, as predicted. But the Braemhors got them settled into their rooms by nightfall and tried to placate their fears of a weather ruined vacation with cheery predictions of a sunny day by the morrow.

After supper, John and Mary retired to their quarters in the back of the Cottage, and John repeated his concern about tomorrow's weather. "I do hope this rain lets up by tomorrow," he commented as he looked out their bedroom window through the water cascading down the pane so heavily that his vision of the outdoors was blurred beyond recognition. He could not even make out the outline of his apple trees, bowing their heads under the weight of the rain.

"Don't worry. Rita will bring her wet weather togs, and she will have wrapped them around her sunny disposition," Mary reassured him as she turned out the reading lamp on her side of the bed.

* * * * *

The surprise of the morning was the sunshine brightening the water slogged landscape surrounding the Cottage. So delighted were the guests that one commented, "You really do have sunshine, don't you?"

"Specially ordered for our guests," was Mary's lighthearted response.

Soon after breakfast, both couples left for their respective sight-seeing, and John helped Mary tidy up the dining area and sitting room before going out to see if his apple trees had sustained any damage from the torrential rain overnight. But like the Braemhors, the trees were a hardy breed, and John settled in with the morning papers on one of the divans in front of the warm morning peat fire.

"Look at this, Mary!" he suddenly exclaimed, handing her the copy of *The Times* with the headline: *Strange Lights Appear Again Over Perthshire*.

"The same sort of phenomena Robert Hayson photographed?" Mary asked as she sat across from John on the other divan.

"Looks very similar. I wonder what it is?"

"Sounds like what we saw in Carterville last spring."

Mary could tell from the tone of his voice that Perthshire may well be their next adventure stop.

That afternoon John drove to Melrose to get Rita. As Mary predicted, she arrived in rain togs wrapped around her bright smiling disposition.

"Good trip?" John asked as he put her valise into the boot.

"Wonderful! I met the most interesting man in the club car. He was a scientist from London. Studies dark matter. Professor Lügner, that was his name, actually had a box of it with him! He showed it to me!"

"What did it look like, Rita?"

"Oh, I couldn't tell you. It's invisible, you know that."

"I see. So this professor showed you an empty box full of invisible dark matter. Did he try to sell you any?" John was incredulous at the apparent gullibility of his wife's aunt.

"Oh, yes. He even offered me a special price."

"Did you buy?" John feared the answer.

"Of course not, John."

"I'm glad."

"You don't think I'd buy such a box of invisible dark matter from just anyone, do you? For all I know he might have stolen it. Besides," Rita explained as she gave her characteristic little pixie grin, "maybe he wasn't even a real professor. You know a lot of people go about saying they're something they're not."

"You've got a good head on your shoulders, Rita," John praised her and smiled as they pulled into the Dunmoor Cottage car park.

While Rita was putting her valise in her room, John told Mary of the adventure Rita had had on the train. "We almost had a box of dark matter right here in the Cottage." John smiled.

"What are you talking about, John? Dark matter is invisible."

"I know, and Rita claims that a professor on the train showed her a box of it! Fortunately, she didn't buy any."

"Really, John, I sometimes think you make these things up," Mary commented as Rita joined them in the sitting room.

"Have you been doing any travelling lately?" Rita asked.

"Not for a while. Why do you ask?" Mary answered.

"Oh, on the train I was reading about strange lights in the sky over Perthshire. I think it's UFOs, don't you?"

"Maybe it's fairy airplanes," John grumbled from behind his newspaper.

"Oh, John!" Mary tried to silence him with a knowing glance.

"Do you really think so? Sir Arthur says they move around in mysterious ways."

"Rita, fairies are mythical creatures despite what Sir Arthur might say. Really, Rita, for an intelligent person like you to. . . ."

"Maybe we should go to Perthshire and find out," Mary broke in before her husband could say something that would offend her aunt, who at times showed a sensitive side.

John was flabbergasted and for a brief moment did not know how to respond. He didn't know if Mary was serious or just trying to head off the conversation. Mary looked at him with a knowing and "stop where you are going" look.

"Fine, fine," John stammered, "maybe Rita would like the trip."

"Oh, and can I be a UFO divining rod this time like I was for the hum?"

"Of course, Rita. You were a big help then, and I'm sure you will be again," Mary replied.

"And a junior detective, too?" Rita blossomed.

"That, too," John joined in.

"Oh, that's wonderful! When do we leave?"

"Well, we'll have to stay here until our guests have left, but we should be able to go on Monday or Tuesday.

* * * * *

Tuesday morning, after three glorious days of sunshine, the ubiquitous Scottish mists once again descended upon Dunmoor Cottage. After breakfast John packed the valises in the boot and he, Mary and

Rita drove north, through Edinburgh, across the Firth of Forth and on towards Perth. They skirted Perth itself and went instead to the small village of Cairn-on-the-Green, set on a hill overlooking the Firth of Tay, where they took rooms at the Tayside Inn.

The Tayside was typical of inns in the region, offering luxurious room accommodations as well as an excellent restaurant and pub. At check-in Rita proudly announced in a voice that all in the common rooms could hear, "We've come to see the UFOs!"

The clerk smiled and said, "Well, you're too early; they don't come out until after dark, but we now have a whole group of watchers who sit on the hill outside the inn and watch. You're welcome to join them. They start gathering around dusk."

"Oh, I'd like that. Can we do that, John, Mary?"

"I think that would be a wonderful way to start our holiday, don't you, John?" Mary said in agreement.

"Of course, but we might see if we can talk with Robert Hayson before supper." John turned to the clerk. "Does he live around here?"

"Yes, sir. He has a farm just northeast of here, along the Dundee road. He's become quite famous, you know. Until recently he spent almost every evening in our pub regaling the tourists with tales of his sightings, though he hasn't been in the last few nights. Somewhat odd, but he seems to really enjoy the attention his photo of the lights has given him. I understand the government boys have been interviewing him pretty intensely of late. And his sighting has certainly been good for the inn. Our pub has been doing very well with all the tourists and the like gathering every night to see the lights."

"So he's not averse to talking about his experience?" John asked.

"Not at all! I'm sure he'd be happy to tell you all about the lights. I understand he's now selling copies of his famous picture to anyone who will buy. We have a few copies here, if you would like one."

"Oh, that would be so nice, to have a picture of real UFOs," Rita gushed.

"We'll take one," John said. "Just put it on our room bill." The clerk handed John an 8x10 photograph, showing the lights, some forming an arc, others grouped in the center of the arc. It was a beautiful sepia toned print. "Beautifully done," Mary remarked as John gave the photo to Rita for a keepsake of the trip.

"Oh, yes," the clerk replied. "Mr. Hayson is something of an excellent amateur photographer. Does his own prints at his house."

"Mr. Hayson a heavy drinker?" John was pursuing a line of thought.

"Not really," the clerk answered. "Maybe a couple of beers a night, not any more."

"Why don't we put our bags in our rooms, then go to Mr. Hayson's farm and see what he can tell us about his discovery," Mary suggested.

Half hour later, the three were on the road toward Dundee seeking the Hayson farm. It was easily found for the entry gate was festooned with signs, garlands and copies of Hayson's picture of the strange lights over the Firth of Tay. "I think this is it," John understated the fact with a chuckle. "Shall we visit the famous Farmer Hayson?"

Rita was literally bouncing in the backseat of the Vauxhall with excitement. After all, she'd never met anyone who had actually seen a UFO. "Do you think he talked with the aliens? Maybe they were from Mars or Jupiter." She continued to bubble.

"Rita, try to stay calm, please. We are not even sure what it was Mr. Hayson saw and photographed. We'll find out more in a few minutes." John parked the car near the stone farmhouse on a rise of ground that overlooked the Tay. John got out and knocked on the front door. No answer. *Strange,* John thought. He looked out over the vista of farm fields surrounding the house. Not a soul or farm vehicle in sight.

As John walked around the house, he rounded a corner on the Tay side and almost bumped into a short, slight, hungry-looking man in his early sixties, whose face wore a perpetual frown which knitted his forehead into a worried look and deepened the crevice at the top of his nose. His eyes were deeply sunken into his face and hidden by wireless glasses which somehow managed to give him an otherworldly appearance. His skin, which should have been ruddy and weatherworn, looked instead as if it belonged to a person who'd spent much of his life indoors, out of the sun and wind. His coveralls were dark blue but spattered with a white dust across his shoulders and chest.

"Help ye?" the man droned.

John was almost overcome with the odor of garlic. Even more striking about Hayson's appearance was the complete lack of hair about his immobile face.

"Mr. Hayson?" John asked.

"The same," was the flat intonation.

"Can we talk to you about your sighting?"

"Who's 'we'?"

John was a bit taken aback by the flat tone emanating from this specter-like person he was having a conversation with, but he charged ahead. "I'm John Braemhor. My wife and I and her aunt came out to talk with you about the lights. Would another time be better? Tomorrow, perhaps?"

"Now's fine. Bring them in the front door." He pointed and turned to go in the Tay-side door. No expression animated his face, and his movements were wooden, made with no more energy than his voice. He hardly blinked. John wondered if he'd suffered a farm injury sometime in the past or possibly had Parkinsons Disease. *There is just something mechanical and unreal about him,* John thought, as he went around to the car park and the front door.

He warned Mary and Rita that there was something very strange about Mr. Hayson, though he had yet to be able to capture it with words. He spoke as he took them to the front door where the gaunt Mr. Hayson awaited their entry.

"Sit," he said and pointed to a divan and an overstuffed chair. Hayson then took the Morris chair that faced the window looking out onto the Tay. On one arm of the chair was an open bottle of antacid tablets which Hayson occasionally ate, two or three at a time.

Beside him on the floor was a black, white and tan sheep dog, and the dog showed no more animation than his master. In fact, he lay stark still, not moving at all, his ears laid back and his eyes having the same immobile rigidity as Mr. Hayson. Occasionally, Hayson reached down and patted the dog's head and still the dog never moved. "What do you want to know?" The smell of garlic was overwhelming. His appearance and manner startled both Mary and Rita, the latter so much that she was reduced to utter silence and actually cowered in her corner of the divan like a frightened puppy.

"We'd like to hear about your adventure with the lights," John opened.

With no animation at all, Hayson began, "I was sitting in my chair after supper enjoying a pipe when I heard a very loud roaring, so loud I thought I had left me tractor running outside. So I went out to see. It wasn't running, but the noise was there all the same. Then I looked up and saw the lights. I came back in to get me camera and took the picture. As soon as I took the picture, the lights were gone." He stared through his guests with his watery, pale blue eyes as he spoke.

"Did they make any other noise, except the roaring?"

"Nope."

"Did they move around at all or change in any way?"

"Nope."

"What do you think they were?"

"Don't know," was Hayson's response.

Rita finally broke her silence with an enthusiastic, "Did you see the creatures?"

Hayson turned slowly, his eyes looking at, yet through, Rita, and he said nothing. After an awkward silence, John rose, thanked Mr. Hayson for his time and led Mary and Rita outside to the car. They drove back to the inn in silence until Mary said, "What an odd person."

"He wasn't just odd. He was creepy," Rita added. "He frightened me. Like he wasn't even human."

"Maybe he doesn't like to talk about his experience." Mary tried to explain the strange evening.

"That's not what the clerk said. He said Mr. Hayson likes to come into the pub and talk to people about the lights," Rita countered, "and did you notice the dog?"

"As strange as his owner," Mary answered. "It didn't move."

"Maybe it was a stuffed dog," Rita offered.

"Or dead," John concluded.

"Dead, oh, John, really," Mary exclaimed.

"I'm serious. It didn't move one hair the whole time we were there. Its eyes never flickered, and if I'm not mistaken, it wasn't breathing."

"Wouldn't it have smelled?" Mary was trying to understand.

"But it didn't."

"Then what was that smell," Mary asked, "like garlic? He reeked of garlic."

"That's another curious thing," John was thinking aloud.

Rita suddenly interrupted, "I know. He was trying to ward off vampires. The UFOs were carrying vampires!"

"Calm down, Rita, we don't know that the lights were anything extraterrestrial, much less something out of a Bram Stoker novel," John said, as they entered the inn's car park. After a short pause, he asked, "How about some supper? I saw they have hard battered haddock on the menu."

Inside, the three saw the desk clerk. "Did you get to see Mr. Hayson?" he asked cheerfully.

"Yes, it was quite an experience," John responded.

"He was creepy!" Rita added.

"Oh, he can be a little odd at times, but usually he's quite friendly, at least after he's had a brew or two." The clerk smiled.

"Maybe he's more friendly with local people. A little shy with strangers?" Mary asked.

"Maybe. Most of our rural neighbors are a little standoffish," the clerk agreed. "Well, enjoy your suppers." Rita, Mary and John went into the dining area.

"What next, John?" Mary asked after the entrées.

"First, I think we should watch the skies over the Tay after it gets dark, don't you think? See if the lights appear."

"This is so exciting!!" Rita bubbled. "Then what?"

"I think we should talk to some of the locals in the pub. See what their view of the lights is. Tomorrow I'll talk with the local authorities, but for now we should go outside and find a good lookout spot."

After retrieving their jackets, Rita, Mary and John walked to the Tay side of the inn's property to find a good observation location. The inn sat several hundred feet above the level of the Tay, which was a hundred yards or so in the distance. The 180° vista looked much like Hayson's grazing fields, punctuated with a few copses of trees and the faint lights of farm cottages sprinkled throughout.

"Beautiful!" Mary exclaimed, as John located the low remains of an ancient cairn on which they could sit and look. Rita was literally shaking with excitement. A half dozen or so other inn guests joined them on surrounding outcroppings as the night descended. But the evening gave all of them nothing but disappointment, until two hours later John suggested to Mary and Rita that they retire to the pub to interview the guests and the locals.

John chose seats at a long table in the middle of the pub where had gathered a mixture of individuals. After John got their tea, the three introduced themselves to the others sitting nearest them and sought out the varied opinions of the lights which Mr. Hayson had photographed.

One older gentleman sitting across from John was the first to offer an opinion. "I think the whole thing's a hoax. Hayson's jest trying to make a pound. It works well on the tourists, but not on those of us who live here. Bah!" His face reddened as he spoke, and his bulbous nose twitched like a hound on a scent.

"But I thought others had seen them as well?" John asked.

"Bah! Some people'll say anything to get attention. For me own part, there ain't no lights. And pretty soon we'll have a bunch of travelers, like they've got over in Halfbrewed, moving in to scam the tourists." The older man harrumphed.

"Ned's right about the travelers, but I seen 'em, too. They jest lit up the sky for a short while and then disappeared," added Ned's friend sitting next to him.

"But I thought they flew away at high speed?" Mary asked.

"No, ma'am. They jest disappeared, like you'd turn off a lamp. One minute they were there, the next they were gone."

"Interesting," John commented.

"Maybe they're aliens set by God to punish us for our sins," the woman across from Rita suddenly broke in.

"She's right, you know," added the man sitting next to her. "It says so in the *Bible*. It's the modern-day locusts."

Oh, good heavens, John thought, *this will get us nowhere.*

Rita looked at the man directly and said, "God has more important things to do." Then she turned to John, "John, let's move to another table." And she abruptly picked up her teacup and stood up. Mary joined her and John followed.

"It's been nice talking with you." Mary tried to calm the encounter.

As they sat at another long table, John took Rita's arm and whispered to her, "Well said, Rita." She smiled her acknowledgment. At this table, the crowd was younger, and some seemed to be tourists rather than locals. The discussion was a bit more orderly.

"Even if what Hayson saw were UFOs, what do we do about them?" was one early question.

"Wait," another interjected, "first we need to find out what it was Hayson saw. Then we can decide reasonably what to do about it."

"How many other people saw what Hayson saw and photographed?"

"I, for one, and the lights looked real enough to me. Bright in the sky and then, poof, they were gone." Three of the half dozen people at the table raised their hands to John's query.

"I still think we have to ascertain if Hayson's photo is authentic," another said.

"Haven't the authorities already done that?"

An older woman answered, "Oh, yes, the local authorities have done. I even heard that MI6 was involved."

"And what did they conclude?" asked one of the younger individuals.

"Nobody knows."

The three who admitted seeing the lights offered three different descriptions of the phenomenon. One said they were white and stationary. Another thought they moved around the sky before suddenly disappearing. And the third swore the lights were multicolored. None heard any unusual sound.

At this point John decided that they had gleaned enough information for the moment and motioned Mary and Rita towards their rooms.

Rita deferred. Her excitement was still bubbling over. "I'll see you at breakfast." She waved to John and Mary and turned back to her tablemates.

"I think Aunt Rita is really enjoying this adventure, don't you, John?" Mary asked after they were in bed.

"Definitely. Maybe she'll get more information for us."

"What next?"

"Perth, I think. I'd like to talk with the local DI and look at back copies of *The Courier* at the library. Think you and Rita can entertain yourselves?"

"Maybe we can do some of the library work? What will we be looking for?"

"I want to know what the weather was like on the nights the lights appeared."

Mary's face was quizzical but she said, "We can do that while you see the DI. Save us time."

"It's a plan," John agreed as he rolled over to sleep.

* * * * *

Next morning at breakfast Rita was as happy and as jumpy as a chipmunk.

"What did you learn, Aunt Rita?" Mary asked as she cracked her soft-boiled, knowing Rita could hardly contain herself with what she'd discovered the night before.

Rita's smile covered her entire face. "First the lights only appear near the area of the confluence of the River Tay and the Firth. No one said they saw them anywhere else."

"Near Halfbrewed then," John concluded.

Rita looked puzzled and a little miffed that John was telling her story. "I guess."

"Sorry, Rita, go ahead."

"One man did say that there was a loud noise. He thought it sounded like an industrial generator, but he was an engineer from Aberdeen. Only a couple of people said the lights moved about. All the rest said they just appeared and disappeared. But everybody said some of the lights blinked on and off at times."

"Some, but not all?" John asked.

"Yes. And one man thought it was only the lights in the center of the arc that did that. The ones at the outer edge of the half-circle didn't blink."

"The blinking might account for some seeing apparent movement," Mary added.

"Right," John concurred. "Anything else, Rita?"

"Oh, yes. They never come on when the moon is out, and they are always low in the sky, like on the horizon. One man thinks they are reflections of village lights across the Tay, but the rest think they are too bright for that."

"Last night one woman said she thought they were multicolored. Did anyone else say that?" Mary asked.

"Yes, two others saw colored lights but only once or twice. Almost all of the time, they were white. Have I been a good detective?" Rita beamed at John.

"An excellent sleuth, Rita." John reached over and patted her hand on the table. Rita's smile broadened. "Now I think we should be off to Perth. I've contacted DI Melville, and he'll see me about half nine."

The morning mist was burning off on the Tay-side hills as the Braemhors and Rita entered the city of Perth. Mary dropped John off at Melville's office and took Rita to the central library for research into the weather conditions in the area for the last few weeks or so.

John introduced himself to the desk clerk, "I'm John Braemhor, here to see DI Melville."

A short, little, round man with a cherry complexion and cheery face appeared at a door in the back. "Come on in, Mr. Braemhor." Melville spoke as if he already knew Braemhor. "Ron Ferguson's a good friend of mine. He's mentioned you several times. Understand you're a private investigator? Ron says you've helped him on a case or two."

"That's right. Over near Ft. Ewen."

"What brings you to Perthshire?"

"Mr. Hayson's lights." John took Melville's offered hand.

"Ah, the UFOs. Fascinated a lot of people. We've looked into them, but they're a mystery to us, too. Even had some boys from MI6 snooping around for all the good it did. I'm afraid, Mr. Braemhor, I'm not going to be of much help to you. We frankly don't know what they are, or if they really exist. In fact, some of us around the office have taken to calling them 'Hayson's Hoax'."

"But I've talked to a lot of people who report seeing them, not just Hayson," John persisted.

"I know, I know. That's the puzzle. A lot of people claim to have seen them, but there aren't many consistencies in the reports. Everybody has a different story about what they've seen. I even had one lady who claims to have seen multiple flying saucers with tiny creatures on the wings waving at her. We think it's a case of general hysteria." Melville broke out laughing.

"But there are some consistencies." John persisted again. "Nobody reports seeing them on moonlit nights. They are always reported as being low on the horizon, never high in the sky. And, so far as I've been able to ascertain, always on the south side of the Tay."

"What you say is perfectly true, but everything we've looked into has been a blind alley. You know, Mr. Braemhor, the United States Air Force put together an extensive project to investigate UFOs. They called it

Project Blue Book and pursued it for over 20 years back at the time of that Roswell thing. Kept unbelievable records. Investigated over 12,000 sightings. Nothing. Finally gave it up."

"They did have over 700 sightings they couldn't explain," John pointed out.

"True, but they finally decided further investigation wasn't worth the effort and costs. Maybe there was something there, but they couldn't find it. Same here in Perthshire."

"You say our MI6 looked into it?" John asked.

"Yes, a Mr. Street and several of his agents, up from Manchester."

"And they concluded?"

"Nothing they could pin down. I think their final conclusion was 'unknown phenomenon' and they went back to Manchester." Melville shrugged. "So there we are. I certainly wish you well with your research, but frankly I don't hold out much hope for your finding anything substantive." Melville rose to indicate that the interview was over.

John, too, rose, took Melville's hand again, thanked him for his time and then walked to the central library. He found Mary and Rita sitting on a bench across the street from the library.

"What have you found?" he asked, noting that Rita was still bouncing with enthusiasm.

"According to *The Courier,* the last two weeks had five clear nights, the rest were cloudy, and five of those were heavily cloudy," Mary informed him.

"And," Rita burst in, "sightings of the lights were reported on the five cloudiest of them! So, don't you see? It has something to do with clouds! Maybe the

UFOs are hiding behind the clouds and don't come out on clear nights because they don't want to be seen!"

"Maybe so, Rita. Maybe so." John tried to contain her enthusiasm.

John told them both about the lack of information he obtained at Melville's office.

"Off to Halfbrewed, then?" Mary asked abruptly.

John was startled that Mary's thinking had anticipated his. "How did you know?"

"It's the nearest place to where the lights have been seen," Mary calmly answered.

Halfbrewed, on the south bank of the Tay, was a smallish village with an inn situated on the edge of the green at its center. On the green were parked a large number of travelers' caravans complete with clotheslines, lounge chairs, barbeques and other assorted camping gear. A number of the automobiles sported foreign license plates from Scandinavia and EU countries.

"With the ease of travel in the EU, it looks like the travelers are going greater distances," John noted as he parked in the inn car park. "Let's get some dinner."

Inside, John approached the reception desk. "See you've got some visitors on your green."

The clerk rolled his eyes. "Oh, yes, sir. They came in about a week and a half ago and just settled in. Nobody seems able to get rid of them. Police Scotland said it was a local matter, and our council hasn't been able to do anything. And that's our public space. People walk their dogs there, and the village uses it for football training. We're very upset I can tell you. We've tried to be nice to them and get them to move on quietly, but a lot of them don't seem to want to make nice. Ever since the EU let down the travel restrictions, we've had more travelers than ever before. We're a very quiet village. Low crime. Low noise. A nice place to live and raise a family. And now this! This group even brought their own power generator with them—huge thing—so all night long the place is lit up like a circus. I guess we should be happy they're not illegally tapping into our power grid. It's a real mess!"

"That's too bad. You say they arrived about a week and a half ago? Do travelers usually stay that long in one place?"

"If they take a liking to the place. We just hope they'll move on soon. You need a room?"

"No, thank you. We thought we'd get some dinner. We're staying over at Cairn-on-the-Green." John smiled and led Mary and Rita into the dining area for a respite. "Where to next?" Mary asked.

"I'd like to go back to Hayson's farm and talk with him some more."

"If you can get any more than a monosyllable or two out of him."

"True, but let's see what we can do."

Hayson's farm was as before. Beautiful but desolate. His tractor was on the Tay-side as was an old mule that brayed at John when he came around the corner of the house. A few chickens clucked their way to his feet, apparently having not been fed recently. But no Hayson.

John went around to the front again and told Mary and Rita to stay in the car while he looked inside, if he could. He rapped loudly on the front door. No answer, so he looked through the front window into the sitting room where Mary, Rita and he had first talked with Hayson. Through the caked dirt on the pane he thought he could barely make out the outline of Hayson, sitting in his Morris chair beside the dog. *The dead dog*, John thought. *Maybe Hayson's asleep.* John pushed gently on the door. It creaked open.

"Mr. Hayson!" John called out. "Mr. Hayson!" Still no answer. *Maybe he's gone out*, John thought as he gently opened the door fully and walked into the entryway. "Mr. Hayson!" he tried again. He went into the sitting room. There sat Hayson, his back to the door and facing the Tay through his back window.

"Mr. Hayson," John strode into the room and walked around the Morris chair to face him directly. John stopped abruptly as he faced Hayson. The man was sitting in the chair, his arms on the two broad armrests, looking—or so John thought—out on the Tay. Then John was struck by Hayson's appearance. His skin, unlike the parchment of yesterday, was now ashen grey, drained of all color. His lipid eyes stared straight ahead, not moving or seeing the image of John before him. John felt for a pulse and quickly confirmed his worst suspicion. Robert Hayson was dead!!

Hayson's right hand held the open jar of antacid he had been eating, as the day before when John, Mary and Rita visited him. And in his rigid left hand was a piece of note paper and on the floor a half sealed envelope. John looked, as best he could, at the writing on the paper without touching it. It was in the hand of a very old individual, one much older than Hayson. It was to a Rebecca Hayson in Dundee. "They're here. They're all around me. I can't escape. They took Scrappy yesterday. I have nothing left. I have seen more than I should. Know that I. . . ." Hayson's thumb covered the rest of the sentence. It was signed "Father."

John took the nearby telephone in a handkerchief-covered hand and called DI Melville. "I've got a real crime for you here in Cairn-on-the-Green." He quickly explained what he'd found and finished with, "We'll need some officers and the local coroner." He hung up and went outside to tell Mary and Rita of his find, and to await the local authorities.

Chapter 12

Melville and two junior officers arrived sooner than John expected. The coroner's van was not far behind. *They must have broken all limits getting here,* he mused as he led the officers into the farmhouse and his grim discovery.

"What time did you find him?' Melville asked.

"About half three. I'd guess he's only been dead a couple of hours, judging from the rigor. I don't see any obvious wounds but that will be up to the coroner. "

The officers quickly ribboned off the farmhouse and car park and had Mary move the Vauxhall out to the side of the roadway. Mary spent most of her time trying to calm Rita who once she'd been told what John had discovered became quite distraught. "You're just not used to what real detective work is like. It's not all pretty and an intellectual connecting of clues together. Try to calm down. Both John and I are here and everything is all right."

"Not for Mr. Hayson," Rita said, tears running down her cheeks.

John came over to Mary after his first meeting with Melville. "I'll have to stay awhile. Take Rita back to the inn and get her to lie down in her room. Maybe a mild sedative would be in order. And for heaven's sake, don't let her talk to anyone. The authorities will make public what we found soon enough, but better the locals hear it from officials, not Rita. I'll call you as soon as I can get away."

With permission from Melville, Mary took Rita back to the inn to await John's call.

While the coroner examined Hayson's body, Melville's officers started gathering up and bagging items from the house. The coroner looked up from his work. "Preliminarily, I'd agree with Mr. Braemhor's guess that death came within the last three or four hours. I don't see any obvious signs of a wound or blows. A sudden coronary is possible, but I'll have to consider other causes."

"Like?" Melville asked.

"Poisoning for one, but that will take a few days to ascertain."

Half an hour later, Braemhor called Mary for a ride back to the inn.

"What did you learn?" Mary asked as John settled into the passenger's seat.

"Very little. Melville and his men are stripping Hayson's home for possible clues. The coroner said he wasn't immediately sure what the cause of death was. No obvious answer. So we'll just have to wait. They'll call me when they have something more definitive. How's Rita?"

"Oh, she'll be all right. Except for squirrels, rabbits and pheasants, she hasn't had to face death. For all of her eccentricities, Rita is a caring, loving person, you know, and she feels terrible for poor Mr. Hayson. What's next on our agenda?"

"I think we should spend some time this evening looking for the lights. We still haven't solved that puzzle yet, and it might take Rita's mind off of Mr. Hayson," John said as Mary turned into the inn's car park.

Rita, looking a little haggard, but brighter than when Mary had brought her back to the inn, was downstairs in reception waiting for John and Mary. "Feeling better?" John asked.

"Oh yes, but I still feel so sorry for Mr. Hayson. What happened to him?"

"We won't know for a couple of days. The coroner will let us know," Mary answered.

"I think we ought to look for the lights again tonight." Rita perked up slightly at her own suggestion.

"Excellent idea, Rita!" John jumped in. "Let's plan on sitting out on the cairn again. Who knows? Maybe they'll come back."

So after supper the three resumed their observation post on the cairn ruin they had used the night before. Rita seemed almost her old self, exuberant at being able to play the role of "little detective" again. While they waited for events, they discussed the plight of Mr. Hayson. "What do you think caused his death, John?" Mary started the conversation.

"Well, since neither the coroner nor I saw any obvious wounds, it had to be something internal. A stroke, a heart attack, or possibly poisoning. I opt for the latter. You know I still can't explain the garlic he reeked of. At least it wasn't an almond scent which would have pointed us toward cyanide. But even if poisoning turns out to be true, I'm still puzzled by the delivery route.

"Oh, look!" Rita virtually shouted as she pointed to the southwest horizon. And there they were, just as Hayson had photographed them. Some of the lights under the center of the arc were in fact blinking but the arc of lights itself was stationary. "It's right over the area of Halfbrewed," John noted. "I wonder if it has anything to do with the travelers? Let's go over there and see." He rose and headed back to the inn and their Vauxhall.

"Wait, John, they're gone!" Mary called him back.

"All right." John returned to the cairn. "Let's take stock. An arc of lights came on suddenly low on the horizon above about where Halfbrewed is. They were all white. No colors, as some have reported. Some of the ones under the center of the arc blinked on and off irregularly. And then, quite suddenly, they disappeared. No rapid speeding across the sky. Either of you two note anything else?"

"I thought the ones that blinked weren't as bright as the others," Rita noticed.

"Good observation, Aunt Rita." Mary wanted to make sure Rita felt a real contributor to their investigation.

"So whatever it is, it isn't 'Hayson's Hoax'," John concluded, thinking of Melville's remark the day before. "Now I think we're on to something." Like Rita, John's enthusiasm was evident in his voice.

"Did you see 'em?" the clerk asked as they re-entered the inn.

"Oh yes!" Rita gushed, "and they were so pretty. Like little dancing elves!"

"Or fairies," John whispered to Mary and they all ascended the stairs to their rooms and a well-deserved sleep.

* * * * *

The next day was one of Braemhor's usual when in the midst of an investigation—pacing and waiting for something to happen. Even though he knew that Melville would have no news for him for a day or two, it did not prevent him from his caged leopard behavior.

"Oh, John, why don't you sit down and read. We can't do anything until tonight when we go to Halfbrewed. Calm yourself, please." Mary had been through this so many times in the past. "I thought I might take Rita to Perth and do some shopping to pass the day."

"Good idea and good advice." John smiled sheepishly, took a book from the inn's guest library and went out on the inn's porch to try to pass the afternoon. It did not come easy for him. He did find a history of the Middle East during WWI and so settled down in a chaise lounge. Ten pages into the tome, he closed his eyes to rest a moment, and the next thing he knew he awoke with a start in the midst of an interview with T. E. Lawrence just back from the front with a coded message from Faisal ihn Hussein. "I need this decoded immediately!" Lawrence told him. "The Arab Revolt depends on it!"

Braemhor retrieved his 5x5 Wheatstone Square and began decoding it as fast as he could, but it wasn't making any sense. Something about troop movements and further orders to come. But the more he worked, the more confused he became. Lawrence grabbed his shoulder and shook him violently. "Hurry man, hurry. Hundreds of Bedouin lives depend on your accurate reading of this message! Hurry!" Lawrence shook John's shoulder all the more vigorously. Braemhor looked up at his tormentor.

"Mary! What's wrong?" he asked through the fog.

"Nothing, John, I just don't want you to miss supper. Rita and I have been back for a half hour waiting for you to wake up." Mary smiled down at her husband. John slowly got up, looked a little sheepish and followed Mary and Rita into the dining area.

After supper, John, Mary, and Rita stayed in the inn's common area off of reception to plan their evening's activities. They decided to arrive in the hamlet of Halfbrewed shortly after dark and to find themselves a good vantage point from which to observe the traveler's campsite. John provided each of them with pads and pencils with which to keep notes. They decided to keep separate notes which they could compare after they returned to Cairn-on-the-Green.

By 10:00 p.m., the three had found a convenient bench on the edge of the green in Halfbrewed and sat down to wait. Heavy clouds covered the sky. "The clerk was right," was John's first observation. Mary looked slightly puzzled. "He said the travelers lit up the green like a circus," John explained. Lights were on all over. Each caravan was festooned with different colored illumination.

At first all was quiet, except for the travelers' laughing and drinking together, but about an hour later the noise of a large electrical generator starting up enveloped the area and then settled back to a constant hum. Around the edges of the multi-lights of the encampment an arc of white lights came to life. They were like miniature versions of the old WWII searchlights used over London during the blitz. In the middle of this arc and interspersed among the colorful caravans were a number of additional white lights. The focus of all of the white lights was reflected quite brightly by the cloud cover. Then the lights in the center began slowly to blink on and off irregularly.

"It's Morse code," John suddenly realized. "Take it down as best you can. Short flashes are dots and long ones, dashes." All three concentrated on the illuminations, interpreting the flashing lights as best they could. After a short period there was a pause and then the lights began flashing again. "They're repeating the message," John announced. "Take it down again!"

In a brief few minutes all of the lights went off suddenly, and the generator noise ground down and faded until again there was silence. John, Mary and Rita stayed for another half hour and then returned to the inn at Cairn-on-the-Green.

* * * * *

Once in their room, John sat down at the small desk with his, Mary's and Rita's pads of dots and dashes. Although there were some discrepancies among the three notations, they matched well enough that John felt he had a reasonably accurate transcription of the Morse code letters the flashing lights were projecting onto the clouds. The first code letters read: PCXRFQBUSY, then,

YOPBYTNPZAHOTUSQDSOTSXYTNPSWMYZ
BDQKCSWUKWEOYYOMH

Initially, John attacked the messages as a series of monograms where the encryption of the message was done with a simple one letter for one letter substitution. That and several other similar attempts failed. "I wonder," he muttered to himself. "I have to assume this is a simple code, nothing too complex. I doubt that the travelers would have an encryption machine. If not, they would want to work with simply paper and a pencil. It also cannot be too demanding an encryption because of the diverse number of travelers they would want to communicate with. Keep it simple, John. Keep it simple."

"How's it coming, John?" Mary asked. "Do you know it's almost 1:30? Maybe you should put it down for now and get some sleep. You know, you always say that the brain asleep solves many problems."

"Maybe you're right. A few hours sleep may help solve the encryption. Let's get some sleep. Rita, we'll tap on your door at 8:00."

Next morning, John was up early pacing and muttering to himself. He'd slept well, though only for an abbreviated period. He dreamt a lot and, as yesterday afternoon, found himself discussing codes with T. E. Lawrence. Suddenly he stopped in mid-pace. "Of course, they're bigrams not monograms!" Quickly, he went to the desk and took the encoded message and broke it into bigrams, thus:

YO/PB/YT/NP/ZA/HO/TU/SQ/DS/OT/SX/YT/NP/
SW/MY/ZB/DQ/KC/SW/UK/WE/OY/YO/MH

He did the same with the shorter, initial message:
PC/XR/FQ/BU/SY

You don't suppose they used a simple alphabet key? Do you? Worth a try. He quickly plotted out a 5x5 square and filled in the cells with the alphabet, omitting J. He took the shorter message first and decoded the bigrams into key-based letters.

"That's it! I've got it! I've got it!"

"John, what are you going on about?' Mary had just stepped out of the shower.

"The code! The code! I've broken the travelers' code! Look here! The short message says, 'News Alert.' All you have to do is substitute bigram for bigram in this Wheatstone Square." He showed Mary the square he had sketched out on his pad:

A	B	C	D	E
F	G	H	I	K
L	M	N	O	P
Q	R	S	T	U
V	W	X	Y	Z

"It was so simple, once I realized the travelers were working with a simple bigram encryption system. And fortunately, they used a simple alphabet key. Nothing complex but something that most all travelers could deal with, with just paper and pencil. I was lucky, Mary."

"You certainly were. But what made you think of this particular system? It's not like you deal with codes everyday."

"Well, I was discussing the Wheatstone Square system with T. E. Lawrence last night."

"Last night! What are you talking about?! Lawrence has been dead for decades. Really, John, you're starting to sound like Rita."

"I had a dream. Remember, I was reading that book yesterday about the Middle East during WWI. Well, in that book Lawrence discussed the Wheatstone Square encryption system with one of his fellow officers. It's a system that the British Foreign Office used off and on in the late nineteenth and early twentieth centuries. You see, the brain really does solve problems while you sleep."

"I suppose so, John, but it just sounds like an awful lot of serendipity to me."

"Whatever it was, it was good fortune for us." He turned back to the desk to decode the longer message the three had taken down last night. In ten minutes he handed Mary a sheet of paper on which was inscribed: 'Time to move. Instructions tomorrow. Weather permitting."

"After breakfast we'll go back to Halfbrewed and tell the village council that their problem with the travelers will soon be at an end."

* * * * *

On the way back to Halfbrewed, Rita looked a bit subdued.

"What's wrong, Aunt Rita?" Mary asked.

"It doesn't look like there are UFOs, after all."

John smiled. "That's right, Rita, but we have to stick with the natural facts. So far as we know, UFOs as alien spacecraft don't exist, and we have just proved it here in Halfbrewed."

"But how will the fairies get around?"

Mary squeezed John's arm to keep him from further destroying Rita's belief in the supernatural. "Oh, I'm sure they'll manage somehow. They do have wings, you know." John managed to answer Rita with a straight face, and Mary relaxed her grip on his arm.

At the town office, John asked if he could see the mayor, as he thought he had some important information for her regarding the travelers now camping on the village green. The mayor, Mrs. Fanning, was a short, round woman in her early fifties with a spherical face and ready smile. "How can I help you, Mr. Braemhor?"

"I hope it's the other way round," John said as he took her proffered hand. He then proceeded to tell her of his attempts to understand Mr. Hayson's photograph of UFOs, complete with discovering that the lights were not extraterrestrial but light signals from the travelers on the green, probably to other bands of travelers, coordinating their movements around the countryside. The signals seemed to indicate that they would be leaving Halfbrewed in the near future.

"Well, I certainly hope you're right, Mr. Braemhor. It's been very difficult dealing with the travelers. We don't like to seem inhospitable to anyone or any group, but these people do try our patience. You know we have set aside some space on the edge of the village for travelers passing through, but this group settled on the green and would not move. It would have taken a major police action to physically remove them, something that would be beyond our small budget." She paused, then, "Well, Mr. Braemhor, I do appreciate your positive news, and I hope you're right."

As John exited the council office, the mayor had one last comment. "Wasn't that a horrible thing that happened to Mr. Hayson?"

"Oh, what was that?" was John's circumspect comment.

"Oh, didn't you know? He was murdered a day ago at his farm near Cairn-on-the-Green."

"Where did you hear that?" John wanted to know how the news had travelled.

"My neighbor saw all the police at his farm and stopped to find out what was going on. Dreadful business. We pride ourselves on being a low crime region. You don't suppose it was any of the travelers, do you?"

"I really wouldn't know, Mrs. Fanning, but I'm sure the authorities will investigate all possibilities." *I wonder if she's right?* John thought as he drove back to the inn at Cairn-on-the-Green.

* * * * *

When John arrived at the inn at Cairn-on-the-Green, Mary and Rita had just gotten back from the small stationer's in the village. "We both needed some stationery. Rita wants to write Dunmoor Castle, and I'd like to write the grandchildren. We thought it would be an efficient way to use our time while we wait for DI Melville to contact you."

"What did you get?" John asked absent-mindedly. He was still stewing over Mrs. Fanning's question about the travelers. Mary showed him the writing tablets and box of envelopes they'd bought.

The early afternoon was passed by Mary and Rita writing various family members. John spent his time on the inn's guest computer looking up some ideas he had developed regarding Mr. Hayson. Later, the inn clerk came into the common room and approached the three. "There's a call for you, Mr. Braemhor. You can take it on the phone in reception." John jumped up and hastily went in to the phone.

"Braemhor here," he said into the receiver.

"Mr. Braemhor, this is DI Melville. Got some information for you."

"And I for you," John rejoined.

"You're going to tell me about the UFOs and the travelers in Halfbrewed." Melville was somber.

"How did you know?" John was again impressed with how fast information moved around Perthshire.

"Mrs. Fanning called me. Said that what the people thought were UFOs were actually lights being flashed from the travelers' camp and that these visitors would be moving soon. In fact, I believe some have already left."

"That's good news. What do you have for me?"

"It looks like you were right. Our Mr. Hayson died of poisoning, but the coroner hasn't determined what kind yet. Another day for that."

"Any suspects yet? The travelers, maybe?"

"First thing we thought of. Particularly with your finding that the travelers had been sending light signals that Hayson photographed as UFOs. Maybe they did not take kindly to his giving notoriety to their project. We're looking into it, but somehow I doubt it. Those types are more given to thievery than murder. I'll let you know if we get anything along those lines. But there's something else."

"Yes," John said, fascinated that Melville would discard a whole group of possible suspects on the basis of past group behavior.

"Our Mr. Hayson was quite an amateur photographer. Not just UFOs. Took multiple pictures of local people. Snapshots, nothing posed. Most of the people probably don't even know they're in his portfolio. Some were through windows at night. Nothing really smutty, but I'm sure would not be appreciated by the subjects. We found the photos in his dark room downstairs. Most of the people are very recognizable by one of our constables who lives in Cairn-on-the-Green."

"None really compromising?" John asked. "Something that someone would want very much to hide from the public at large?" John was thinking very rapidly with thoughts flashing through his brain so fast he could not capture all of them. *What if he caught a local in a very compromising situation? And that someone was so angered he became violent toward*

Hayson? If that someone did murder him, wouldn't he or she search Hayson's house for copies of the photo or photos?

"None that we found, but the place, particularly his dark room, was a shambles. I think it had been searched before we got there." Melville was now tuned into John's line of thought. "I think we'd better search his place again."

"Can I meet you there and go through the house with you?" John was on the scent now.

"If you would like, Mr. Braemhor, but my boys are pretty thorough." Melville sounded a bit hurt at what he took as an accusation from John.

"I'm sure they are. I meant no offense, Melville, but the more eyes looking, the more we might see." John hoped he had placated the DI's miffed feelings.

"You're right. Sorry. It's been a busy two days. I'll send Sgt. Richards. 'Bout 4?"

"That's fine. I'll meet him at Hayson's farm." John hung up and went to inform Mary and Rita that his late afternoon was taken up.

* * * * *

Four o'clock sharp both John in his Vauxhall and Richards in his green and white pulled into the car park in front of the Hayson farm.

"Mr. Braemhor." Richards shook John's hand. "Heard a lot about you."

"Oh?"

"Yes, Ron Ferguson told me about your work over near Loch Ness. You have a very fine reputation with Ron."

"That's nice. I was happy to help him out. Now about Mr. Hayson's house. Let's go through each room together so we don't miss anything. Okay?"

"It's a plan." The tall, slender, blond officer smiled. He seemed to be especially happy to get out of the routine of smash and grabs and paperwork and into something more like what he was trained for. He and John went slowly, room by room, opening every drawer, pulling knick knacks off of shelves, even looking inside the lampshades for anything Melville's men might have missed on their first go through. Nothing. Even in the dark room they looked behind the bottles of chemicals and under the packets of photographic paper. John also took apart the photo enlarger to be sure that no negative had been left in the film carrier.

"We're coming up blank, Mr. Braemhor." The young Sgt. sounded disappointed. "DI Melville told me to turn the house upside down."

"Of course, that's it." John's abrupt statement startled Richards. "Let's go through it again and look *under* everything. Turn every piece of furniture upside down. If necessary, we may even slice open the upholstery on the chairs." John felt a certain frustration coming over him. *There's got to be something here. From what Melville said, none of the pictures they found were incriminating enough to precipitate a major crime. A few minor embarrassments maybe, but not murder.* He flopped down in Hayson's Morris chair in disgust.

"We need to turn that chair over, too, Mr. Braemhor," Richards reminded John.

"Right." John got up and turned the Morris chair over. And there it was, a small, slender envelope taped to the underside of the chair's left armrest. John looked at Richards and smiled. "As they say in the Colonies, Bingo!" John said as he pulled the envelope from its hiding place. After putting on some gloves, Braemhor looked inside to find several photos of a man and woman in passionate embrace in a grassy cove beside what looked like the Firth of Tay!

"Tst, tst, tst," Richards tutted, looking over Braemhor's shoulder. "Mr. Lewis, of all people!"

"You know him?"

"Yes, sir, he owns the stationery shop in the village. But that's not his wife."

"I didn't imagine it was. Do you know who it is?" John asked.

"Never seen her, but we'd better put the photos into an evidence bag so I can take them back to DI Melville."

Later, after Richards had gone back to Perth, John placed a call to Melville and informed him of his and Richards's find. "Right, I'll have Lewis picked up this evening." Melville was quick off the mark.

"Wait!" John spoke sharply. "Can I suggest that you wait until we have the coroner's report on the cause of death? Lewis is still here in the village. He's not going anywhere, if I'm not mistaken. No sense stirring up the whole village by the arrest of one of their own."

"Well, I don't know." Melville was very hesitant to take profound advice from a man he considered an amateur, despite his reputation with other police agencies. "I can't let a prime suspect stay on the loose on your word."

"I know. I know. And I understand your hesitancy, but I don't think Mr. Hayson died from the type of poisoning we usually see in crime scenes, like cyanide or arsenic. Tell the coroner to look for cirrhosis of the liver and pulmonary edema."

"What's your thinking?" Melville wanted more.

"Look, Hayson was an amateur photographer. Printed a lot of his pictures in sepia. Mishandling of some of the chemicals used in the sepia process can cause severe illness, even death. This is particularly true of selenium which is used in processing sepia prints. Tell the coroner to check for selenium poisoning—it's called selenosis. He'll know. It could be that Hayson inadvertently killed himself by a misuse of his chemicals; if so, we don't have a murder after all.

"True, he caught Mr. Lewis in a compromising position, and if Lewis found out or saw the photos, he may have been very angry. But if he did want to murder Hayson he probably would not have known of selenium poisoning. If Hayson died of selenium poisoning, then Lewis is not your man and you would do him and the community a service by not picking him up on suspicion of a heinous crime. My advice is to tell the coroner to look for selenosis and don't jump to arrest Lewis. Can you give it 24 hours?"

"But if you're wrong, I'm the one who's going to look foolish. And a killer will still be on the loose."

"I know, but life is a series of taking chances, isn't it?" John tried to be persuasive. "Twenty-four hours?"

After a protracted pause, Melville sighed and said, "All right. I'll take a chance on your theory. I'm probably being a fool, but it won't be the first time. Only 24 hours, no more. I'll call as soon as I have Dr. May's report." Despite his misgivings, Melville had taken a liking to Braemhor and felt a connection to him he'd not felt with other private investigators.

"Thanks. I don't think you'll regret this," John said.

"I hope you're right."

John hung up and went back into the dining room to have supper with Mary and Rita.

The next day was real agony for John, and by his agitated pacing, for Mary as well. They and Rita took walks around the village and along the Tay trying to make the time go faster. By dinnertime, John's agitation had reached the point where it interfered with his appetite. As they were finishing their dessert, or what John could eat of his, the three looked to see DI Melville enter the dining room.

John hopped to his feet. "Well?"

"Relax, Mr. Braemhor. Both of our reputations are safe." John visibly relaxed. "Dr. May's report confirmed your suppositions. Hayson died of advanced selenosis. His lungs were virtually full of fluid and his liver was in terrible shape. May said he was surprised he lived as long as he did. So it does look like his death was self-inflicted over years of misuse of selenium while making his sepia photographic prints. Mr. Lewis has nothing to fear except possibly the wrath of his wife and the disdain of his neighbors. And I can write off this case to my good sense in taking your advice." He smiled and held out his hand to Braemhor.

"Well, I'm pleased it worked out well for all concerned, except, of course, Mr. Hayson. We'll be going back to Daraichburn later this afternoon. I'm glad I got to meet you and Sgt. Richards, and if I can ever be of any assistance again call me at our B&B, Dunmoor Cottage. John shook Melville's hand, and the latter exited the inn on his way back to Perth.

"Shall we pack our bags and go home?" John turned to Mary and Rita. "We should be able to get there in time for supper."

On the road south, the three reviewed their latest adventure.

"Well, Rita, what do you think of detective work?" John opened.

Rita squinched her nose and gave her signature giggle. "It's very exciting, but there are some parts of it I don't like much." Her smile dissolved into a look of sadness. "Poor Mr. Hayson."

"But you see, Rita, Mr. Hayson's death wasn't a crime after all. Just a case of the misuse of the chemicals he used in his hobby."

"And he did such beautiful work, too," Mary said. "He could have made a career of his hobby, if he'd been more careful."

"Just goes to show that you have to have the proper knowledge to do much of anything well. . .and safely," John concluded. "But there is one thing you have to remember about detective work."

"What's that?" Rita asked.

"That sometimes it's just as important to find out what a person hasn't done as what he has."

"Like Mr. Lewis?"

"Yes, Mr. Lewis. And something else, things happen because of natural causes, not supernatural ones, even if it seems otherwise. Take the UFOs. We've demonstrated that supernatural interpretations always take a backseat to the natural. UFOs can be explained by attention to natural events."

"But what about those lights we saw in Carterville on our last visit?" Mary asked.

"Just another mystery yet to be solved," John smiled.

THE END

ABOUT THE AUTHOR

Owen Magruder is the *nom de plume* of a retired college professor. He has authored three professional books and a small volume of remembrances of the American Civil War. In addition, he and his wife have co-authored a brief biography of a little known abolitionist from upstate New York for the National Abolition Hall of Fame. From 1989 to 2005, the couple ran a small publishing house that specialized in original letters and journals from the American Civil War.

Magruder's ancestral home is a castle just north of Glasgow given to the family by King Robert [Bruce] III of Scotland, hence the Scottish link to his mystery novels. One of his ancestors was Alice Edmonstone Keppel, mistress of King Edward VII of the United Kingdom.

The Lost Pipers of CraigDhuin is his fifth book in the John and Mary Braemhor mystery series. Owen Magruder resides in upstate New York.

Other Owen Magruder Mysteries:

The Strange Case of Mr. Nobody
The Case of the Hidden Dentures
The Feud at Glencoe
Death at Beggar's Knob